ABOUT THIS BOOK

Three paranormal fantasy novellas (books 22-24) in this multi-author shared world of Havenwood Falls, home to sexy men, strong women, and neighbors who bite.

The Ward & the Wanderers by T.V. Hahn

Sequel to *The Winged & the Wicked*—Teeny Weeny Tahini's life had always been quiet and simple, just the way she liked it. At least, until her owl-shifter nephew Mat came to town with trouble on his heels. She and her extraordinary friends saved the day, but their happily ever after was short lived. Now, the spring faerie has been haunted not only by nightmares but also her past. Coralie, her long-time mermaid friend, is in danger, and the only way to save her is to bring her to Havenwood Falls. But traveling with a mermaid isn't easy.

Toil & Trouble by Melissa Wright

Circe strikes out on her own in Havenwood Falls, far away from the constant reminders that someone wants her blood. Evan is that someone. He's a shifter—a truth he's hidden his entire existence—and now, thanks to a binding deal, he's charged with locating Circe. This job is all he needs to resolve his bargain with the Council, yet Evan can't seem to follow through. When the council tires of waiting, though, they take matters into their own hands. And Evan must decide: step out of the shadows to save her, or keep his own skin.

Of Salt and Stars by Seven Jane

For as long as she can remember, Maris Heilen has been haunted by dreams of a beautiful woman beckoning to her from beneath the water. When her dreams take on a new sense of urgency following the mysterious death of her estranged father, Maris knows it's time to uproot and move on, her soul pulled to the west, toward the water—toward *her*. Instead she finds herself drawn to a surreal little town high in the Colorado mountains, where she discovers her past is linked to a legend even more haunting than her dreams.

HAVENWOOD FALLS VOLUME SEVEN

A HAVENWOOD FALLS COLLECTION

MELISSA WRIGHT   SEVEN JANE   T.V. HAHN

HAVENWOOD FALLS BOOKS

Forget You Not by Kristie Cook

Old Wounds by Susan Burdorf

Fate, Love & Loyalty by E.J. Fechenda

Covetousness by Randi Cooley Wilson

The Winged & the Wicked by T.V. Hahn & Kristie Cook

Alpha's Queen by Lila Felix

Ink & Fire by R.K. Ryals

Lose You Not by Kristie Cook

Tragic Ink by Heather Hildenbrand

Nowhere to Hide by Belinda Boring

Flames Among the Frost by Amy Hale

Rock Me Gently by Susan Burdorf

From the Embers by Amy Miles

Defying Gravity by Kallie Ross

Gypsy Heart by Randi Cooley Wilson

Break Me Not by Kristie Cook

How the Dead Lie by Stacey Rourke

The Lurkers Within by Danielle Bannister

The Collector: Awakening by Kristie Cook, R.K. Ryals, Belinda Boring & Nadirah Foxx

Addicted to You by Belinda Boring

Affliction Mine by C.J. Pinard

The Ward & the Wanderers by T.V. Hahn

Toil & Trouble by Melissa Wright

Of Salt and Stars by Seven Jane

Redefined by Morgan Wylie

Betrayal Among the Frost by Amy Hale

Forever Loyal by E.J. Fechenda

Fate's Demand by Emily Cyr

The Wu & the Wand by T.V. Hahn

A Demon's Redemption by JD Nelson

THE WARD & THE WANDERERS

T.V. HAHN

~ A Havenwood Falls New Adult Novella ~

Havenwood Falls

The WARD AND THE WANDERERS

T.V. HAHN

This book is dedicated to my husband "Bob," whose patience with my pixie life and endurance of reading everything I write (even the drafts) makes me adore him even more.

PROLOGUE

"FATHER, NO!"

"Siobhan, stay out of this. Your brother has disobeyed the code, and for that he must be punished."

My mother stood beside my father, crestfallen and bereaved.

Grenfold stood firm, silent, accepting of his fate. If he only knew.

My father chanted the code. "We, this family of fae, are of earth and air. When sea mixes with earth, it becomes mud. When sea mixes with air, tears fall from the heavens. You have brought both to this family. To be true, from this day hence, no longer are you fae, a prince. For your crime I extol, from this day forward, your life, a troll."

With that, King Ian—for he acted as king now, and not as a loving father —waved his royal wand above my brother's head, and the glowing orb at its tip touched my brother's brow. The first sounds Grenfold made since the commencement of this ghastly ceremony—which was unfairly replacing our usual festive Rites of Spring—were of such pain and agony that nothing human could compare to what my once beautiful brother was suffering. I knew this because over the years, as an empath, I had felt human pain, and this was something far beyond it.

The decibels and frequencies of my brother's cries were otherworldly as his body was transformed. The graceful, perfect frame of the handsome prince made a grotesque crunching of bones as his back disintegrated into a warped spine. My brother's cries and the horrific crackling of cartilage rocked the Isle of Gwynf'l to its core. His hands and feet became gnarled and twisted. His gorgeous golden locks fell in clumps from his head to be replaced by a wiry configuration of corkscrew strands, and even those had a resonance that I could taste as acrid and fuzzy on my tongue. His bright hazel eyes became like lumps of coal placed in a bed of gray clay, as his handsome features distorted. His nose became a long crooked probe with crusty warts, and his mouth turned and twisted, totally malformed, filled with protruding and decayed teeth.

After this horrible transformation was complete, my father, the great King Ian, ordered the troll to find a rock to crawl under.

And so he did.

My mother, the kind and generous Queen Rose, was so heartbroken, she turned ill and died within a few short months after Grenfold's departure.

Such is the price one pays for love. It didn't seem right that a gift of love should be so painful, so costly.

CHAPTER 1

$\mathcal{T}$he tinkling of the shopkeeper's bell rang sweetly in the dining room of Broastful Brew as I entered and slowly closed the shop door behind me, accidentally allowing a brisk March wind to add a bit of chill to the café. I trudged into the toasty coffee house and made my way to the back table, where my best friend, Barbie Stuart, the mayor of Havenwood Falls, sat sipping a simmering cup of coffee.

Havenwood Falls was no ordinary Colorado town. Oh sure, it looked like your typical frontier Victorian village one could find nestled in just about any canyon in the state, with the sun rays glistening off the golden aspens' fluttering leaves and the scent of pine wafting in the cool breeze. I could assure you, however, that was just a façade. Behind the brick and mortar, wood shingles, and gingerbread lattice work was a town full of supernaturals, from vampires and demons to werewolves and angels. In fact, I was one of them, a spring fae.

Not all of the townsfolk were supernaturals. The ratio varied from time to time, ranging between forty and sixty percent supes. I think it depended on how the stars aligned, but I could be wrong. There could be something much more mysterious behind the mix.

Regardless, the town was founded by the Old Families, one of which was mine. We were—and yes, some of us are still quite alive and kicking—supernaturals looking for a safe haven, where our supernatural abilities would not subject us to prejudice, as we discovered would happen just about anywhere else.

The founders created the town and the government known as the Court of the Sun and the Moon. All of the Old Families had one member sitting on the Court. I held my family's seat, although I was basically the wallflower of the group most of the time.

The Luna Coven created most of the magic that protected Havenwood Falls, including something the town referred to as the "memory ward." As soon as a visitor traveled outside of the twenty-five mile radius of the town's limits, their memory of our little haven vanished. The residents got a bit of a reprieve on this mystic cloak, in that we could exit town for one complete moon phase—twenty-eight days—before our memories of Havenwood Falls disappeared.

I found Havenwood Falls serene and comforting, and really never had any reason to go anywhere outside of its protective borders. Others—a Roca here and a Bishop there—seemed to have a necessity to come and go frequently.

I withdrew the chair from the table when the mayor looked up at me. She was visibly startled at my appearance.

"Siobhan! You look dreadful! Is it the spring equinox that's bothering you? I've never seen you look so . . . well, so bad." Barbara, a dear friend and a member of another Old Family, invited me to join her.

Barbie had listened to me recount my family tale every spring for what seemed like a hundred years, and may very well have been. We met regularly at Broastful Brew. Unlike the bustling Coffee Haven, where the younger folk liked to hang, Mabel's coffee shop was quite sedate and the perfect place for us two to congregate.

Barbie's stature was so starkly different from mine, me being only four foot five, the town's mysterious palm reader and potion mixer, lovingly (I think) known as Madame "Teeny Weeny" Tahini. By contrast, Barbie's six-foot frame was not enough to intimidate, her bouffant beehive hairdo—which she sometimes dyed in various pastel colors according to her whimsy so it looked like a wand of cotton candy—added at least six more inches to her height.

Tahini was not really my surname. It was McFeeny, but being a palm reader and all, I felt Tahini gave it a much more exotic allure for my trade, and it rhymed with McFeeny. For that matter, it rhymed with Teeny Weeny, too.

Normally I was very cheerful and lighthearted, or so I'd been told. Barbie always said I had a childlike nature of wonderment drifting about me. However, this day my faerie glamour wasn't sparkling, dark circles rimmed my eyes, and my generally shiny long brunette hair was in a fizzled mess around my shoulders. I'd noticed the ghastly reflection in the glass door before I entered.

"I haven't been sleeping well, Barbie. I've been bombarded with nightmares. I can't make anything of them. It's just so weird for me. The Rites of Spring dream—I'm used to that. For so long, I've relived that moment, and I have wished I had the power to break my father's curse."

Barbie nodded with understanding, but she raised one eyebrow, as if she thought differently about my wish.

She wrapped her large soft hands around my tiny wringing fists, trying her best to comfort me.

"You poor dear," she said soothingly. "Maybe these nightmares stem from that awful incident with that Pisik cat-shifting witch and your poor nephew Mat. You are not so accustomed to commotion."

I smiled weakly at my friend's attempt at assonance—word play had always been one of my favorite forms of dialogue. But not so much today, or for the last week or so, for that matter.

"Tell me about the nightmare. It might help to talk it out. Maybe between the two of us, we can fathom its meaning," she prodded.

"Well the first one—" I started.

"First one! There's more?"

"Nightmarezzz," I exaggerated wearily, emphasizing the plural, then continued. "The first one starts out in the dead of winter. The snows have already fallen heavily in the canyon. I have effervesced and flown up to Peacock Lake. The triplet falls are frozen solid, and the lake is like a shining mirror. I'm barely able to discern any of its radiant colors. I am enjoying the crisp, fresh smell of the whiteness. The air is so clean, the scent of the pines is outright singing to me at Small's Falls. I am listening to the soft chords of the sunlight passing through the icicles on the falls' ledge, spraying the colors like a prism, a harp strumming angelic psalms across the lake. It's peaceful and serene, and I am enjoying the scenery."

I paused, then continued, "Suddenly, black irregular spots begin to appear across the snowy landscape. They grow bigger, dripping upon the land, as if something black and evil is clawing at the snow-laden mountains. The blackness runs like spilt ink, and the spots begin to run into one another, growing larger. The smell is so acrid, sticky, like the smell of crude oil, but worse, like deeper than those bowels of the earth. It is a smell so strong that I wake up drenched in sweat, unable to shake the odor from my nostrils and way too afraid to try to go back to sleep."

Barbie sat unblinkingly as she pondered the dream's description and sipped her coffee. Mabel had brought my usual pot of hot water and favorite chamomile tea in a bag. I half-heartedly bounced the teabag up and down in the pot, but I was just not really inclined to actually pour the tea into my cup.

"Not sure I can make much of that. *Yet.*" Barbie went on, "Normally, it doesn't sound like much to make such a sweat over —sorry, no pun intended. However, you do have that ultra-synesthesia thing going on. You know, where you *feel* smells so strongly, and *hear* colors so vividly, and a bunch of other mixed up senses, that it's perfectly understandable. Maybe it's connected to the next dream. Tell me about that one?"

There were not too many folks in town who knew the mayor

had a talent for interpreting dreams. Maybe it was just her curiosity in netherworldly ways, or maybe an inheritance she had yet to expose.

Barbie was supposedly human, but I had my doubts, having known her for so long. Even with our long friendship, I had just learned some of her secrets at her last Thankshannamas gathering, when she thought she had lost her dragon pendant, a family relic that evidently gave her strength and agelessness when she wore it. I had noticed long before that she never changed, except, of course, for the mound of cotton candy that topped her crown. From time to time, her hair color had been pale blue, pale pink, pale yellow, pale purple, pale whatever, a pastel rainbow of sorts. The pale yellow must've been her favorite, at least when in public, but every now and again, she would get a little adventurous. And each color smelled like . . . well, pale blue like blueberry, pale yellow like lemon chiffon, etc. At least to me, which was yummy.

I remembered when she had it almost a lavender color, but lavender was not the scent I'd picked up. I'd had a hard time identifying it.

"Welch's grape juice," she'd remarked.

That was it! It smelled like grapes. Did she soak that magnificent head of hair in a vat of Welch's grape juice, or was it just her inspiration? I didn't know. Maybe someday she'd tell me.

But like I said, Barbie had never changed—other than the color of her hair—for decades. On the other hand, she had never exhibited any supernatural powers either, in public or to me, other than that ancient talent of dream interpretation. Then again, she did seem to have some superhuman strength, or I could be imagining it. Since she's so much larger than I am, her own human abilities might just be that strong in comparison to me having to use my faerie dust to accomplish something similar, like picking up beings twice my size, as an example.

She'd held so many different positions in town and on the Court, but had always been a major presence. And she was never without the dragon pendant (which most folks thought represented the high school mascot) that hung precariously from a silver chain around her neck, with its tail always pointing to a voluptuous cavern of cleavage, as she was very well-endowed.

As to her requesting me to tell her about the *next* dream, I obliged.

"So the next time, I dreamed I was sipping a delightful cup of tea in front of the blazing fireplace in the parlor of Whisper Falls Inn. Madame Luiza is sitting with me in her ghostly form, and we are having one of our lovely chats about the town's ancient history, and the miscreants that once inhabited our wonderful village, and the few who still do. You remember what it was like? We are having such fun, as Luiza describes so many of the colorful characters and their doings and misdoings. She saw and knew so much. It is always fun talking with her."

Barbie nodded her lemon-chiffon head, recollecting those chats herself, but waved her large beautiful hands in a come-forward gesture, begging me to continue.

So I did.

"The fire in the hearth suddenly crackles loudly, and fiery sparks fly out of the fireplace. We stand up immediately, trying to bat at the tiny sparks that could alight and place the entire inn in peril. Of course, Luiza is a ghost, so her batting is totally useless. A swirl of black smoke emits from the embers and circles throughout the room, thickening the air, making it nearly impossible to breathe. I am grasping at my chest, trying to gasp at least one more ounce of oxygen into my lungs before the horrific smog-like smoke takes over. There is a similarity in the smoky stench and that oily odor from the previous dream. At this point, I wake up, once again dripping with sweat, the pungent smell still burning in my nose and an ominous, dull ringing tone tolling in my ears."

Barbie sympathetically shook her head and patted my hands. "It's interesting that these dreams start out so . . . well, so dreamy. Then they kind of catch you off guard and take a sudden turn. So that's something to keep in mind. It might be that your dreams are foretelling the fortune teller something. Maybe you need to keep your guard up. Seems like you need to be on the alert."

"Yeah, you might be right, because the next one is like that too," I confided.

"Next one? You mean there's even more?" The mayor grimaced, realizing suddenly why I looked so miserable.

"One more, actually."

Barbie's brow raised higher than I thought capable, so I continued.

"I am back on the Isle of Gwynf'l with my parents and my brother, before, well, you know, before Father changed him. It is a beautiful day, and we are having a faerie picnic on the shore by the Bay of Gwynf'l. Mother has baked our favorite faerie cakes of honeysuckle honey and daisy flower flour. The pixies are skipping along the mollusk shells scattered on the beach and breaking out into their familiar wrestling matches in the sand. The waves are bright aqua topped with marshmallowy sea-foam, and they are gently lapping the shore. There are mountainous fluffy clouds in the sky, and they send sound waves of comforting lullabies and happy Irish ditties toward the sandy dunes that buffet the beach.

"I spot a waterspout forming out in the sea, and I am mesmerized by the sight of the swirling funnel, so magnificent in its perfect Fibonacci spiral. The funnel, though, is moving quickly closer and growing darker and larger. It is suddenly totally black as it reaches the shore, and a giant wave crashes over all of us, smelling like . . . Well, like before—oily, inky, black. And I awoke as soaked as if the wave had actually hit me, and this time I began to vomit from the odiferous air that surrounded me."

"This is not good, Siobhan! You should have called me earlier. We will have to be vigilant, since I am sure these are *warning* signs."

"But there's something else, also," Barbie continued. "I don't know if it's the smell or the black thing, maybe both. I will have to think more about this. No matter what, if you have another dream, you are to call me pronto, regardless of what time it is, understood?"

I nodded in acquiescence to Barbie's order, but my hands were still wringing one another and my teacup still remained empty.

"Drink your tea, hon. It'll help calm you. I have to run. I have a meeting at City Hall with a new visitor. I mean it about calling me!"

I shakily tried to pour the steeped tea from the pot into my cup as Barbie bent over to kiss the top of my head. I struggled to wiggle a few fingers in toodle-oo style, but it probably looked like a very disheartened farewell.

I did finish my tea at the Brew, albeit slowly, since my cup rattled every time I tried to lift it from the saucer, and I was fearful I would spill tea all over the place. I thanked Mabel for letting me sit so long, brooding. I guess today, it could be called Brooding Brew.

CHAPTER 2

I found myself mindlessly wandering through town square, as drab as my mood now that the Into the Mystic Psychic Fair had come and gone, the colorful tents and banners only a memory now. I wound up on the southeast corner, next to the gazebo, and decided to stop into Callie's Consignments, since Callie usually had something unusual in her inventory that could cheer me up a bit. Unfortunately, this morning I had difficulty concentrating on any of the fascinating items that always seemed to present themselves on the shelves and nooks of Callie's shop.

I did spot a new painting of a mermaid sunning herself on a rock as she preened her long red hair with a pearl-studded comb. The painting brought back the bittersweet memories of Gwynf'l and my friend Coralie, the beautiful sea maiden who, unlike her fellow merfolk, preferred to chat with the faeries rather than swim amongst her school.

This memory saddened me, though, as did my annual spring equinox recollection. I recalled how heartbroken Coralie was when she lost her love, my young faerie prince brother Grenfold. If only poor Coralie knew that Grenfold was not completely lost, just not a faerie prince any longer. I wasn't sure which was worse.

"Sorry, Callie, I'm a little distracted today. I'll come back when I'm in better spirits."

Callie Montgomery, the stunning-beyond-words olive-skinned gypsy demon, gently patted me on the shoulder, her multi-bangled wrist clinking a melody that looked like stars shooting around the room.

"No worries," she said as I exited the store.

I turned in the opposite direction from my own shop, Madame Tahini's Potions, Lotions, Palm Reading, and Other Extra-Sensory Services, and proceeded to the corner of the block, where the Haven Saloon loomed over the corner of the square.

I stopped and gazed at the frontier-style batwing doors of the saloon, and the sound of shattering glass and wooden chairs cracking on the floor of the saloon pierced my memory, as I reminisced about the brawl that Sheriff Ric Kasun broke up one of the last times I was there. The sheriff had a nose for trouble brewing. Must have been the wolf in him, literally. This did make him the perfect sheriff for our little town.

Maybe a shot of Irish Mist in my tea would fix me up . . . Tea and Sympathy. Maybe later.

Turning up Eighth Street, back in the direction of Broastful Brew, I strolled to the alleyway that led to Nina's Dress Perfect tailor shop. I climbed the steps that led to the second story tailor, but was greeted by a sign on the door that read *Closed*. I pulled my wool vest closer to my chest as I turned and descended the stairwell, not too disappointed, as I really wasn't in the mood to visit anyone, but was just trying to keep myself distracted. Besides, I knew in the back of my mind that it was unlikely Nina would be up at this early hour anyway, since she was quite a night owl.

I reluctantly returned home, as it was getting too cold for me to just wander about aimlessly. The winter winds started to whip up through the town square—even though it was already early spring—after all, these were the Rockies.

Retrieving the onyx-colored key from my vest pocket, I unlocked the front door, pulling the heavy engraved wooden plank toward me as I stepped into my townhome shop. I removed the vest and hung it on the coatrack in the foyer, then headed to the kitchen, which I always had decked out like a mad scientist's laboratory, with Bunsen burner, beakers and flasks, and an ancient apothecary's scale sitting on the kitchen counter where most people had their coffee maker and canisters. After all, I was a potion mixer, and these were essential tools.

I looked out the window over the kitchen sink and saw Cyllene, the dryad of Maximus. Maximus was an eight-hundred-year-old bristlecone pine that had been struck by lightning a decade or so ago, and the dryad was his soul. Cyllene was perched on the spearmint plant that still thrived in the window box, even throughout the harsh winter. A bit of a gift I had.

I opened the window, and the luminescent moth-like creature flew in gracefully, humming an indistinguishable buzz and whirr. I set up a funnel and clamp at the kitchen table, the little megaphone contraption I invented, and the nymph took her place of honor before the small end of the funnel.

"You're a sight for sore eyes, Silly Annie," I told her.

"Siobhan! It's Cyllene!"

"Yeah, yeah. See-Lee-Nee. Whatever, Silly Annie."

"Well, you are definitely *not* a sight for sore eyes! You look like a Terrible Teeny Weeny to me. In fact, you look like you have sore eyes. Are you sick? I haven't seen you for over a week. I've been worried about you."

"I've just had a few nights' bad sleep is all. Not for you to worry about." But I was concerned. Even more now, given Barbie's warning, but not knowing what I was supposed to be keeping my guard up against.

I SPENT a few hours that evening in my salon reading my first edition of Hans Christian Andersen's *Eventyr fortalte for børn* —*Fairy Tales for Children*. It was one of my favorites, and I'd been contemplating donating it to the Havenwood Falls Library, since the fire at the library had destroyed so many of the wonderful books that had been housed there. Many of the lost books had been contributed over a century ago by the founders, and since I was among the founding families, it seemed right to renew the tradition. But before I started getting all charitable and everything, especially with this prized possession, I thought I'd want to read it a couple more times.

I knew people thought these were fairy tales, but there was a lot of history and truth in the stories, and I was always reminded of one thing or another. I'd treated this book more like an encyclopedia of my family culture than a storytelling compilation.

Getting ready for bed, I picked out the pink flannel nightgown Nina had made for me. The flannel was so soft and thick, it felt like velvet. Only Nina could have found such a material as this. I finally felt a glimmer of coziness come over me as I climbed onto my thick feather mattress and pulled up the quilted duvet overstuffed with warm down.

A big yawn escaped my mouth as I reached over to turn off the Tiffany stained-glass lamp by the bedside and prayed to the spirits that tonight, at least one night, I would have a dreamless slumber.

That wasn't to occur.

I found myself walking into an unfamiliar village. There were thick oaks, maples, and pines surrounding the town. I could even feel the syrupy scent of maple in the air. It had the quaintness of a charming New England town, but no beings, human or otherwise, could be found, not even a squirrel or moose. It was so quiet and serene. As I entered the village, a wooden sign painted green and held up by two white posts greeted me. The gold lettering read *Welcome to the Historic Village of Fishkill – Settled in 1714.*

Near the center of the town stood a large two-story building of Georgian architecture with a cupola-topped turret attached on the right side. The lower story was white clapboard, while the upper story had brown wooden shingles on its walls. Beveled lettering above the entrance read *Van Wyck Hall.* There was a tall ladder that stood on the lower stoop of the entryway, leaning against the railing above the doorway, as if it was going to be used for restoring the sign.

I walked up the sidewalk to the town hall and ducked under the ladder that stood in front of the double doors of the building. On the left-hand door hung a small mirror for no apparent reason. As I reached to open the door of the hall, the mirror suddenly swung erratically, then flew off the door and shattered on the stoop into a dozen sparkling shards. I turned around to pick up one of the shards, and a small black cat with lime green eyes crossed my path. That bitter, pungent odor pierced my senses.

I sat up abruptly to find myself back in my feather bed, but the thick flannel nightgown was now sopping wet. I could barely catch my breath as I fumbled to turn the light on. I groped around some more on the nightstand and felt my cell phone on the stand. The phone read 5:11 a.m., but Barbie said anytime, "pronto," and that was an order, so I dialed 9-1-1.

The phone did not ring at the fire station, nor did it ring at the sheriff's office. My 9-1-1 was a direct hotline to the mayor, and of course, she picked up immediately.

"Siobhan, did you have another dream?" she asked without even saying hello. She could probably hear my labored breathing over the connection.

"Oh yes, and it's like the others, dreamy at first then . . ." I went on to recite the details of this newest nocturnal haunting.

"Hmm . . . I think I've got it. Meet me at the Brew at seven o'clock sharp," Barbie told me, and hung up without waiting for a response.

CHAPTER 3

I pattered around the kitchen and salon for the next couple of hours, as the stench from that wicked dream would not dissipate enough for me to go back to sleep.

As it neared seven, I went back up to my room to dress, still feeling the dampness from the nightmare sweats. I pulled a black woolen long-sleeved dress from the armoire and placed a few ribbons, a dainty embroidered handkerchief, my ebony key, and a small silk packet of faerie dust (just in case—my personal motto) in the large blossomy pocket on the left hip of the dress. I bundled up a woven neck scarf and shoved it into the right hip pocket.

Downstairs in the foyer, I grabbed my wool vest with the fur collar from the coat rack. The fur pelt that Nina had fashioned into the collar was given to her compliments of Ranger Rusty, a bit of a lone wolf, but a very kind soul, from one of his hunts.

Pushing the door open to face the cold dark morning in Havenwood Falls, I stepped out, turned around to shut the door behind me, and locked it with the ebony key, dropping it back into my left pocket. I was keeping my guard up.

We both arrived at exactly the same time as Mabel was unlocking Broastful Brew's door.

"You two are earlier than usual this morning. It will take me a bit of time to get everything heated up. Sorry I'm so late, but I couldn't decide if I should put my thermals on this morning or if I was jumping the gun. Don't want to get overheated, you know, but then it's not worth catching a cold either." Mabel greeted us in her typically long-winded manner.

The shopkeeper's bell rang loudly as all three of us entered, and a brisk breeze blew through the door, throwing the small bell into a tizzy.

Barbie and I, looking much like the female versions of Mutt and Jeff, walked to our usual table, which should have a sign that said *Property of Mayors and Palm Readers*.

I was kind of hoping the black dress might detract from the dark circles under my eyes, but I don't think it helped very much. Barbie, on the other hand, looked stunning, perfectly manicured and made up as a model of Amazonian beauty would be, regardless of the early hour. A trait I admired about the mayor.

"Siobhan, do you remember right before we sent that Wicked Witch Pisik to her Carpathian rock, she said something?" Barbie began, shortly after the two of us had taken our seats. She wasn't wasting any time with small talk this morning.

"Sorta. I don't know that I caught all the words. It was a poem. Something about altitude and fish, didn't make any sense to me. I just figured it was her evil ranting madness."

"It was a poem, so to speak. Just as the black swirl of obliviation was about to whisk her away, she said, 'Altai's death I shall avenge. The fish will die as my revenge.'"

"Okay, I give. What's Altai? What's with the fish?"

"Altai was her lover, a snow leopard shifter. That's your ink spots on the snowy landscape in your first dream, remember?"

"Oh! Oh, my!" The skin on the back of my neck began to crawl.

Barbie continued to interpret the dream. "I believe the black smoke swirling in your Whisper Falls Inn dream and the black funnel cloud swirling in your Gwynf'l dream is the Pisik being swept off to her fate."

Now my entire body was beginning to get goose bumps, which for me felt like an extremely excruciating itch.

"I see. That makes sense, especially the smell. Remember when she first arrived, and I caught that awful scent when she came into Broastful Brew? I thought it was from the boys behind her, but they turned out to be her half-blooded brothers."

"Speaking of those two half-bloods—after they were defrocked, or should I say de-furred, by the Peacock Lake water and looked like two hairless sphinx cats, they were put up for adoption. Biddie Half-Moon, or maybe it was Irene Beckett, told me one of the hellhounds adopted them."

"Well, that's fitting—hounds and cats, ha! Okay, what about the other part of the Pisik poetry? 'The fish will die'? What do fish have to do with anything?"

"Ah, dear Teeny, your last dream put it all together for me. Your dream took place in a town called Fishkill. That's how I remembered what that wretched feline said. You hit three bad omens, just like your first three dreams. So the bad luck omens are walking under the ladder, breaking the mirror, then of all things a *black* cat crossing your path. Remember Shayin's evil background that Mat had shared with the Court? That the mermaid at Gwynf'l had drowned her precious Altai? So sad for Pisik," Barbie said with feigned sympathy for the terrible temptress, then she sighed again, knowing the heartbroken fate of poor Coralie. Barbie went on. "Not 'fish' plural in her little verse. It's *the* fish, meaning the mermaid," Barbie emphasized.

I nearly fell out of my chair as soon as I put two and two together—or three and three (omens and dreams), in this case. That wicked Shay was planning on killing my friend Coralie! The obliviation spell that the Court cast upon Shay would make her unable to remember Havenwood Falls, but it could not protect Coralie in Gwynf'l.

Oh my gods and goddesses. I felt so guilty! I pled with the Court that day to obliviate, not obliterate, the Pisik. I hated to destroy anything, and through the centuries I'd come to realize that even when you did the right thing, there were unintentional consequences. Now it looked like my "right thing" had its unintentional consequences, this time another of Pisik's diabolical plots.

Here I go again. I began to wring my hands nervously, this time worried about how to keep Coralie safe from any gross ritual that creepy she-cat could concoct. *Keep my guard up? I'm going to have to* become *a guard.*

Barbie seemed to read my mind, as old friends often did. She patted my hand in that familiar gesture that I usually found so comforting.

"Maybe I should bring Coralie here to Havenwood Falls. That would certainly protect her from Pisik. Do you think I could? I'm not sure how, but maybe I can figure it out. Do you think the Court would allow it?"

Barbie smiled reassuringly. "I am sure the Court would allow it. Sounds like the only bad thing Coralie ever did was a good thing—get rid of a bad cat named Altai."

I brightened up for the first time in over a week and leaped up from my chair before Mabel could even come over with my tea bag and a pot of piping hot water. I couldn't help myself. I started jumping up and down with glee, like my normal faerie self, which made the mayor grin even wider.

"I've got to get to my salon and figure out what I will need for this adventure. Barbie, I love you!"

I had to pull out my handkerchief from my pocket to dab my eyes as they filled with tears of joy. I gleefully pulled on my winter vest and practically skipped out of Broastful Brew in such a delightful dance that Mabel didn't even scold me for not closing the door behind me.

~

I WILL HAVE *to contact Seamus. He's the only one who can get a hold of Coralie through her pearl. There is so much to do,* I thought to myself, as I unlocked my door and entered the townhome. I lit the candle on the foyer table, and almost immediately the pumpkin-spice scent wrapped around me like a cozy blanket. I pushed through the draped beads and entered my palm-reading salon.

Nestled atop the large round table that was located in the center of the room and covered with a maroon brocade cloth was a glass sphere with a mysteriously whirling mist inside. I sat down in my overstuffed chair directly opposite the shop's storefront window. Gazing into the multi-colored orb, I began to chant, slowly and deliberately, taking deep breaths. "Tahini McFeeny, Famous Seamus," I repeated, over and over again.

The whirling colors inside the crystal ball began to turn into various shades of green, and a face came into view amongst the swirling mists of the globe.

"Ah, Siobhan, how is my dearest niece and favorite fae queen?" The baritone voice of my uncle Seamus came booming from the glass ball. I flinched at his use of *fae queen*, but I hoped he didn't see it.

"Good morn, Uncle Seamus, much better now, especially to see and hear you again. I need your help with a little communication, I think."

"Go on, little one."

"I need to bring Coralie to Havenwood Falls. I'm pretty sure she's in danger, and I think it's the best way to protect her."

"I am guessing that is probably true, since you saved my boy Mathew, and as we know, they both have a common enemy. But what about Grenfold? Will he be all right with that?"

I ignored his mention of my brother, as my only immediate thought was to protect Coralie from Pisik.

"Do you think you can contact her with your orb and her matched pearl? Let her know I will be coming for her within the fortnight?" I pleaded.

"For you, Siobhan, anything. I have not contacted her in very many moons, but she is never without her pearl, so I'm sure I can let her know. She will be so happy to see you. Just be careful. There may be more to protect against than just a demonic witch. Let me know if you need any other assistance. Make sure you take your sphere with you in case you need to get a hold of me."

"Thank you, Uncle! I will put the ball on the top of my to-do list. Kisses to Aunt Abigail. Speak soon!" I bade him farewell, blowing kisses at the rounded glass, as the face in the globe grew fainter and the green hues began to return to the myriad of rainbow colors it originally contained.

I swiveled my chair around to face the back wall and pulled on the tapestry that hung on it. The tapestry was like a pull cord for the drop-down door, revealing a recess in the wall that housed my computer. I tapped on a few keys, and the computer sprang to life.

I logged on to the Havenwood Falls residents' website and clicked the button that said *TW Only*. The browser re-directed me to the password reset page, to which only I and the other members of the Court of the Sun and the Moon had access.

I thought I'd better reset the password now, since I wasn't sure when my next opportunity would be. *Let's see. I'll be gone a couple of fortnights, so end of April or beginning of May. A May Day theme would be appropriate. I got it!*

I quickly typed out "mA¥pØ£€fA3R13f€5T"

That reminds me. I need to make some faerie cakes to leave for the pixies, just in case I'm not back before Spring Fest.

I created a new file on the computer called TO DO, and typed in:

1. Google Earth
2. Calendar
3. Faerie Cakes
4. Tell All Ball
5. Faerie Dust

Then I clicked save, logged off the computer, and closed the tapestried access door.

CHAPTER 4

I awoke after the first good night's sleep I'd had in weeks. I felt so refreshed in the morning and was anxious to put together the plan to rescue the endangered and forlorn Coralie.

I wasn't terribly creative, but I thought what I'd plotted out wasn't half bad.

I checked out Google Earth and estimated how far I would have to fly to get to Gwynf'l. Over 4,600 miles! Even though I could fly nearly 800 miles an hour, once I effervesced, I would need to make so many stops to replenish myself, as speeds that high eat up a lot of my energy. Shimmering was out of the question for that leg anyway, as the time warp is way too unpredictable—the Stipple in the Ripple. It was most likely best for me to take a plane to Belfast. Maybe the Court could supply me with a passport. I was hoping so.

I still had some family in Belfast, so I could ship whatever I needed to them first, like the Tell All Ball, and of course my stash of faerie dust. I needed to travel light and not mess around with airport security and all, so the shipping was better. I'd see if Addie could put a spell on the package, just in case it was scanned, so it appeared as if it only contained papers and books.

I could catch a fishing boat in Belfast to take me to the Isle of Gwynf'l.

This was going pretty well. Until I got to the point of how the heck I was supposed to get Coralie back here. I certainly couldn't expect her to swim all this way, especially in unfamiliar waters, and with so many waterways, rivers, and falls to maneuver.

I thought I might need the mayor's help on some of this, so I texted her a message to see if she could meet me at Broastful Brew.

So once again, we were at our table in the cozy coffee shop. This time I felt much perkier, and I was swinging my feet under my chair, because my legs were too short to meet the floor.

"Barbie, it's a long trip there and back again. I can fly like a faerie, but I doubt I could do the whole trip, especially over the Atlantic Ocean. There would be no place for me to rest. Let alone the fact that I'm not sure I can do it and be back again within a moon's full cycle. I may never be able to find Havenwood Falls again. But if I could get a passport, I could fly to Belfast. That would certainly speed things up a bit. Is that possible?"

"Not a problem. Come in to the Court and ask if they can give you some magic that will delay the effects of the wards. And yes, you can get a passport. After all, we are a government agency, don't you know?" Barbie said with a sly smile.

"Okay. I've already reset the internet password." I handed my dear friend a little slip of paper with the new secret phrase. "I'm pretty sure I've worked out getting there, but I'm not sure about getting Coralie back."

"Teeny, I have always believed that you underestimate your faerie magic. You will be able to do something to get Coralie back, I'm sure of that. Just don't forget to get the ward magic in place before you leave. The passport is easy. You can come over to City Hall anytime."

I wasn't so sure if she was right about my faerie magic. After Grenfold was turned and Mum died, I didn't want to have anything to do with fae magic or curses. Then when my father died, I only sprinkled a little dust now and then, since the pixies counted on me for that.

"You're probably right, Barbie. I'll just think positive."

I was even beginning to feel more positive. Barbie had already made arrangements for my upcoming departure. Now I had to get things packed up and ready to go.

≈

WHEN I RETURNED HOME from Broastful Brew, I found four yammering pixies at my door. Enya was yanking on Ushka's hair, while Tierri was rabbit punching Aieri's arm. I opened the door as quickly as I could and shuffled them in before they could cause a scene on Main Street by breaking out into one of their notorious wrestling matches. Then Sheriff Kasun would be on their case and mine.

"Stop that, all of you! Where is your glamour anyway?"

Aieri shuffled her foot shyly in circles with her head down. "Oops, sorry, we forgot."

For the pixie sisters, their glamour was the closest thing they could come to manners.

"I have a lot to do today. I have to pack for a trip."

"A trip? Great! Where are we going?" Tierri asked, now jumping up and down, all excited.

"Is it a vacation?" Aieri, excited as well, rubbed the arm that Tierri had just moments ago used as a punching bag.

"Let's go to the Bahamas!" cried Enya, quickly joining the enthusiasm.

"Yeah! We could take the yeti too. HimaLaLa's in the Bahamas!" piped in Ushka. And of course, that little rhyme sent the pixies into a roar of laughter, rolling on the floor in my foyer. HimaLaLa was what they called the yeti that secretly lived in a cave with Gruff.

"It is *not* a vacation! And it is *not* we!" I stomped my foot to get their attention.

Suddenly, four small disappointed faces looked up at me. My heart dropped, but there was just no way I could risk their little lives on this strange journey I was about to embark on, especially when I was unsure how it was going to turn out.

I explained to the pixies that I had to go back to Gwynf'l, their homeland too, as it were, but it was too dangerous a trip for them to take, and I was going to be on a very tight schedule. I told them there was nothing there for them anyway, just sad memories.

"I should be back before the May Day fest, but I'll make some faerie cakes, and keep them in the freezer, just in case. Cyllene can let you in. She can get through the keyhole to unlock the door. And Mat has a key, so he can, too. Now why don't you help me pack?"

They all gleefully nodded their heads and scampered off into the kitchen.

I got a large box, some tape and string, and sent the pixies to gather bundles of loose paper to pad the box. Gathering things was a specialty of theirs: ribbons, strings, paper, and sometimes, carelessly, other people's jewelry.

I had printed off a calendar and marked what I thought would be a fairly accurate timeline. Even though the Court could help delay the ward's effects that would otherwise wipe my memory of Havenwood Falls, I didn't want to take any chances. Besides, I felt uncomfortable leaving the pixies for more than a month. I had a few ideas of what kind of trouble they could get into without supervision.

I placed the calendar in the box and went to get my crystal ball. I wrapped the brocade cloth that the ball sat upon carefully around the glass orb. There was plenty of cloth, but I said a small prayer to the spirits anyway that it would be protected.

When I returned to the box in the kitchen, the little sprites had already filled it halfway with balls of crumpled paper. I placed the covered sphere gently into the bed of padding.

Next, I went up to the attic to retrieve my stash of faerie dust. In the northwest corner of the attic sat the expertly handcrafted box made of various woods, smoothly polished and gleaming in the ray of light that cracked through the attic window. It was about fourteen inches long, five inches wide, and three inches deep. I passed my hand over the keyless latch of silver and abalone. The latch snapped open, and I inventoried my silk pouches of faerie dust, moving the small sachets about, and noticing the empty crevice in the bottom of the felt-lined box. The crevice seemed to have held something there long ago, but it was empty when my father gave me the box, telling me it was for my fae magic stuff. So I was never sure if that indentation was just a time-worn element or it was meant for something. Anyway, I was satisfied the dust was sufficient for my journey, so I closed up the box, passed my hand over the latch again, and it abruptly snapped shut.

I climbed down from the attic, released the access door, then went into my bedroom to get a silk scarf to wrap around the box and a few articles of clothing I would need for the trip.

By the time I returned, the packing box was now completely filled with paper balls, and there was no room for the items I had come down with.

"I need to put these in there too," I told them, holding up my armload of essentials in emphasis. "You will need to take some of this packing paper out."

With that, eight small hands began picking out the crumpled balls, and the next thing I knew they were lobbing them at one another, first as a game of catch, then they were throwing them at one another, then, yes, you guessed it, they were on the floor wrestling.

It's a pixie life. I sighed and shook my head. Once all the items were in the box and it was ready to close up, I realized I should cover it in craft paper, and went back up to the attic to get the large roll of brown wrapping paper. I could hear the pixies giggling and whispering, and could only hope they didn't make more of a mess before I came back down.

While up in the attic, I heard Enya holler up that they were leaving, and Ushka wishing me a safe trip, then Tierri's "me too" and Aieri's "me three." Of course, Enya added "me four." Another squeal of laughter, and I could hear the door slamming closed behind them.

Now where did I put that roll of craft paper?

I checked all the usual storage bins, and generally I was very organized, but it had been a very long time since I'd used it. At last, I found the cylinder under the bed that my "nephew" Mat had made his for a time.

I carried that back down the attic ladder, then down the stairs to the first floor. The kitchen was still strewn with paper, most of it in shreds now, but the pixies were gone, and a little peace and quiet was restored.

I sealed up the box, wrapped it in the craft paper, then tied it all securely with the string. With a black marker, I wrote my name on the package, then "c/o Rebecca Smyth" and her address. I would call her first to let her know to expect it.

The Smyth family was my second mother's family. I kept in touch with the family line through the ages, but because they were human, each time I had to tell the next family I was a descendant of Ian McFeeny and their great-great-great aunt, who was also a Rebecca. Mother Rebecca unfortunately died in childbirth, with a stillborn no less. It was great sadness for the Smyths, but each family had always been gracious to me, nevertheless.

After my father's marriage to Rebecca Smyth ended with her death, he found his next wife in Toronto, my third mother. After my mother's death and our exodus from Gwynf'l, the great King Ian was not so much the faerie king anymore. Once he met Rebecca, he found he had a penchant for the touch of human flesh, and just continued to marry one human woman after another, including my fifth mother, Tess, whom he had met in the States, and finally settled in Havenwood Falls. After Tess died, I guess my father just gave up, or maybe he really did love her, but he died only a few years later.

Cripes! I have to tell Gruff that I'm bringing Coralie to Havenwood Falls. Ugh, this is not going to be pleasant.

Father was going to leave Grenfold, now known as Gruff, under his rock when we were leaving Gwynf'l. This was the one and only time I stood up to my father. I refused to leave without him. Gruff would always be my family, even if Father disowned him. Even if he was a troll.

~

I picked up the package and carried it out the door, headed toward Addie's house. I was greeted by one of her familiars, a small dragon named Leia, who sniffed me up and down, then hopped off to get her mistress.

Oh my gosh, she's so adorable. I hope they're right, and she doesn't grow very big.

I explained to Addie that I needed to ship this package overseas, but it needed a spell so that its contents could not be detected. She asked me why didn't I just do it myself, since I could glamour anything with my faerie magic.

"I have to be in its presence to work the glamour. This package will be out of my powers' reach."

Addie was a whiz at all kinds of spells, being a Beaumont *and* an Augustine. Saundra, her grandmother, sat on the High Council of the Luna Coven, and had been grooming her for that position. Addie accepted the challenge, so I left the package with her and set off to see Gruff.

Once behind Addie's house, I looked around to make sure there were no humans that could see me, then I shimmered. The air around me began to waffle, and I started to become translucent, waving into that shimmering air, until I was more and more translucent, then completely gone.

My entrance at the front of Gruff's cave was the same as my exit from Addie's yard, but in reverse. As soon as I was opaque and the air stopped shimmering, I called out for him.

My dear malformed brother hobbled out of the cave. That little glimpse of light that flashed in his eyes when he saw me appeared briefly, before the black sullen lumps of coal took their place.

"Gruff, I have something to tell you. Please don't be mad at me." I could barely face him, but I mustered up the courage. "I'm going to Gwynf'l to bring Coralie back here."

That agonizing moan of centuries ago I had to endure again at this moment as Gruff's response echoed throughout his cave. The painful roar bounced off every rock and crevice in the hole.

He grabbed his head as if it were about to explode and could only say "NO NO NO," with his poor malformed mouth chock full of disfigured teeth.

"Gruff, I have to! Coralie's life is in danger. I have to . . . *We* have to protect her!"

Gruff's black eyes became glossy. Although the poor troll could not cry, it was evident he was weeping inside. "NO SEE ME!"

"No, I won't let her see you. I won't even tell her you're here, if you don't want me to. She doesn't even know you're still alive. I'm going to place her in Peacock Lake, so you may want to stay away from there. But we have to do this, okay?"

I felt my brother's heartache, his shame, his loss. I so wished there was some way I could help him. Some potion I could make to relieve his anguish.

Gruff just nodded reluctantly, sadly, and hobbled back into the cave.

I couldn't shimmer out of there fast enough. I felt so guilty, a lump caught in my throat, and my stomach knotted into a giant hard ball.

The shimmering knocked out a couple of hours in my day. That's a little problem with shimmering—there was stipple in that ripple—and I never knew if it was going to be a few minutes lost, or hours, or possibly even days. On occasion, it worked the opposite, and I would be given time to spare, or just have to wait until the rest of the world caught up with me. But not often, and I never knew which way it would go.

I had to get to the Court of the Sun and the Moon and get my passport before City Hall closed, and of course to request a delay in the memory ward, if possible.

I walked down Stuart to Eighth Street, then north to get to the entry behind City Hall. I pulled the heavy metal door emblazoned with the Court's insignia open, and pushed myself through the opening I had managed.

Lucky for me, Addie, or Adelaide Beaumont to the snooty old people, was at the door to the courtroom. She looked over her black-rimmed glasses, smiled, and waved at me to come over.

I still can't get the vision of her dressed up for Halloween as a sexy Stormtrooper out of my head.

"Okay, your package is spellbound!" she said, delighted with her own word play.

Even I laughed. "That's pretty good, Addie! I'm really running short of time. Could you possibly take this over to the OutPost for me?"

While the OutPost projected the image of a normal postal and overnight delivery store for the humans, Cerberus Delivery Inc. did the actual shipping in and out of town. CDI was kind of like Havenwood Falls' very own import/export company, owned by the leaders of an outlaw motorcycle gang, but we tended to ignore that little tidbit.

"Sure thing, Madame Tahini. Anything else you need?"

"I need to get a passport. Mayor Stuart said I could pick it up here."

Addie pointed to a door behind the Court's podium, and I followed her fingered direction. The courtroom was a "charming" place. Doors appeared and disappeared depending on their necessity.

Barbie was standing in the hallway, whispering with a ravishing caramel-skinned woman, whom I recognized as Qadira, the djinn that Roman Bishop had enslaved, though of course, I was not supposed to know that.

Barbie raised her right index finger to her lip when she spied my entrance. That was my signal that I never speak of this.

Yes, the scene looked a bit like a conspiracy. Barbie bade the amazingly sexy Qadira farewell, and I swear I heard both of them snicker, you know like that girlie confidante kind of snicker. Quadira poofed—vanished—and Barbie escorted me into a small room stationed just to the left of the door I had walked through just a few moments before.

As I entered, Roman stood up and held his arms out in a welcoming gesture, which was pretty scary, if you asked me. Like Barbie, he was perfectly manicured, and exquisitely suited to the max in what must have been a hand-tailored coat, probably Italian, but then his enterprise reached all over the world, so who knew.

Roman welcoming (and I used that term loosely) anyone other than a Bishop was more than just weird. He was usually surly and had no compunction to use his powerful mage abilities, even over other Court members. I was not about to offend him, so I walked into the small room to his opened-arm greeting, and gave him a perfunctory hug, as he wrapped his arms around my tiny frame in response. He was creeping me out.

Maybe he's on drugs?

"Barbara has been filling me in on some needs you have to make a trip across the pond. All we need now is a picture for your passport. We are quite up to date on the Homeland Security requirements, and since you've never had one issued to you, we of course have to alter a bit of your information, say like your date of birth! Haha!"

Roman making a joke was beyond a little eerie. But okay, though I did catch a little twitch under his left eye. *Is he lying or is he just uncomfortable?*

Barbie cleared her throat in an attention-getting way. It worked.

"Oh yeah, and I believe we have a little spell we need to expel so the ward doesn't get in the way of your wandering," he added, with another little strange chuckle.

He's definitely on drugs!

Roman had his own family, and they had their own issues. But this was sooooo out of character for him to be pandering to me with his play on words that my skin was beginning to break out in those tiny foretelling bumps all over again.

Barbie rolled her eyes, gave me a quick knowing wink, then nodded and smiled. I wondered if she had made a pact with the devil here. However, the nod and smile was my cue that I was good to go.

Roman then instructed me to go to the room across the hall, where I could to take a "glamour shot" for my passport. Ugh, another pun from Roman?

It must've been Qadira. She had to have put a spell on him.

BRAND NEW PASSPORT IN HAND, I was practically skipping home. As I crossed Town Square Park, I tossed a penny into the gold-flecked fountain and made a wish, just in case.

I was now ready to make my airline reservation. As soon as I got home, I went straight to my computer, pulled the tapestry access door down, and fired up the hard drive. I found a flight and booked a one-way ticket, since I wasn't exactly sure yet how I intended to get back home with Coralie. I then emailed my itinerary to Barbie.

In the parlor next to the kitchen, I lit a cozy fire in the hearth, sat down in the plush chair across from the fireplace, and pulled my cell phone out of my pocket. I dialed the overseas number for Rebecca Smyth. I hoped I wasn't calling too late, as it would be about nine p.m. there.

A lilting voice with a heavy Irish brogue answered the other end. "Smyth residence. Rebecca here."

"Hello, Rebecca! This is Siobhan McFeeny calling. How are you?"

"Siobhan, how lovely to hear from you. I'm doing quite well, thank you for asking. And you?"

"A bit busy lately. I have to make a trip to Belfast, and I'm on a tight schedule. I've sent a package to your home, if that's okay. Could you hold it for me until I arrive? I should be arriving Wednesday."

"Well, of course, my dear. It will be delightful to see you. Will you be staying here?"

"Oh no, just passing through, unfortunately. But I can certainly stay long enough to share a spot of tea."

We continued with a few pleasantries and catching up with her family tree. I bid farewell and placed my phone back in my pocket.

Closing my eyes for a moment, I basked in the warmth of the fire on my face, feeling pretty satisfied with my arrangements.

Yikes! I almost forgot. I still have to make faerie cakes for the pixie sisters.

Barbie called me first thing the next morning and offered to drive me to Denver International, knowing how likely I was to get motion sickness on the bus. I gladly accepted the offer, relieved but aware the canyon trip was still going to be a white-knuckled ride for me.

CHAPTER 5

$\mathcal{T}$he flight to the UK was uneventful and far more relaxing than the ride in Barbie's Maserati through the mountains. I had no idea how Barbie got the Maserati (and was sure I didn't want to know), or even how she managed to get her long legs and tall hair into the vehicle, but she did, and it seemed to suit her.

I was actually able to sleep some on the plane, with it being a red-eye flight. It worked out perfect for me landing at Heathrow. I only had a short layover, enough time to grab a breakfast tea and scone, before I picked up the second leg to Belfast.

Addie had downloaded the Uber and Lyft apps on my phone and showed me how to use them, so I wouldn't have to bother with exchange rates while moving around in a foreign country. The apps were so easy to use, and I had no idea there was such a thing, even though Addie said we had our own Luber in Havenwood Falls. How cool was that?

The apps came in handy when I arrived in Belfast. Only moments after going through customs, I was picked up by Evan, a blue-eyed redhead. I gave him Rebecca Smyth's address and was whisked off from the airport to a little section on the edge of the city. The driver said he couldn't take me all the way to the door, the road being one-way in the wrong direction, but it was only a few steps away from this intersection. I only had my carpet bag with me, and that was pretty lightweight, since most of what I needed was hopefully sitting in a carton at Rebecca's flat. I let him know I could easily walk it, and thanked him for the ride.

I rang the bell at Rebecca's door, and a diminutive young woman answered. She was just a few inches taller than me, unlike most of the Irish I had seen on the ride to her place. But it was no surprise, as my father had the small stature of the fae, and his tastes ran the same way when choosing his human brides, so that he appeared taller and stronger than those wonderful women.

Rebecca had the unblemished pale skin of her great, great ancestor, with just a small sprinkle of freckles across the bridge of her nose. She wrapped her arms around me, giving me a generous hug, then led me into her hallway.

I spied my package on the floor next to her entryway table, and was relieved that it had arrived safely.

Rebecca and I sat in her parlor for about an hour, sipping tea and reminiscing about our families. She pulled out an old family album, and all the women seemed to resemble the Rebecca I recalled as my second mother. It was so sad she died in childbirth along with her baby. Fortunately, she had a large family to carry on her memory.

After tea, Rebecca asked if I wanted to open the package. I told her it only contained papers and books, and nothing I really needed right away. It was light enough for me to carry, so I just needed to get to the fishing marina. I told her I had been researching my genealogy and discovered my father still had kin on the Isle of Gwynf'l, and I was headed there next.

Rebecca offered to take me to the marina, and I welcomed the invite, as I already had to deal with enough strangers in a strange land as it was. She dropped me off at the fisherman's pier, and I toddled my way down the deck with my carpet bag slung over my shoulder and my package in my arms. I asked a few of the fishermen if they knew where the Isle of Gwynf'l was. The first two just looked at me dumbfounded and shook their heads.

The third one, however, said, "Aye, go see Patrick at slip thirteen. E's gotta partner 'oo fishes outta da Bay o' Gwynf'l. Goes there of'en."

I thanked him profusely and scurried down to the slip numbered thirteen. Fortunately, Patrick was just loading up gear into his skiff.

I asked him if he could take me to the isle, and he informed me that it just so happened he was headed there today, and I could join him, no charge.

For his kindness, I slipped a little faerie dust onto his fishing rods while he wasn't looking, to give him some extra luck with his catch today.

The salt breeze was refreshing as we sailed through the Belfast harbor, down the strait and across the Irish Sea to get to the Isle of Gwynf'l.

Patrick had barely placed a hook into the waters when a great fish grabbed his bait and took off with what the poor fish thought would be a delightful breakfast. He even caught a huge king mackerel that was nearly half the size of me. Someone was eating well tonight.

The weather was cooperative, and the sails set just so to glide us toward our destination. It was truly great luck, since Patrick spent most of the expedition reeling one fish in right after another.

"Are you a leprechaun?" he asked me. "You even look like one, and you are certainly my lucky charm today."

I just smiled and wished him continued good luck.

Patrick sailed his small fishing boat up to the rickety pier in the small fisherman's village located on the Bay of Gwynf'l. His partner was waving at him, and Patrick was waving an overloaded skein of fish back at him, showing off his fantastic luck.

I again thanked the young fisherman, then daintily stepped out of the boat and onto the pier, my tapestried satchel over my shoulder and craft-paper-covered carton in hand, as his friend took my elbow to help me out.

I quickly made my way through the little village and wandered toward the hills in the north, where the shamrock glen bordered upon my ancient family home.

Alone in the glen, I sat on a large rock and began to untwine the wrapped package that held my precious items. Slowly, I pulled the tape off the packaging and folded back the craft paper to lift the lid off the box.

I was knocked off the rock by Enya and Tierri, who jumped out of the box screaming, "Surprise!"

Next, I found Aeiri and Ushka doing a jig around me, and all of them chanting, "I'm the Belle of Gwynf'l in the Dell of Gwynf'l!"

Wow! Did that bring back ancient memories. I taught them that little rhyme over half a millennium ago as they used to dance through the thick shamrock fields that flocked this glen.

"What have you done, you sneaky little stowaways? I have so much to do and so little time. How am I going to get back home in time, now that I have you munchkins to deal with?"

"We can help!" cried out Ushka.

"You need us!" stated Tierri, as she stomped her little pixie foot firmly on the ground.

The other two just mimicked the first two, then they all went back into their little jig and chant, as they picked through the field of green clover, sticking clumps of the three-leafed plants into their hair.

How I could use a four-leafed clover just about now, or maybe even a leprechaun to rein in these imps.

"I'm going to look around. Don't dare leave the glen!" I commanded the unwelcome travelers. They all giggled at me, then started a rumpus in the patch of shamrock. Okay, that would keep them busy for a while. And, generally, they were pretty good at following my orders; well, at least for a few minutes.

I was planning on heading up to my family's cottage, if it was still standing, which to our clan was the Crown Seat. Then I realized the rock the unexpected and exuberant pixie sisters knocked me off of was the same one my dear brother Grenfold, then turned into my poor Gruff, had crawled under as my father had ordered.

I thought maybe there might have been something under the rock that could ease some of poor pitiful Gruff's pain. Even after all these eons, I carried such tormented grief that there was nothing I could have done to stop my father from his cruel sentence. If I could have, then maybe Grenfold would still be my handsome, talented faerie brother and maybe the king of our fae, or my mother Rose and even my father might still have been alive. My heart ached so badly, I could hardly breathe.

The rock turned out to be, well, just a rock. There was a small gulley furrowed under it, which I assumed was formed by my brother's clawing and crawling. Just the thought of his damnation made my own fingernails hurt. I looked down at my hands, and there was blood and dirt crusted around my nails.

The empath in me returns.

The sun began to set in the west of the isle, but just as the glazing ball of gas was approaching the tips of the western mounts, a ray of light shone on something that gleamed in that gulley.

I forced my aching fingers down to the tip of that shining piece and felt a smooth round stone. It felt like there was some rod or branch attached to it. Regardless of the pain, I dug deeper with my bare hands into that gulch, and was able to grab the stick attached to the spherical rock that sat atop it.

I had to push my shoulder against the boulder, and I prayed to my faerie spirits to help me move it just enough.

I heard a thunderclap in the distance as the stone budged a centimeter or so, but lo, it was enough to get a grip on the handle of that stick and pull it out from where it had been buried for hundreds of years.

Thank you, spirits!

My shoulder ached, inflamed with the effort of pushing

against that blasted boulder, but I held in my hand something I had not seen since that fateful day my father placed his curse on my brother.

The tip of my father's faerie wand! His king's scepter shone brightly in the fading sunlight, as if never encumbered by centuries of earth and rain. The staff was of finely polished ebony, a gift from his brethren of Belize, and that too remained unmarred.

Such is the way of fae wonders.

Some of my history started to make sense. After my mother Rose died, my father, other than gathering his clan and moving westward to the newfound land, never used his wand again. A bit of faerie dust here and there, when necessary, but I never saw his wand again.

I held the charmed scepter in my hand, knowing inherently that no one, other than I, could use it. I was the last of this fae family, not including Gruff, of course, but since he had been cursed to be a troll, he was no longer Grenfold, the would-be heir to the throne of McFeeny fae.

Damn my father!

Then I had this sinking feeling, like my heart had just dropped into my stomach. I couldn't really identify it, but suddenly my heart ached for my father. I didn't have time for him. There were two souls damaged by that cursed curse—Grenfold's and Coralie's.

Once again, I was thrown into this turmoil of wondering if there was something I could have done. Maybe my failure to act was what really brought all this pain to my family.

Stop wallowing in self-pity, Teeny Weeny! You've got work to do.

I pulled out a silk scarf from my skirt pocket (all of my clothes have wonderfully deep pockets, thanks to Nina), carefully wrapped the heirloom in the scarf, and placed it back in my pocket.

The pixies were heavily engaged in dancing and rolling around in the shamrock, and I was grateful it kept them occupied. Gwynf'l, unlike most other lands in and around the Irish Sea, still remained charmed. The weather was quite mild for early April, the spring spirits obviously favored the land, and spring seemed to arrive much earlier than in most parts of this world.

I dug around in my carpet bag and pulled out my "crystal ball" to summon Seamus. He needed to connect with Coralie and let her know I was here. I would meet with her tomorrow at the point.

It was weird that I'd never thought to pair my ball with her pearl. Maybe I was afraid Father would then turn me into a troll, too. Maybe I was always *too* afraid.

I started, "Tahini McFeeny, Famous Seamus," praying to the spirits that he was receptive to my call. After several chants, the ball began to swirl into shades of green, and my dear uncle's face appeared through the rounded glass.

"Ah, Siobhan, my favored niece!"

Sheesh, I'm his only niece.

"Uncle Seamus! I'm here on Gwynf'l! Have you connected with Coralie?"

"Ah yes, lassie, that I have. She has been anticipating your arrival."

"Please let her know I will meet her at the point of the isle when the sun is directly above."

"I will do that, my dear! Stay safe! We all look forward to your return."

That was strange. What did he mean by "we all"? Only his son Mat was in Havenwood Falls. He must've meant it as a universal.

I whistled—well, it was sort of a whistle. It was a sound I could emit through my lips and teeth that only the pixie sisters could hear, kind of like a dog whistle, and generally they responded. Fortunately, as the sun was beginning to set over the mounts of the west side of the isle, they actually did respond, and the four little imps were by my feet in a matter of minutes.

I led the girls to the east side of the glen, where a thatched cottage sat, a bit dilapidated with a mountain goat perched on the roof, noshing on the few strands of decaying hay that still remained.

Ha! This is my family's castle. Our throne, our kingdom. So much different from Havenwood Falls, yet in so many ways, so much the same.

"Leave the goat alone!" I warned them. "We need to eat and get some rest. There is a lot to do tomorrow, and we have to head back home."

"Home, home sweet home!" Tierri started a chorus. Suddenly, the humble abode was filled with the shrill shrieks of four pixies competing in rounds, like a frickin' Christmas carol, "Home, home sweet home."

Dear gods and goddesses, spirits of the glen, give me patience and guidance.

Just in case, or just because I love faerie cakes, I'd also packed a few of them in my carpet bag (it was going to be a long flight, but since I slept through it, they went uneaten). I had also stashed some scones, compliments of Rebecca. This was the fare and sustenance of my people, and so we were well nourished for the night.

CHAPTER 6

The morning greeted me with a bright ray of light from the eastern opening that posed as a window, sans glass. I blinked several times, trying to adjust my eyes to the new day's dawn.

Extremely loud snoring exuded from the far southwest corner of the cottage's single room, where the pixie sisters were all cuddled together, arms and limbs wrapped around one another in a faerie knot that no human could untie. I was glad my little sprites slumbered, unencumbered with the prospect of what might lie ahead.

I calculated that I had about four hours before the sun would peak above the point.

Stepping outdoors, I surveyed my surroundings. The glen was a few miles northwest of the point, and I could shimmer there easily, with few repercussions, but it wasn't worth taking the chance, *just in case*, since time was of the essence. Especially since the pixies didn't have any extra protection from the wards of Havenwood Falls, as they had stowed away unknowingly.

While the pixies slept, I donned the outfit I had on yesterday, since I was traveling light and didn't need to impress anyone. For that matter, I could glamour or affect anything or anyone I came across, but I had already become honed to the human nature of the world.

I checked out the carpet bag and remembered there were silk pouches of magic flakes that I must certainly have with me. This was the magic I knew. It may not have been strong, but it had served me well through the ages.

～

THE TIME HAD COME. My pixie wards had filled themselves on faerie cakes and goat's milk (don't ask).

I led them down the glen and to the shores of the Bay of Gwynf'l. We took a sharp left to the east, to avoid the village. The pixies, apparently satiated, followed me as if they were a small regiment following their leader. Here's the crux: I *was* their leader; at least that's what they thought. And they could think no different, spirits bless these little souls.

I saw the sun rising above the point. Tierri, Aeiri, Ushka, and Enya were on the shore, partly picking through shells and mostly wrestling in the sand, but totally engrossed in the semblance of a family picnic at the beach.

As I cautiously worked my feet over the rocky precipice leading to the promontory, I noted a storm brewing to the south. The edge of the southern sky was beginning to darken as if someone was taking a paintbrush filled with black ink and splaying it across the southern hemisphere.

I began the song. My voice was weak and tired. I was not very much of a singer, at least not anymore, but the words and the melody were the same, and Coralie was expecting me.

Of fish and reef and coral down under
Of shells and earls and Oceana's wonders
A fair maiden with hair a blaze of red
Lives here amongst this watery bed
With magnificent tail she swims the sea
I call to my dear friend Coralie

I watched as a great wave gathered, with aqua-colored sea-foam atop, moving fairly quickly toward the point. That would have been Coralie preceded by her glorious ancestor Neptune's regalia.

Out of the blue-green waters that lapped the point, a pale, almost pearlescent face, poked out of the ripples, followed by a cascade of rich orangish-red wavy tresses of hair that took hold of each wavering ripple and seemed to follow them.

Big bright green eyes like emeralds blinked at me, as the long reddish eyelashes batted back the bright sunrays that blazed upon the sea and rock. Her large pearl hung at the base of her neck, shimmering in the sunlight.

Neither of us knew who should speak first. Coralie had once been my closest friend, centuries ago. My brother Grenfold would never have known her, if she had not been my ally, my confidante, the sister I did not have.

Oh great! Another wave of guilt to deal with.

"Coralie, it's time to come home. You need to be with those who love you most. Are you ready?"

Unexpectedly, Coralie replied, "I've always been ready."

Relieved that she didn't protest, I pulled a small silk packet of faerie dust from my bag, along with my Tell All Ball. I waved my hand over the ball, and a hole developed, about three inches in diameter. I knelt over the rocky jetty and scooped up a batch of seawater into the ball. I had "divined" a fishbowl out of my crystal globe.

Before I could sprinkle any fae powder onto the dear forlorn mermaiden, the storm that came beckoning from the south approached briskly.

A small fishing boat in the distance tried vigorously to paddle ashore. A tall, lean, well-endowed woman with stark black hair stood at the bow, barking orders at the poor sailor trying earnestly to fathom the impending storm. Her stance and demeanor were familiar to me. Although she and the small boat were nearly a mile down the shoreline, my keen sight and smell detected that it was none other than Shayin Pisik, the vicious cat-shifter-witch who had been sent to her place of origin in the Carpathian mountains, after trying to slay my dear nephew Mat. Or so I thought, but here she was. A huge lump grew in my throat at the sight of her, nearly choking me.

No sooner had the vessel reached the beach than Shayin, with supernatural strength, grabbed the unwitting rower by the collar, lifted him off his feet, and ruthlessly slung him far into the cold deep waters of the bay. The taste of bile rose from my churning stomach, from either fear or the awful scent of the cat-woman, or both, making me retch.

The sight of her, the smell of her, so like my dreams, made me shake uncontrollably. My dreams—my omens—were true. Had I arrived only a little later, I would have been too late. In fact, my trembling caused me to believe I may still have been too late to save Coralie. I was certainly no match for the likes of the Pisik.

The witchy creature caught sight of us, too. I could see her visibly twinge—not exactly recognizing me, because of the memory wards of Havenwood Falls, but a twinge of something. Then I realized—it wasn't me she was reacting to, but Coralie.

My heart began to pound relentlessly, filling my eardrums with the roar of its fast-paced rhythm, outmatching the speed of my shaking hands and knees.

She broke into an Olympian sprint across the sandy shore, and as she did, her long legs shifted into those of a large wild cat, and she continued to shift up her svelte upper body. As her arms became the front powerful legs of a feline, she moved to all fours, and her head became that of a black panther. Her speed increased astronomically with her new form, and she was nearing the point where I stood near Coralie rapidly.

So determined to "kill the fish," she obviously did not realize she was crossing the paths of the pixie sisters building little sandcastles on the beach, completely unaware of the invader. My stomach took another turn at seeing my dear wee ones in danger of being trampled by this fierce beast.

I swallowed back the acrid taste and gave out a sharp whistle. The pixies raised their tiny heads in time to see the large cat approaching only feet before them.

Immediately, the four sand covered imps jumped onto the furry back of the creature and sank their sharp little teeth into her back and shoulders. Enya threw sand into her eyes, and Aeiri hung on to the Pisik's tail for dear life—with her teeth. I was suddenly filled with so much pride, seeing these small creatures with such enormous bravery.

However, it did not take long for Shayin to regain her composure as she reached back and grabbed Aeiri off her tail with her fangs, and with a swift turn of her head, she tossed the pixie into the rolling waves. My little white-haired wonder bobbed helplessly, as Pisik's muscular tail swatted Tierri and Ushka off her back and stomped them into the beach with her large paws. Now these two were clawing fearfully to get out of the sandpit that Pisik had just fashioned for them.

She then batted Enya on the top of her head, sending the hotheaded pixie into the rocks that lined the shore. Enya appeared dazed at first, then began to get her footing back as she lifted herself from the rocks. But the she-cat swerved back to go after Enya, and I could see the fire in Pisik's eyes far outburned whatever little Enya could muster, as she sped toward her to put an end to my poor little ward.

That was enough.

I grabbed my father's wand out of my pocket and pointed it at the vile vixen.

"To Hell with you, Shayin Pisik!" I screamed at the top of my lungs as a bolt of lightning flew from the tip of the brightly glowing wand. The recoil from the wand was so strong that it knocked me off the point, and I was flailing backwards into the icy depths of the sea.

As I was falling, only one thought filled my mind:

I've failed! I've failed! I can't save anyone, not even myself.

I closed my eyes to accept my fate, as my poor brother did

centuries ago. But other than a spray of sea mist, I never felt the frigid grip of the waters. Instead, warm soft hands were holding me above the waves. I turned to look deep into Coralie's dark green eyes, and her beautifully soft smile shone upon me as she gently placed me back upon the rocky crag.

While a dark plume of black smoke rose high into the sky, dissipating into the jet stream above, I saw Tierra and Ushka brushing sand off of one another, and Aeiri twirling around as droplets of seawater flew from her pale pink skin. Enya was rubbing a blood-soaked spot on her head, but a huge smile on her face denied any pain. Then the four pixies broke into cheering and began dancing around in a circle.

I could almost hear the pixies singing "Ding-Dong! The Witch Is Dead" from *The Wizard of Oz*, but of course, that was my imagination. They were singing some faerie song of glorious joy.

I whistled once more to summon them to my side, and the four wandering minstrels came skipping toward me.

"You all were wonderful! So brave! I could not have done this without you!"

The pixie sisters beamed with pride and began patting each other on the back. Then the happy patting became a rabbit punch to one another's arms, and before one could count to three or four, they were all wrestling in the sand once again.

"Brother! Well, it's time to go," I said, so totally relieved that everyone was safe (if not exactly sound) as I tossed a sprinkling of faerie dust on the pixies just as a gentle wave lapped up to the shore, and the four wee women turned into four miniature minnows. I scooped them from the foamy remains of the retreating wave into my makeshift aquarium. I pulled a second packet of dust from my pocket and sprinkled that upon the waiting Coralie. She transformed into an iridescence of orange and white, with translucently flowing orange fins and tail, much like her hair appeared as a mermaid, becoming an elegant oriental Koi. She leapt out of the water and landed expertly in the Tell All Ball.

I waved my hand over the ball once more, and the opening

that had appeared to allow the water in now disappeared, the ball becoming a globe once again.

I plopped the ball and the wand into my carpet bag and headed back toward the glen and the thatched cottage, once my family home.

I lay down on a small cot that I covered with one of my oversized scarfs. Setting the carpet bag beside me, I took stock of the now five wards I was charged with.

Good night, my little sea urchins.

I fell into a deep sleep, so exhausted from it all, and so relieved my swimming serpents were all safe.

CHAPTER 7

I had no idea how long I slept, but I awoke with a sense of overwhelming urgency. The Isle of Gwynf'l is filled with mystery and magic, and time on the isle is among those wonders. Years could flash by in a heartbeat, and days could last forever. So much time had passed since last I was here, I had forgotten its many mysteries.

I could not waste any time getting home. I decided I would shimmer to Boston. At least I would be back in the States without dealing with customs, TSA, and Homeland Security, especially with a freaky ball of fish in my luggage, and a flashing wand that would not stop glowing.

It was risky. That was a far distance to shimmer, especially with the load I was carrying, but I had to take a chance and hope that the Stipple in the Ripple would work to my benefit. After all, I was heading west, and the time zone would be five hours earlier. Maybe this time I would get lucky and so would the days be earlier in this ripple.

~

IN BOSTON, my shimmering landed me in front of a People's

Bank near the pier. A digital sign at the top of the bank scrolled bright red letters reading, "TIME TO SAVE! IT'S MAY 13, 2019, 8:27 P.M."

Oh jeez and jezebel, I've lost an entire month with all this shimmering! How long was that magic supposed to last?

The stars above the bay sparkled in the velvety night sky as their reflection glittered upon the waters. The smell of fish and salty spray filled my nostrils as I took in the surroundings. I passed my hand over the water-filled ball, and the opening reappeared. I went to the end of the pier and sprinkled a little faerie dust on the graceful white and orange koi that was swimming in the ball of water. The koi leapt out of the ball, and as it splashed into Boston Harbor, she became the lovely sea maiden Coralie.

"Take a few minutes, Coralie, and stretch your tail. But we'll have to be leaving very soon."

A few more sprinkles on the guppies, and the pixies once again became their jabbing and jabbering selves.

"Where are we?" they all chimed in unison.

"We're in Boston. Back in the United States," I informed them.

"What's a Boston?" asked Aeiri.

"It's a cream pie!" answered Tierri.

As was their little pixie style, they all started jumping up and down, and ran around hollering, "Pie! Pie! My oh my!"

Now I had four tiny pixies rolling and wrestling down the pier. Before they could make enough ruckus to attract attention, I threw a handful of faerie dust at them, and the wrestling turned into a flapping of tiny fins and tails on the wooden deck of the pier. I scooped the four small fish into my hand and plopped them back into the crystal globe.

I sang out a few bars of Coralie's favorite song into the night, certainly not as beautiful as Coralie can sing, but sufficient for her to hear the call. The stunning mermaid, her scales looking diamond-studded as they glimmered in the moonlight and the reflecting stars, appeared in the ripples right below where I stood.

"Thank you, Siobhan! I needed that swim. Now let's go home."

Home? Where was that again? Ugh! I hope I'm heading in the right direction.

A dash of dust sprayed upon Coralie's lithe figure, and the mermaid jumped out of the harbor and transformed into the small oriental carp once again in mid-air, splashing into the globe in a perfect dive.

All my wards safe and sound in the Tell All Ball once again, I shimmered to Logan Airport.

Wards? There's something about that word. It nagged at my memory, but I couldn't seem to put my finger on it.

I had a ticket stub in my carpet bag that showed Denver as the place I had left from, so that must be where I had to go to get back to Heavenbark Springs. *No, that's not it. Haven Tree Waters?* I wasn't sure what my town's name was anymore! How could I not know that? Could the ripple have scattered my memory chip?

I had to get back to the beginning. That was all I knew, and the plane ticket was the closest I had to know where that was. So I went to the same airline that was stamped on that stub to book a flight.

The next one wasn't until morning, but it wasn't too costly—a couple of hundred dollars, and I still had a little over $450 in my pocket. It would give me a chance to rest and arrive early enough in Denver to figure out where I was supposed to go.

THE FLIGHT HOME was very turbulent. My stomach was so queasy, and my head was swimming in a storm of confusion. Speaking of swimming, I checked on my ball-turned-fishbowl to see how my little friends were doing. They appeared unaffected by the rock and roll of the plane's maneuvering through the turbulent skies, probably because their watery surroundings just flowed with the movements of the airplane.

A flight attendant caught me handling the aquatic crew, and questioned me about the ball.

"Oh look, it's like a snow globe. The fish are actually made of silicone, but they look so real, don't you think? I just had to have it." Hoping my response would be enough to satisfy the attendant's curiosity, I grinned up at her.

She nodded in agreement, and went to check on a passenger a few aisles back—I could hear retching and the rustling of a barf bag being manipulated.

My sentiments exactly, fellow traveler.

At last we landed, but my head did not stop swimming, and I wasn't even sure where we were. As I walked down the gangplank with my carpet bag held tightly to my chest, a large sign appeared that read *Welcome to Denver International Airport.*

Okay, good, I was in Denver, and on land, thank the gods and goddesses. But I wasn't completely sure why I was in Denver or really where Denver even was in connection with my home. I was still confused, but relied on that used plane ticket I found in my bag. The mountains I'd seen in the morning sun as we landed somehow felt right to me, too.

A brightly lit poster hung on the wall ahead, displaying a quaint town surrounded by mountains decked with ski runs. It looked almost familiar, but not quite. The sign advertised *Ski Aspen*. I wasn't sure where I was supposed to go—I still couldn't remember the name of my town—but this picture on the poster seemed to come so close to what I could recall that I thought maybe it was near my home.

I went to the restroom and ducked into one of the back stalls. There I pulled out the Tell All Ball turned fishbowl, and sprinkled some faerie dust onto the four circling minnows. One at a time, each minnow jumped out of the bowl and landed on the bathroom floor as a pixie. A little more dust on each of their heads, and they glamoured into four small, seemingly innocent children.

"Okay, we've got to get moving. Any of you have an idea of

where we need to go?" I asked, hoping maybe one of them would remember our hometown. I didn't even know why I thought any of them would remember, especially since they left home as stowaways, so they didn't get even get a smattering of ward magic to protect them.

Ah, that was it—ward, ward magic. That has something to do with why I can't remember home. I think.

While I was bending down to put the ball that still held koi Coralie back into my carpet bag, the four pixies crawled out under the stall door and took off.

Criminy, I need to run after these little imps like I need the hole I already have in my head.

As I exited the ladies' room, I caught sight of the men's room door closing, and what looked like a small pixie foot scooting inside. I looked around to see if the coast was clear, then ducked into the men's room to find Aeiri under the hand-dryer letting the warm air blow her cumulus locks around her face. Ushka was flushing the urinal and splashing around in the water.

"Look, Siobhan! I've never seen a fountain like this one before. Isn't it cool?"

"That's not a fountain! That's disgusting!" I pulled her out and placed her under the sink to soap her up.

Right at this moment, an older gentleman walked into the bathroom to find me and my tiny wards washing up.

"Sorry, sir. The girls can't read. We'll be out of here in a jiffy."

I pushed Ushka under the hand-dryer. Once dry, I grabbed both Aeiri's and Ushka's wrists and dragged them both out of the restroom.

"You two stay with me. We have to find Enya and Tierri."

Ushka pointed across the large corridor filled with rushing travelers heading to or from their gates. I spied Tierri at a café concession, licking the apples and oranges in the refrigerated bin.

Oh, for Heaven's sake and Hell's fury!

I grabbed Tierri's hand and yanked her away from the fruit

selections, and gave the cashier, who looked aghast, a ten-dollar bill to cover the Tierri-tainted treats.

"Where's Enya?"

Tierri, still licking her lips, pointed down the corridor to a large glass room, where Enya had her face pressed up against the glass.

Naturally, she's at the smoker's lounge, mesmerized by the curls of smoke and the little flames that fired up briefly and dashed out in an instant from the loungers' lighters.

Finally having rounded up all the wandering sprites, with my carpet bag slung over my shoulder, I followed the sign that directed me to ground transportation.

"Where to, lady?" the driver of the taxi we were ushered to asked.

"Umm, Aspen?" I responded.

"Wow, lady, that's a three-hour drive. Pretty steep fare for a cab ride. You don't want to take a bus?"

I looked down at my wayward wards and knew a bus ride with the four of them was out of the question.

"How much?" I gulped out the question.

"It'll be about half a K."

"Half a K? How much is that?"

"Five hundred, but the kids can ride for free, okay?"

Kids? Ha, if he only knew they were the ones he should be charging extra for.

"Yikes! Hold on." I fished around in my carpet bag to see what cash I still had left after the purchase of my plane ticket in Boston. I only had a couple of hundred dollars left, and that had to last me until I got back to the beginning. I felt around the bottom of the bag, and my fingers caught a plastic card lodged in the corner. I pulled it out and found what looked like a credit card, with the words *Havenwood Falls Savings & Loan* emblazoned on the shiny front of the card.

"Ah! Havenwood Falls, that's where I want to go! How far is that?"

"Sorry, ma'am. Never heard of it."

"Do you take debit cards?" If not, I could go back into the airport and find an ATM.

"Sure, not a problem. Still want to go to Aspen?"

"Absolutely!" I tossed the carpet bag into the backseat and guided the pixie sisters in along with it. I had a vague memory of a mountainous ride to Denver when I had left. The ride was eastward as the sun had begun to set behind us, and that trip seemed to take at least four hours, so Aspen just might have been close enough.

I handed him the debit card, as this was a trip he needed to be sure was prepaid.

The rugged looking cab driver—he kind of had that *I'm an ol' cowhand* look about him—ran the card, got the approval, and we were on our way.

CHAPTER 8

*T*he pixies had settled in the backseat right away, wrapped themselves around each other, and fell fast asleep. Except for their horrendous snoring, the long ride to Aspen was relatively peaceful.

The driver asked me about this unknown town of Havenwood Falls. Little clips of memories flashed in my mind, kind of like a movie reel with most of the frames skipping or missing. I couldn't tell him much really. It was a little like the picture I saw of Aspen, about the same size. The buildings were similar. I recalled gingerbread latticed Victorian homes, a town square with a large gazebo and a sparkling fountain, and thickly forested mountains surrounding the town. I started to tell him the people were very different, but my tongue got tied up before I could, and I wasn't even sure what exactly that meant.

Like me and the pixies, maybe?

He stopped in the center of town, next to an antique store. A good place to start, where I could ask people how to get to Havenwood Falls. I nudged the pixies awake, and they rubbed the sleepy sand out of their eyes. They tumbled out of the cab as I thanked the driver for the pleasant ride. He informed me he was going to check out some of the hotels and see if he couldn't pick up a fare back to Denver. I gave him a couple of twenties for a tip and wished him luck. The bills, having been nestled among some of my faerie dust, were likely to get him that fare in short course.

It was a bit of a risk, but I asked the pixies to split up in pairs and go into the shops to ask about Havenwood Falls. We were to meet right back here at the antique store in an hour. I pointed to a large vintage street clock at the corner of the sidewalk, and they eagerly nodded and headed in opposite directions, Tierri with Ushka, and Enya with Aeiri.

Earth with water, fire with air. May the spirits guide the sprites.

I started my inquiries in the antique store. There was a familiarity about the shop packed with old pieces of furniture, paintings, a rack of old-fashioned clothing, and bric-a-brac of all sorts and sizes. As I finagled my way through the boisterously positioned articles, trying not to knock anything over with my carpet bag, I came across a large painting of a rock jutting out of a tranquil body of water. The gold filigreed frame accented the sunlit sky reflected in the waters. Another ping in my memory banks— *Callie's? A picture of Coralie?*

An elderly shop attendant walked up to me and asked if she could help.

"Uh. Oh, sorry, by any chance do you know of Havenwood Falls? I think it may be somewhere near here."

"Havenwood Falls? Sounds intriguing, but I've never heard of it, and I've lived in these parts all my life. Hence the antiques." She giggled at her own joke. "I go out every weekend, generally a hundred miles or so in every direction, looking for that special treasure, but I don't recall ever being in a Havenwood Falls. Maybe I have, but I certainly have no recollection of it."

My disappointment was apparent to the kindly shop owner, so she suggested that I try the tourism bureau. Maybe I could locate the town on one of their various maps. She walked me out of the shop and pointed out the direction to the tourism bureau across the street and down two blocks.

I eyed the clock on the corner. I had another thirty minutes before meeting back with the pixies, gods willing. I headed toward the tourism bureau.

I passed by a pastry shop filled with delicious-smelling baked goods, by the scent emitting from its front door. My stomach rumbled, and I realized the pixies would be starving too, so I popped in to buy a few croissants and some sweet teacakes for the girls.

The dark-haired clerk at the counter had an interesting dragon tattoo that ran down her neck. A nose ring dangled from her left nostril in unison with another ring positioned on the end of her right eyebrow.

Maybe that's the kind of different I might've been telling the cab driver about?

After the clerk brought back a white paper bag filled with warm croissants and fondant covered treats, I took a chance and asked her if she knew of Havenwood Falls.

"Me and my guy take runs out on our bikes quite often. We love traveling through the mountains on the motorcycle, but really, I can't remember a place called Havenwood Falls. Maybe we did, but you know, so many little towns, they all kind of run into one another. Sorry, I can't remember it if we did."

Well, I tried. I paid for the pastries and headed out toward the Chamber of Commerce, where the tourism bureau was housed.

As I entered the three-story brick building angled on the corner, I spied a large map of Colorado hanging on the entryway wall. I went straight to the map and focused on the *YOU ARE HERE* marker. I ran my index finger along all the roadways through the area, looking for a star, a circle, or at least a dot, that signified a place called Havenwood Falls. There wasn't one.

A dark-skinned older man, a worker in a uniform with an embroidered *Aspen Chamber of Commerce* patch on the left side of his shirtfront, approached me and offered his assistance. The badge on his chest read *Brad*.

"Havenwood Falls? Sounds familiar, I think. There may be a bus that could take you there. Check it out at the bus station."

My eyes lit up, and I spun around with glee. When I completed my full circle, he was gone. I looked around at the other visitors, but Brad was nowhere in sight. I went to the visitor's desk and asked if they could find Brad for me, but the lady there said no one by that name worked here.

This was getting frustrating, to say the least.

A wall clock above the visitors desk warned me it was time to get back to the meeting place, assuming of course the pixies were paying attention to the time rather than fighting or playing amongst themselves.

Wonders of all wonders, I found four little tots punching each other on the arms when I arrived back at the antique shop. They stopped immediately upon the sight of me, and ran to me, grabbing my legs and hugging them so tight, I nearly lost feeling in my lower limbs.

"Okay, okay! We're all here! Anyone find out anything?"

Four mop-heads shook their tiny heads *no* in unison. Well, at least I had ghostly Brad's suggestion to go on.

So the five of us—well six, counting Coralie still housed in the fish-globe, smuggled away in my *rug*-ged bag—made our way down the aspen-lined street, heading for the bus station.

As we turned the corner, we came across an old-fashioned firehouse. A Sparky look-alike Dalmatian lay at the front door, licking his private parts.

How nice!

A small white sign with red edging and red lettering read *In an Emergency, Dial 9-1-1.*

Oh my gods and goddesses, why didn't I think of that? This is an emergency!

Once more, I fished into my carpet bag, no pun intended, and felt for my cell phone.

Although I really wasn't sure who would be on the other end when I called, there was something about 9-1-1 that rang a loud bell in my head, which probably sounded like the big red bell that was positioned over the red-lettered sign.

I looked at the phone, and three bars showed in the upper left corner.

Great! I have a signal!

I immediately dialed 9-1-1.

A worried woman's voice picked up and said, "Oh my gosh, Teeny Weeny! Are you okay? I've been worried sick about you!"

Teeny Weeny? This was no emergency operator, no "What's Your Emergency?" question. In fact, it was a much more informal answer, and the person on the other end seemed to already know what my emergency was.

"Who is this?"

"It's Barbie, Barbara Stuart, your best friend! Siobhan, are you okay? I think the memory spell kicked in, and the extension magic may have worn off!"

Well, she did say Siobhan this time. So I'm guessing she knows me.

"Where are you, Siobhan? We need to get you back to Havenwood Falls ASAP!" the voice on the other end added insistently. "You have family here! I mean more family, and then there's—" and she cut off.

Now she said that town name, Havenwood Falls. I must have known this Barbie woman. I was feeling like maybe I could trust her. Right now, there weren't many people I thought I could.

"Okay, assuming I know you, assuming you are my best friend . . . I'm in someplace called Aspen. But no one seems to know where or what Havenwood Falls is or how to get there."

"Well, of course not! You are so way out of the twenty-five mile ward radius around Havenwood Falls. You stay put! I'm going to send your nephew Mat to get you. You can all fly home as soon as he finds you."

"Havenwood Falls—no one seems to know where or what it is —but you are telling me this town has an airport?"

She did mention my nephew Mat, who was really my cousin, son of my aunt and uncle in Canada. It sounded like she knew something about him—that he was an owl shifter.

"No, silly, I mean Mat's owl will come and get you, and you can faerie-fly yourself home."

She knows Mat! She knows me!

I agreed to the plan, and she directed me on how to get to the Aspen National Park entrance. Mat would pick us up there.

⁓

IT WAS NEARING dusk as the pixie sisters and I arrived at the entrance to the park. I found a park bench to sit down on and let the pixies go climb the tall pine trees. This was the kind of environment that suited them well.

The sky darkened, and a sliver of moon shone in the night sky like a Cheshire cat's grin. Across the inky black sky, I saw a white bird coming nearer and nearer, with the pale moonlight bouncing off its outstretched wings.

Mat! Mathew! Mateus! Mathieu! (That last one is always pronounced like a sneeze, like Ma-choo!)

The handsome snowy white owl alit beside me. His amber eyes, like glowing Japanese lanterns, acknowledged me with such a sense of affection, it overwhelmed me.

I wrapped my teeny weeny arms around my rescuer, then noticed coming right behind him, out of the dark night sky, a glowing, iridescent green moth, the moonlight fully accentuating her glorious wings.

Mat turned his owl head in that eerie, nearly full-circle manner to eye the beautiful creature that trailed behind him, and nodded as he stretched out his wings and began to morph into the tall, bronzed beautiful human of himself.

He's amazing!

"Aunt Siobhan!" Now his large muscular arms wrapped around my whole body and lifted me well off the ground. Hearing his voice, the pixie sisters scrambled down their climbing posts. "And the pixies, too?" He shook his head, his white locks swinging as he chuckled. "Why am I not surprised?" He gestured at the beautiful moth. "I brought Cyllene along with me. She is one of your oldest friends. She always knows the way home. After all, that is where she was born, long before any of us ever came to Havenwood Falls. I'll take the pixies back to Havenwood Falls on my back, and carry your luggage for you. Effervesce, and Cyllene will guide you home."

Mat laid out the instructions for getting back to the *beginning* —back to *home*!

After Mat transformed himself back, in his glorious manner of turning from hair and muscle into feather and wing, I disenglamoured the four tots into their wee selves, and they all crawled through the down of the wings of this magnificent bird and onto his back, eager for the flight of their lives.

I'm pretty sure it is the flight of their lives!

Mat took flight into the moonlit sky with his four tiny passengers, grabbing the handles of my trusty carpet bag in his strong claws as he lifted off the ground.

Cyllene, who Mat had explained was a minuscule dryad, the soul of a tree, was buzzing and humming in a nagging way, urging me to effervesce. Although I could not really understand her, I knew instinctively that if I effervesced, I could become my flying fae-sized self.

I nodded and then my long brown hair began to turn solid white, starting from the ends and moving toward the roots. Once my hair became totally white, my skin paled, and the forest lit up with a light so bright that prismatic colors from all that whiteness bounced off the dark green needles, throwing the light into this small glade, making it like a ballroom with one of those mirror-type chandeliers. Thousands of small, effervescent bubbles began to rise from my neck, arms, and legs, and then I heard the familiar fizzle and a pop.

I now stood next to the mothy nymph who was perched on the park bench. I was just a head taller than her—my now teeny weeny head—but I was ecstatic to be able to look her in those stunning multicolored eyes of hers. I gave her a kiss on her colorfully pallored cheek. I couldn't help it; I felt so happy to be with someone who truly felt like a dear friend.

"Ready to go home, Siobhan?"

"Oh yes, Silly Annie!" *That* Silly Annie *just popped out of my mouth from nowhere.*

"I mean Cyllene," I added, making sure I pronounced it properly. *The Rain in Spain . . .*

She smiled, assuming I corrected myself purely for her benefit.

CHAPTER 9

*I*t felt as if we were sailing as Cyllene and I floated through the deep dark velvet night. She did indeed know exactly where she was going, and though I could fly much faster than her, I trailed back, allowing her to be my pilot and navigator. After all, I was the one who was lost.

Her bright luminescent wings were sails against a calm, unfathomable blue sea of night. I could never be so happy to follow those beautiful flowing tails of her wings, glowing in the incandescent moonlight.

The two of us flew through the protective ward of Havenwood Falls. Cyllene was unaffected, as she had predated by eons the founders who created the wards in the first place. I, however, felt an *almost* imperceptible squishy feeling, as if I had pierced a bubble, which was accompanied by a nearly inaudible *pop*. It was a sensation that I could only describe as a combination of my shimmer and my effervescing, if they could be combined. As soon as we passed through, my memories of my home returned fully, as though they'd never been gone.

Weird!

I would have expected Cyllene to lead me back to my townhome and shop on Main Street, but she did not. A little turn to the left past City Hall, and we arrived in front of a large Victorian style mansion. I recognized it immediately as the mayor's home. My mayor, my Barbie Stuart, my best friend (not counting Cyllene—or Coralie, for that matter).

How many "bests" can one have? Regardless, I must be home, because now everything is familiar.

As I alit on the bottom step of those leading up to the front porch of the mayor's mansion, Cyllene perched on the post of the railing. I effervesced with that same pop and fizzle, only now those clear bubbles were filling up with colors and growing much larger, as I morphed into my Madame Tahini, Teeny Weeny, Havenwood Falls demeanor. The voice I had heard on my cell phone in Aspen preceded the tall, large-haired Wonder Woman–looking person who stepped out onto the front porch.

She stooped down and immediately hugged me and lifted me off the stoop with ease, raising me way above her head, as if I were nothing more than a carnival toy.

Okay, granted I'm of small stature but REALLY? Barbie still hasn't told me everything, dragon pendant or not!

It was so good to be home. Now I felt like Dorothy in *The Wizard of Oz*. Yet there was still so much unfinished business. I still had a poor mermaid that was trapped in the body of somebody's pet fish. I still had my poor brother, trapped in the body of a troll. I still had this uneasy feeling that my father's power sat in my bag, uncomfortably vibrating emissions that I couldn't even grasp.

I now needed to just go to my home, my shop, my little townhome, my bed, my most comforting surroundings.

I begged Barbie's forgiveness for needing to leave so quickly. She never said a word, just set me down and turned me toward the direction of my shop on Main.

Now that is the definition of a true friend. They know what you need when you need it.

I opened the heavy wooden door to my townhome, feeling so exhausted that even pulling it closed seemed to be a great exercise.

I heard familiar snoring resounding from the living parlor and found the pixie sisters all nestled in the overstuffed chair in front of the hearth. Mat was fast asleep on the settee, with his long legs dangling over the arm of the sofa. Even Cyllene had found a spot on the back of the settee to rest her weary head.

I went upstairs to my bedroom, where Mat had already placed my carpet bag. I would have to unpack, but not tonight.

Donning my comfortable flannel nightgown, I fell back on the down-filled mattress and was out.

~

I AROSE the next morning to find Mat in the kitchen, already brewing a cup of tea for me. He had sent the pixies back home to their forest haven with the faerie cakes from the freezer and sent Cyllene back to Maximus, her soul tree. The young owl shifter wisely knew I could use a little peace and quiet.

The two of us sat down at the kitchen table. I gave Mat a recap of the beach brawl with Pisik, and what I hoped was her final destiny. His amber eyes opened wide with amazement as I re-visualized the scenario for him.

"By the way, Aunt Siobhan, my father and mother will be arriving in Havenwood Falls in the next few days. They are on their way!"

"They are? That's terrific! I miss Seamus and Abigail so much! Seems my little family here in Havenwood Falls is getting bigger and bigger."

After we finished tea and Mat took off to start his day shift at Broastful Brew, I padded around the house for a bit, really doing nothing at all, until I could motivate myself to go back upstairs and unpack.

I placed the carpet bag on the bed and began removing items one by one, examining each.

The Tell All Ball was first, of course, and the brocade tablecloth. I set Coralie's temporary housing on the bedside table, under the Tiffany lamp. Next, I removed the sleek wooden box with the keyless lock, and set that down on the bed next to the bag.

A scarf here, scraps of paper there. The plane ticket stubs to and from Denver.

My cell phone, a few loose faerie dust packets, and my very handy Havenwood Falls Savings & Loan debit card.

A small light glimmered from the bottom of the case. My father's wand. I pulled it out and held it up in the dimly lit room. The tip on the end began to glow brighter, almost to the point that I could not even look at it, like looking into the sun.

The wand began to dim, my hand shaking nervously, as I held it reluctantly. *I'd better put this away.* I opened the box of magical stuff, moved aside the little packets of mysterious powders, and went to place the wand in the bottom of the box. That's when it hit me.

The crevice in the bottom of the box! That's for the wand! I could've realized years ago, when my father gave me the empty box for my faerie dusts, that he no longer had his wand.

"Coralie, I will have to take you to the Court later today so we can get you a tattoo to protect you. But right now, I think I need to see my friend Madame Luiza."

The small decorated carp flashed her translucent orange tail at me in acceptance.

I exited through the back door that led from the kitchen into my overgrown garden (I liked it that way). Even in winter, it seemed to flourish in abundance. I walked through the wooden gate attached to the old stones that father, Tess, and I had stacked meticulously.

I turned left down Beaumont Crossing—*Memory Lane, as Tess had dubbed it, from walking hand in hand with me and my father on our way to Danzan Park*—and headed to Whisper Falls Inn, a block away.

Whisper Falls Inn was a glorious three-story Victorian-style mansion, with a wraparound veranda, all the bells and whistles of the intricate lattice work for which that era was notable, and a large intriguing glass conservatory in the back filled with exotic flora, like a botanical garden. It occupied the entire block of Beaumont Crossing between Eleventh and Petran, as it included small cottages, similarly latticed, as independent suites for some of the guests.

Most folks referred to Luiza as Madame Luiza, and her nieces and nephew and their friends called her Mammie. For me, she was Luiza, the friend I had chatted with since coming to Havenwood Falls, over 120 years ago.

I did not have to ring the bell when I reached the front door. Michaela knew instinctively that I was on the porch (such is the Petran way), swung the door wide open, and held her arms out just as wide.

This beautiful child—well, not a child anymore—was as much my family as so many of the Old Families in this town. I knew their parents, their grandparents, and in some cases their great grandparents.

"Michaela, so good to see you, dear." I pronounced it *Mihaela*, like Luiza did. After all, I'd known Luiza, Mihail, and Irina long before this dear child was a twinkle or spark in their unique moroi eyes. "I think I need a visitation with Luiza," I informed her after our formalities were complete.

Michaela obliged graciously and escorted me to the familiar parlor with the fireplace where Luiza and I had spent so many hours, years really, confiding in one another.

"A cup of tea, Madame Tahini?"

Before I could even finish saying, "Why yes, thank you," she had moved swiftly out of the parlor to brew a fresh pot.

I knew she thought Mammie's favorite place was in the room upstairs, but for Luiza and I, this was our "girls' night out" place, or as we called it, "Girls' Night Inn."

A cool breeze circled the room with a hint of lavender whispering upon it. A blurry vision began to appear, and then took full shape as the woman I knew for more than a century, dressed eternally in her favorite lavender-colored gown.

Madame Luiza.

"I see you found it." The apparition spoke—the deceased Whisper Falls Inn keeper, and Michaela Petran's aunt.

"Found what?"

"Your father's wand. His scepter."

"I did. It's strange. I never knew that he had left it behind."

"Your father was a very interesting man. He was stalwart, strict, and extremely stubborn. I suppose having to rule his fae may have accounted for some of that. But when your mother, Rose, died, a large part of him died with her. Your father was heartbroken."

"My father? He always seemed so ambivalent."

"Oh no, my dear! His guilt ran very deep. He felt great remorse for punishing your brother so harshly. Unfortunately, he could not find it in himself to reverse the curse. Maybe it was his stubbornness, or maybe he just didn't know how to undo what had been done. To add to that pain, his beloved Rose died of heartbreak over your brother's fate. Tess and I were very close friends. She confided a great deal to me."

"I never in a million years would have thought my father felt bad about cursing Grenfold."

"There's more, dear. That was his curse on your brother. The sins of the father are visited on the son and vice versa. Your father Ian, as hard as he tried to have another son, was cursed to lose all in childbirth. Each of his subsequent wives all lost their only child, a son, in childbirth. In fact, only Tess survived the birthing, though the baby boy did not."

"I don't think I was ever told that the babies were boys."

"Now you are the heir to his power. You have the wand to rule your fae."

"Rule my fae? There are not many of us left to rule over. Not sure even what that means."

"Things are ever changing, Siobhan. Already your nephew Mat

has come to Havenwood Falls, and maybe more? And I know you have brought someone home with you."

"Ah, yes, that is true, but she is not fae. That was the whole trouble in the first place."

"Things are ever changing, Siobhan."

Now she sounds like a broken record.

"You have the power to break what was broken. Seek it within yourself."

Power! Bah! Everyone wants power, but it only seems to bring heartache.

A scent of lavender still trailed in the room after Madame Luiza's departure.

That sinking feeling I had at Grenfold/Gruff's rock came blasting back at me. With Luiza's recitation, all of a sudden, I realized what my father gave up. He traveled thousands of miles from our homeland, with his small clan in tow, but without the power he normally would've wielded if he'd had his wand with him.

I feel like such a dunce. A loser. So much time wasted, angry with my father, not ever caring that this man who tried to protect me and so many others, all these years, had so much love and grief in his heart.

All this time, I never thought of my father having feelings, of him loving anything but his power. Had I been that wrong about him? Was there really something I could have done to change things?

Ever changing?

∼

AFTER I FINISHED my tea at Whisper Falls Inn and thanked Michaela for her hospitality, I returned to my own home to prepare Coralie for her tattooing.

I opened my wooden box with a wave of my hand, the latch snapping open instantly, and took out a pink silk packet. Placing the makeshift aquarium on the bed next to the wooden casing, I poured a small bit of a pale pinkish powder into my hand and sprinkled that into the glass sphere.

The water in the bowl began to churn, and bubbles began to rise in rapid succession, filling the entire room with floating spheres of pink and purple that threw off the rays of light from the Tiffany lamp into a profusion of multicolored beams.

Within seconds, a beautiful woman appeared, with skin the color of fresh cream and bright red hair that flowed and waved like an anemone crowning her head. She was completely naked and was stretching out her new legs that had replaced her familiar tail.

"These are interesting," Coralie said as she wiggled her brand new toes.

I explained to the lovely sea maiden that I would need to take her to the Court of the Sun and the Moon to have Adelaide Beaumont give her a protective tattoo, one that would be infused with magic, the kind of magic only Addie would know was needed.

I took out one of my shawls from the armoire and wrapped it around this gorgeous creature, sarong-style. Although mid-May was still quite cool in our parts, Coralie was a cold-blooded animal, and it should suit her well. The shawl should be all she needed.

She followed me out of the bedroom and down the stairs, and I could hear her mutter oohs and ouches all the way down the steps.

"What's wrong, Coralie? Are you okay?" My healing instincts kicked in.

"I don't know. It feels like I am walking on nails and hot coals," she replied.

I hadn't thought about that. She was a fish, not a human. I recalled Hans Christian Andersen's story of the Little Mermaid and how she had to suffer the thorny pangs as she walked in her human body. I would have to get this over with as quickly as possible in order to transform Coralie back to her natural form and place her in a more comfortable habitat than the painfully rough surfaces she would experience on this earthly ground.

I led her straight across town square, keeping an eye on Coralie as she gingerly tiptoed through the park, around the fountain and to the other side. She winced at every step, and I could feel the prickles in my own feet. I felt so bad that she had to endure this.

Opening the heavy metal door to the Court, I led the aching woman toward Adelaide's office.

Introductions and background provided, Addie asked Coralie if she had any idea what kind of tattoo she might like.

"Maybe a heart with an anchor? That's how I have felt for so long, like my heart was dragged to the bottom of the sea."

There's that knot in my stomach again. So much heartache.

Addie said she didn't believe that would always be the case, and felt a design like that would only serve to keep it that way, a self-fulfilling prophecy, so to speak. She proposed a heart with wings and fins, and Coralie's eyes brightened, the pair of emeralds shining nearly as bright as they once did so many moons ago.

I told Addie that I intended to take Coralie to Peacock Lake at Small's Falls, especially since it was so close to my cabin, and I go there so frequently, especially in the spring and summer. The Court's manager reminded me the lake water there was toxic.

"Well, definitely to humans, and yes to some supernaturals, but I think since Coralie is a water-bound creature, she should be safe."

Addie said she would infuse the tattoo with magic that would protect her from the bear shifters and cat shifters, as they both were very fond of fish, and of course the humans would never be able to see her, even though most of the human folk didn't go near Peacock Lake, its legend being quite famous around town. But you never knew about the wayward tourist. And she would add a spell that would protect Coralie from any of the toxicity the waters may have for her.

"Just in case," she added with a wink.

I smiled at her comment. Addie, like a few others who had

known me most of their lives, knew that "just in case" was my tag line. I was surprised they didn't call me Just In Case Teeny Weeny.

Coralie, with her new enchanted tattoo, stood up, and with a grimace, began to step toward the exit. Addie sensed her pain immediately, and with a flick of her fingers, tossed a spell at Coralie's feet.

Thank goodness Addie is so good at what she does. I've cast so little magic for so long, I didn't even think of it.

"Thank you! This is wonderful! It feels like I have little bubbles around my feet!" Coralie exclaimed joyously.

"Well, now you are sarong-wrapped, bubble-wrapped, and ready to go. Let's get some lunch," I said as we walked out of the Court of the Sun and the Moon, and she shook those bright red locks vigorously in agreement.

Back in my kitchen, I found some leftover faerie cake dough in the freezer and thawed it out, adding a little cherry Jell-O mix to the batch. I made small round balls of the cherry flavored dough and let Coralie suck on those while I brewed a pot of tea.

As soon as we finished filling ourselves up on most of the delightful doughballs, I gathered up some packets of faerie dust and placed them in one of the ubiquitous pockets of my skirt. Again we headed out of my townhome, this time through the back garden.

I instructed Coralie to hold on to me, as I would shimmer us up to Peacock Lake, and hold on to me she did, as she lifted me into her arms and cradled me like an infant.

The wavering air surrounded the both of us as we flowed into a translucent wave, then vanished, to reappear again at the edge of the lake.

Peacock Lake was so named as it fanned out from the triplet of falls that fed into it, known as Small's Falls, and the waters were mesmerizing bands of teal, green, blue, and turquoise. It looked like a peacock's tail in its fabulous array of colors.

I explained to Coralie, "You won't be alone in the lake. There's a sweet young water nymph, Mallory Dorian, who has an affinity to the lake, I've noticed. I think you will like her. I have a good feeling about her. There are also a few other water nymphs who may or may not show up, but I am sure you, of all mermaids, can handle the likes of them."

Coralie shed her sarong and sat on the edge of the lake, dangling her feet into the cool waters of the lake. I pulled out a light blue packet of dust and sprinkled a pale aqua powder upon her head.

The delicate toes at the end of her feet began to web together. She crossed her ankles, and a parade of glimmering green scales started to crawl up her legs, enveloping them into the full tail of the alluring Coralie.

She pecked a kiss upon my cheek, and in an instant, splashed into the waters of the lake, flipping her tail with glee, as she bid me good night.

I heard a baleful moan coming from the direction of Gruff's cave.

Forgive me, my goddesses, gods, and Gruff.

That sickening feeling overwhelmed me once again as I shimmered back home.

ANOTHER LONG DAY, and I went to bed that night completely worn out. I pulled out a light flannel set of pink pajamas scattered with dragonflies, to help drift me into a peaceful slumber. Crawling into my welcoming bed, I curled up with my favorite down pillow and cried.

I wept for Coralie. I wept for Grenfold and Gruff. I wept for five mothers and would-be brothers. I wept for my father, the king of our fae. I cried and cried until at last my teeny weeny head could cry no more and fell asleep.

I awoke at dawn, my pillow completely tear-soaked, the dream I had during the night still mysteriously rumbling around in my head.

This is ODD!

I retrieved my trusty cell phone and dialed none other than 9-1-1. And my trusty friend on the other end answered before the second ring could even start.

"Siobhan! Don't tell me, another dream?" the mayor's inquisitive voice started the conversation.

I nodded, as if she could see me, and asked her to meet me at Broastful Brew, as usual. Nothing too urgent—we could meet at our regular time.

And so it was, Barbie and I sitting at our familiar table a little past eight, with Mabel chatting away, and Mat behind the counter, preparing our beverages.

"So spill it! You have me stayed in suspense, Siobhan," Barbie said, accentuating every *s*.

That's my best friend, doing her best to alliterate for me.

"It's so odd, Barbie. I mean, I'm sure it's because of bringing Coralie back here and knowing how hard this is for Gruff."

I gave her the rundown on the adventures in Gwynf'l, finding my father's wand, the wicked witch of a Pisik and her near total destruction of us all, my crazy confused trip back home to Havenwood Falls, and even my chat with Luiza.

"Well, that was quite a trip. Even Bent Brent would be proud of you! But you still haven't told me about the dream last night. That is why you called, right?"

"Yes, actually. See if this sounds familiar. My father chanted the code, 'We, this family of fae, are of earth and air. When sea mixes with earth, it becomes mud. When sea mixes with air, tears fall from the heavens. You have brought both to this family. To be true, from this day hence, no longer are you fae, a prince. For your crime I extol, from this day forward, your life, a troll.'"

"That's your spring equinox dream. I hear of it every year, so yes, very familiar."

"Yeah, well I had it last night! Long past the spring equinox. In fact, we're coming up to the summer solstice shortly." Ha, I got my alliteration in there, too.

Oh no! I missed May Day and Spring Fest for the pixie sisters! I will have to make it up to them this coming solstice.

Barbie looked pensive, then she got her invisible detective's cap on and said, "Was it the whole dream or just that part?"

"Just that part, why?"

"Siobhan, I told you before, you have more power than you give yourself credit for. Even Luiza is trying to tell you that! You told me she said, 'You have the power to break what is broken.' The answer is in your father's curse. You have to seek it."

So many broken records around here. Break what was broken? Seek it?

I just nodded as I dipped my teabag in and out of the tiny teapot in front of me.

How come my friends can see what I can't? I mean, I'm not surprised by Luiza. After all, aside from her supernatural life, she is in the land of spirits now. But Barbie, my human (maybe) friend? How can even she see things that should be as clear as the nose on my face, as small as that might be?

We finished our little café klatch, and bid each other a good day.

I wandered down the blocks of town square heading back to my place, but the only thing that kept ringing in my head were the words: *break what was broken.*

Come on! How do you break something that's already broken? It really didn't make any sense, but apparently it did to some people and apparitions. Okay, maybe I needed to parse the words, so to speak.

Break! Break! Break! My father placed a curse on Grenfold. I had always wished I knew a way to break the curse.

Wait! Didn't Luiza say he may not have known how to undo what was done?

So the first word was break—I needed to break the curse. Okay, that was easy to figure out, kind of like the nose on my face. But if the curse hadn't already been broken, then what was broken?

Broken? Broken? Broken?

By the time I got home, my head was breaking. I went straight to my bedroom to lie down, even though it was only mid-morning. I looked around the room, realizing it was still totally in disarray. I had been so occupied with getting Coralie to Court, then to Peacock Lake, I hadn't straightened up the mess. I had just gone to sleep last night with everything still piled up on my bed.

I went to pick up the Magical Stuff Box, and the wand, now sitting comfortable in its customary place, began to glow brilliantly.

The wand cast these words into the air, and they hovered like a neon sign over the center of my bed.

We, this family of fae, are of earth and air.
When sea mixes with earth, it becomes mud.
When sea mixes with air, tears fall from the heavens.
You have brought both to this family.
To be true, from this day hence, no longer are you fae, a prince.
For your crime I extol, from this day forward, your life, a troll.

THAT'S IT! Broken! Hearts are broken. Grenfold's, Coralie's, even my mother Rose's! I know how to break the curse! Thank you, my souls and spirits!

~

I EFFERVESCED TO PEACOCK LAKE, my father's wand—*No! my wand*—in hand.

Once re-effervesced into my Teeny Weeny self, I threw a few of the cherry dough-balls that I had kept in reserve into the lake. That's really all it took to summon Coralie to the surface.

Fish! Really, they are so easy to please.

"Coralie, I am sure I can fix this! Break the curse, bring Grenfold back to you! But I need your help!"

She looked at me with those curious emerald eyes, a little

glimmer shining. Maybe the rising sunlight from the east catching a reflecting ray—or maybe more?

"Whatever you need, Siobhan. Tell me."

"I need you to sing your love song. The one that Grenfold and you have cherished for an eternity."

That reflecting ray in those emerald eyes disappeared. Her shining smile that greeted me at first turned to a fretful frown.

"It's okay! You can do this! I can do this! I need you to sing!"

Coralie lifted the giant pearl that always hung from a golden chain around her neck and let the rays of sunshine catch its special glow. And then it began.

Coralie, like the being she was created to be, began softly, soulfully, sounding like a true torch singer sitting on the top of a grand piano in a smoky bar, feeling the notes at the bottom of her heart, but emitting from the bottom of her lungs.

"My true love. My Grenfold, forever.
It's you I want, now and forever.
To be of your world, or you of mine
Love's magic would make it shine.
Alas, my beloved but it seems to be
My heart always anchored at the bottom of the sea?
My poor dear lover, do you see?
Are we destined never to be?
Neptune knows I'll never love another.
Grenfold, my soul mate, my only other.
My other half
My rod, my staff"

The tune, so mournful yet so loving, wafted through the forest of Mount Alexa. As I suspected, dear Gruff, the poor misshapen being, could not resist their song of love, his heart's desire that Coralie sang.

Gruff emerged from his cave and stumbled through the dense forest and pine-needle-strewn path down to the water's edge on rickety legs and gnarled feet. But the painful expression on his face told the truth that it was not the grotesque arrangements of limbs and bones, but his heartache that tore that slash of a mouth on his face into an excruciating grimace.

Gruff's tears fell like tiny pebbles running from a river brook. They hit the edges of the lake as he stepped up to the ledge and pondered the woman in the pond. His recognition of the water-bound woman as his true love Coralie made him cover his face with his arthritic-looking hands. He did not want his lilting love to see him, though it appeared that he doubted she would recognize him like this.

I thought he was about to plunge himself into the poisonous waters of Peacock Lake, but Coralie's first look at Gruff, at Grenfold, said it all.

Her emerald eyes sparkled, then softened, and her luminous smile grew wider. One could almost feel her rapid heartbeat as unaccustomed waves began to form in what was always a very still body of water.

Coralie did not see Gruff. What she saw was her beloved Grenfold. She knew and felt his soul. This creature of true beauty did not see a mottled skin, warted, and malformed troll. She saw her own true love.

I knew this was the moment of truth. I pulled out my wand and placed its glowing tip upon Gruff's forehead and said:

"We, this family of fae, are of earth and air.

When sea mixes with earth, it becomes clay with which to build.

When sea mixes with air, it becomes rain with which to grow.

Let sea, earth, and air become the love that builds and grows.

The spring spirits bless us all."

I watched and listened to the transformation of poor Gruff becoming Grenfold once again. This time it was not the horrific crunching of bones, nor the sad transformation of a spirit's ethereal fae eyes turning into lumps of coal. It was a symphony of such astronomical proportion that it seemed as if all the angels of the universe were strumming their golden harps in unison and all the songbirds of the forest joining in joyful harmony.

The next moment, Gruff had become Grenfold once again, my beautiful, handsome fae brother. But something had changed. A softer look in his eyes, not like the arrogant bright hazel ones of yore. They were still hazel, but softer shades of gold and green folded into the browns of his irises. Perhaps his years as a troll had humbled him.

By my side stood four little pixies staring at the wand in my hand, and Cyllene on my shoulder, just nodding in a self-righteous sort of way.

Grenfold kissed me on my forehead and said, "Thank you! Make amends with Father! I love you always, sister!"

And with that, he dove into the lake, and the two lovers, who were always meant to be, swam into the depths of the precarious waters of Peacock Lake, now protected by their own hearts.

"Wait! Coralie, I have one more thing to fix!"

Coralie popped her head out of the water with an immensely joyous smile taking over her fair face.

"Your pearl. Hold it up."

Coralie did so, and with that, I tapped my wand on the lustrous orb and chanted,

"Spirits above and beyond, unite our call
The Whirling Pearl and the Tell All Ball"

By now, the four pixies were jumping, jiving, and oh yes, wrestling for glee over this way-too-romantic scenario.

"Well, now what are we supposed to do?" said the eternally grounded Tierri, after all the romping and raving.

"Well, Gruff, I mean Grenfold, is going to live with Coralie happily ever after in Peacock Lake, as they were meant to be."

"No, I mean what happens to HimaLaLa, the yeti that lives with Gruff? And what happens with his cave? Who's going to take care of HimaLaLa?"

"I wanna live with HimaLaLa!" piped up Aieri, interrupting Tierri's wave of questioning.

"Me too!" said Ushka. And so the numbering followed.

"Well, it only makes sense that you should all move in to

Grenfold's—I mean Gruff's—cave, and care for HimaLaLa. After all, you are the ones who wanted HimaLaLa to stay here in Havenwood Falls."

Out of the clear blue sky, four tiny brooms seemed to have fallen into the pixies' hands, and the next thing I knew, they were headed off to the hole in the mountain, to sweep up and groom the gruffly honed ground into a home for the pixies and a poor unsuspecting yeti.

And that, Dear Diary, is just one of the reasons Havenwood Falls lives magically ever after!

Love and joy to all,

TW Tahini McFeeny

That's strange. I never sign my name so curly. Hmmm . . . Ever changing, Siobhan, Ever changing.

~

READ the next installment of Teeny Weeny's story in *The Wu & the Wand* by T.V. Hahn.

ABOUT THE AUTHOR

T.V. Hahn has loved the fantastical and whimsical since she was a child, which may or may not have been that long ago. A creative soul, she enjoys making art with her hands, her voice, and her words. She finds humor in everything and is the first to laugh at her own jokes. During her downtime, you may find her tending her floral beauties, writing poetry, working on her faerie gardens, or watching *The Dark Crystal* or *The Princess Bride*. All of this, combined with her petite stature, has made more than one person wonder if she is, indeed, a faerie. It may be no accident that her first published book is about Teeny Weeny Tahini, a Spring Fae living in Havenwood Falls. Hahn is self-employed and lives in Florida with her husband and pup. She can be reached through her publisher, Ang'dora Productions.

ACKNOWLEDGMENTS

First and foremost, I want to acknowledge my publisher Kristie Cook, who believed I could really write in this genre, and led the way skillfully and gracefully. My editor Liz Ferry, who endures my incessant rhyming and alliteration and now has to deal with me writing in first person.

I'd like to thank Randi Cooley-Wilson for her allowing me to play a joke on Roman, suggesting how to do it, and cracking me up in the process. I also want to thank J.L. Weil for not only writing about Peacock Lake, but for discussing the story with me long before either of us had started our books.

Brynn Myers, an angel in her own right, who trustingly accepted my talisman. Tish Thawer for being *Witch and Famous*, and all the other wonderful authors in Havenwood Falls who collaborate and enrich my stories.

TOIL & TROUBLE

MELISSA WRIGHT

~ A Havenwood Falls New Adult Novella ~

Havenwood Falls

Toil and Trouble

Melissa Wright

ALSO BY MELISSA WRIGHT

THE FREY SAGA
Frey
Pieces of Eight
Molly (a short story)
Rise of the Seven
Venom and Steel

DESCENDANTS SERIES
Bound by Prophecy
Shifting Fate
Reign of Shadows

SHATTERED REALMS
King of Ash and Bone
Queen of Iron and Blood

HAVENWOOD FALLS
Toil & Trouble

Double, double toil and trouble;
Fire burn, and cauldron bubble.
—William Shakespeare, *Macbeth*

PROLOGUE

*H*e was supposed to take her. He hadn't. Five weeks and he hadn't. And now she'd gone into hiding, in a secret town nestled in the mountains of Colorado. Havenwood Falls: a haven for supernaturals. A place where she could have stayed safe indefinitely, if only he hadn't followed her.

He was a fool.

CHAPTER 1

*C*irce was cursed. Alone. And that was the way she liked it. Love was for fools, not someone like her. She had better things to do, she thought as she shoved her dirty clothes into two machines at the back of the local laundromat. She'd spent most of her life not needing to remind herself of the ancient edicts holding her magic and love life for ransom, but after a few days in Havenwood Falls, suddenly she was surrounded by shifters and supes with Adonis bodies and secret, sexy-times smiles. It was getting hard to stay focused.

A shifter of some sort leaned against the machine beside her, his thick arms flexing as they crossed over his chest. She couldn't tell what kind, but he radiated otherness, and everything about him tried to draw her in. She reached up to amp the volume on her earbuds and slammed the door on the washing machine a little too hard. *Fools*, she reminded herself. *Love is for fools.*

And dirty sexy-time was how you got there.

Laundry Playlist blaring in her ears, Circe turned to go. She'd grab coffee while she waited on the wash; that would at least get her away from the half-dressed blond who liked to practice stretching his quads during the spin cycle.

The apartment she'd moved into at Havenwood Village wasn't

quite ready when she'd arrived, but if she could only hang on a few more days, she would finally be able to close herself in and introvert the hell out of it. As it was, a nice man from McCabe & Sons was banging and hammering around four or five hours a day to whittle down the extensive list of damages left by the previous occupant. Whatever had happened there hadn't been an easy thing. Circe couldn't be sure if it'd been caused by one supe or two, but signs pointed to a violent and unintentional shift in the center of a crowded apartment—and it hadn't gone well. Being exposed to new species was turning out to be a good reminder to Circe to be grateful for what she had—at least her magic wouldn't tear her apart.

She strolled down the sidewalk toward Coffee Haven, tugging her new puffer jacket tight around herself. She wouldn't miss the soul-scorching heat of an Arizona summer, but this "cool mountain breeze," as her new hosts had called it, was a pretty harsh swing. Piles of snow edged the town where the streets and sidewalks had been cleared, and Circe imagined there would be long stretches of winter where she did not even leave her home. Havenwood Falls had something else that desert town didn't have: a hefty population of supernatural beings.

Thanks to a nasty curse, Circe's mother had died during childbirth, leaving Circe orphaned. Well, that hadn't exactly been what had orphaned her. Circe had been told that once her mother was gone, her father couldn't stand to look at the child they'd created. He'd apparently abandoned Circe, left her on the steps of on old church inhabited by witches. Circe might have understood if he was too distraught to deal, but it was kind of hard to forgive something like that. Even now that the passage of time had given her distance from it.

Her father had dumped her, simple as that, and Circe had been left with nothing but a hand-me-down hex and a bad outlook.

So the witches who raised her became her guardians, and she counted the days until she was finally old enough to look out for herself. They'd insisted she call them all aunts, and she did love them, but some days they felt a lot more like jailers than kin. She'd played in the courtyard behind the church as a child, locked inside by invisible wards. The aunts had attempted a few play dates, but it was hard to find children who fit into a world so filled with magic, who would play among the church's crypts and lofts. So the cats and crows became her only friends.

She didn't know her birthday, but Circe had watched the calendar since she was big enough to read, and every March during the spring equinox ritual, she'd mark another year's passing. Eighteen of those ceremonies had come and gone without freedom.

And then, only weeks ago, a distant relative of one of the aunts had come for a visit. Lyra Beaumont had been pretty and petite, and pale enough it was clear she'd not lived through a recent Arizona summer. The aunts had met privately with her for long hours, and then they'd brought Circe in to be introduced. Circe had stood frozen in front of Lyra where she sat in a plush velvet chair, and it was gently explained that Circe would finally be allowed to leave their home.

Her heart was in her throat, but she still heard the truth of it. The offer came with a condition: she would be trading one set of wards for another. Circe could leave the coven, choose her own vocation, and live a real life, but only if she would come to Havenwood Falls, a place where she and her secrets could be protected. Lyra and the Beaumont family were apparently locals and members of the Luna Coven. Their coven and the governing body of the town—the Court of the Sun and the Moon—had been told of Circe's curse and her unusual situation.

The problem with not having a family is that you've got no one to ask what the hell you are. Circe's father had left her when she'd been no more than a baby. The aunts had found out what they could about him, and about Circe's curse, but it wasn't much. No one could be certain what might happen in her future.

Sure, the aunts had given her shelter until she reached an age where she could legally go out on her own—and even longer. They'd shown her what not to do. They'd shown her who to stay away from. They'd warned her of the curse, that she could never fall for a man or she would be doomed worse than her mother. But aside from that, aside from the constant assurances that she was a witch and that was all that mattered, they'd no idea where Circe really came from—what sort of beings her parents were. Circe knew she wasn't part shifter or vamp like some of the locals here. Not fae. But even though she hadn't come into her full power, something potent was inside of her. She felt it—the magic that ran through her blood, strong and dangerous.

Capable of decimating the shadows that followed her.

And, unlike the aunts, Lyra and her coven were not keeping Circe tucked away.

A chime dinged on the street in front of her, the door to Shelf Indulgence opening as a tall brunette came out. The woman smelled of herbs and tonics, and something like home. Circe didn't want to go back, but it was hard not to miss a place she'd been for nineteen years. Circe smiled, and the woman gave her a friendly wave, fumbling her books and packages before regaining control. One door down, and Circe was at Coffee Haven, near the center of a line of shops that faced the town square.

It was lovely inside, with worn hardwood floors and a long marble counter like an old-fashioned ice cream parlor. The walls were covered in art, hanging plants and crystals were scattered around the space, and Circe was comfortable despite the press of the crowd. She leaned against the counter, deciding on a sweet orange tea before being talked into a blueberry scone by a petite blonde whose name tag read "Willow." Circe had encountered the woman the previous day and noticed she seemed exceptionally good at reading people, that she had an uncanny intuition. There was a sense of otherness about this Willow, and Circe wondered if she had empathic abilities. Circe had been a bundle of nerves that first day, and Willow had immediately offered a selection of calming teas and sweet cakes.

Circe had liked her right away.

Today, Circe took her purchases to a small table against the wall and was immediately glad she chose the scone. Her gaze wandered over the crowd, taking in a myriad of supernatural tells and what appeared to be simply normal human beings, all going about their lives as if this wasn't an entirely epic event. Circe being alone. On her own. Thoroughly without the watching eyes of her many, many aunts.

Her gaze trailed over the wall of art, pencils and acrylics and oils, all varied in style and skill, and she realized they must have been the work of local artists. Her stomach dipped at the idea of the possibility, and she added it to the growing list of potential thrills: someday seeing her own watercolors on display. In public. She caught herself grinning like an idiot and bit the edge of her lip against that grin. Didn't want the residents of Havenwood Falls to think she was one of *those* witches.

And then a shadow moved at the edge of the storefront window outside, and Circe's mood fell. She wasn't under the watchful eye of the coven, but that didn't mean she was alone.

It didn't mean she was safe.

Circe grimaced, keeping her head down as she finished her scone. The tea was sweet, with just a little bite, and it warmed her all the way through. She thought she was brave enough now for her meeting with Addie, so she picked up her handbag overstuffed with elixirs and charms thanks to the vigilant aunts, and left the safety of Coffee Haven to tick off one more task.

Adelaide Beaumont, youngest of the Beaumont witches and Lyra's daughter, was not what Circe had expected. The aunts had called her a business manager and court liaison, but here she was in a hoodie and ripped jeans, legs crossed at the ankles with a worn pair of Chuck Taylor All Stars propped on the edge of the desk.

She snapped her gum, sitting up to give Circe a knowing smile as she spotted her in the doorway.

"Do I look that nervous?" Circe asked.

Addie chuckled. "It'll be over in a jiffy."

Circe managed to smile back as she looked at the woman, searching for signs of familiarity. Addie was a Beaumont too, which meant she was some distant relative of Morgan, one of the many "aunts." Morgan had never specified the exact relationship, but it was apparently close enough that the Beaumonts would do her this favor, that they would allow Circe a safe haven even knowing she would soon develop dangerous powers.

Circe cleared her throat. In truth, it wasn't the needle she was afraid of. "So this is permanent?"

Addie glanced up from the supplies she was laying out on the table, her wrists layered in bracelets and stones. She cocked a brow behind her black-framed glasses. "Already planning on running away?"

Circe took a deep breath and stepped forward. "No, I'm here for good."

She reached a hand out to Addie, cementing her independence from the aunts, committing her soul to Havenwood Falls.

CHAPTER 2

*E*van followed her as she walked alone through the town, apparently unaware of the danger she was in. Circe Alexander—nineteen years old, five foot four, brown hair, brown eyes, no identifiable markings—had been under the protection of thirteen women since the moment he'd found her, and now suddenly she was strolling around on her own, like she didn't have a care in the world. She'd been doing laundry, having coffee, browsing books, and now it looked as if she was sporting a brand new tattoo. So much for no identifiable markings. It was utterly baffling. And yet, here he was, watching her still.

Tattoo still fresh and pink, Circe sauntered along the town square, rubbing her hands and blowing a breath to warm them. It wasn't overly cold, but she was a transplant, and that made all the difference. Evan wore a jacket over his henley, but only so he could turn up the collar in an effort to blend in. The magic in his blood kept him warm enough, and the jacket had done little to keep him under the radar. This was a town scattered with supernaturals. They could sense their own. They knew he was something different.

Nothing about this bargain was going the right way, and every fiber of Evan's being told him to run. But Evan couldn't run. He'd made a deal. The thing about deals with mages is that they're unaccountably binding. Impossible to break. And, more often than not, started and ended in blood.

Evan ran a finger over the scar at the base of his thumb. He'd been desperate when he'd sought out the mages, desperate enough he hadn't thought about how dangerous they were—and foolish enough to think his life could get no worse. And then they had marked him, ran a ritual dagger across his palm before he realized what they'd done. They had his blood.

They wanted hers.

Circe turned into the laundromat and a cat shifter—probably Evan's least favorite kind—held the door for her, leaning too close and giving Circe a pointed smile. She ducked her head and pressed the earbuds into her ears. Evan waited as she folded her clothes and tucked them into an oversized tote, tugged the straps onto her shoulder, and headed back for the door. She had one more stop: the vet's office, where she would be picking up what might have been the ugliest bulldog Evan had ever seen.

When she finally stepped out of Havenwood Falls Animal Hospital, Circe knelt beside the beast, cooing and babbling and carrying on about how wonderful he looked. "He's got the prettiest trimmed nails and the softest coat, and he's such a good boy." And then she kissed him. Full on, right over his big slobbery mouth. The dog smiled, or appeared to, his maw going wide and his tongue lolling out as he panted. Chompers, it seemed, was also not too cold in the mountain climate.

Circe appeared to suddenly realize she was kneeling on a public sidewalk, her recently washed tote of clothes in danger of spilling and her purse abandoned in her haste to lavish praise upon this dog. She gathered her bags onto her shoulder and gave Chompers one final *good boy* pat. He waddled to standing, following obediently on his purple-patterned leash. They walked down Petran Street the few blocks to her apartment, and Evan found an alcove on an adjacent building, settling in to watch the door.

His cell phone buzzed in his pocket, but he did not check the screen. He knew what it was going to say.

There were no more excuses, no more chances to buy time. He was going to have to do it. Tonight would be the night. The mages were on a deadline, and there was no way he could wait any longer and remain alive. It was her or him, and as much as it turned his stomach, Evan wasn't stupid. If he didn't hand her over, someone else would.

And they might not be as gentle about it.

He ran a palm over his face, thinking through his plan for the dozenth time. Second floor window, while she was asleep. Tainted rag over her mouth, band of herbs around her wrist. The mages had sent him with an arsenal of spelled weapons for one single woman. *She's dangerous*, Lucius had told him, the head of the powerful council taking the time to warn Evan himself. *Do not give her a chance.*

That was the thing that had stuck with Evan the most. The thing that had made him hesitate that first day. Dangerous, they'd said. A killer, no mercy, no code. Evan knew about witches. He'd had firsthand experience with the way they could destroy lives. He had been fully prepared to do what the council had asked, and then he'd seen her in the yard of the old church that housed the coven, and he'd wondered if that could ever be true. If Circe the witch could really be dangerous.

She had been reading in the morning sun, legs crossed over a blanket in the landscaped yard out back of the old church. One of their many cats sat beside her, preening until its black fur glistened like wet lacquer. Evan had watched as a small bird alighted on the stepping stones, not ten feet from that very cat. Circe's gaze had flicked to it, and the bird became hidden by a cloud of gray smoke until it lifted once more into the air. Spared from the keen eyes of the cat, just like that.

Dangerous. A killer. Eater of the hearts of men.

Savior of tiny birds.

Reader of historical fiction.

It wasn't as if Evan had trusted the mages to begin with, or even wanted to do their work, but when he made the bargain, he'd had no other choice. If he didn't do something, the magic inside of Evan would destroy him. He'd meant to gain freedom from a drawn-out, torturous destruction in exchange for completing a single task for them. Taking down a witch—a ruthless killer—seemed less an offense than stealing a harmless girl. So he'd waited. He'd watched her. That day, and the next. Nothing had ever changed in her, not even when under stress. Circe had never used magic again, aside from that first day, and Evan began to wonder if he'd seen it right at all. When she'd found herself in sticky situations with her guardians, when she'd been caught out in the rain, troubles large or small—never once did she reach for that power, never once did she use it to help herself or to hurt a soul.

Evan had made a bad bargain. He knew that much for sure. And now it was time to pay the piper.

Now, he was afraid, he was about to kidnap an innocent girl.

CHAPTER 3

*C*irce opened the door to her apartment just as the contractor was wiping his hands on an old strip of cloth. He tucked it into his back pocket and nodded in greeting. "Afternoon. Looks like we've got you all finished up."

Chompers jerked on his leash, pulling Circe closer so he could snuffle at the poor man's boots. Circe smiled up at him apologetically. Ryker, he'd said his name was. He was well over six feet tall and built of muscle. His blond hair was pulled back while he worked, his blue eyes bright. When Circe was this close to a man who seemed capable of snapping a person in two, she couldn't help but think of the aunts' warnings. But while Ryker was certainly dangerous, he didn't actually make Circe feel scared.

"Thank you so much," she said. "For everything." She took a cursory glance around the apartment. "It looks great."

It did, really. It was barely decorated, but what was there was hers. The apartment might have been small, but it felt like Circe, and it felt like home.

He picked up his tool bag and tipped his hat. "It's nothing. Sorry you had to wait." He turned at the door, and as Circe bent to unsnap Chompers's leash, he added, "Don't forget to lock up behind me. Better safe than sorry, you know."

"Yes," Circe said, ignoring the chill that ran over her skin. "I'll be sure to remember."

The latch clicked as he closed the door behind him, and Circe moved to lock both the deadbolt and chain, and then check the windows. She'd not heard of any break-ins in the community, but common criminals weren't what she was worried about keeping out.

"Right," she told herself. "Back to the old bag of tricks."

She moved down the short hallway to the kitchenette, opening the pantry that held her stock. The aunts had made her promise to set wards, and she supposed now that she was truly alone, she should do at least that much. She took down the bottles and jars, and though they were unlabeled, she knew what was in each and every one. She felt silly singing with no one else in the apartment, so she hummed the tune and mumbled the words where they needed to strike. She was eager to heat up water for tea, but that would have to wait. It was never a good idea to mix cooking with casting.

Circe thought about her afternoon while she worked, specifically her visit to the Havenwood Falls Animal Hospital. One of her aunts had secured her a position there as a groomer and after her meeting with the owner, Isa Hilton, Circe had never felt better about the prospect of a job that would be fulfilling, something she actually enjoyed and could be proud of. It might not be the job she'd always dreamed of, but it was working with animals, and Circe had always been good at that. She knew it was something that made her happy. Something that might start to heal the empty place inside her. For now, she didn't have the required degree to become a vet tech, but the beauty of Havenwood Falls was that so many of its residents were like Circe. It would give her the opportunity to use her gifts to help in those special circumstances, licensed or not, when it was a risk to ask those who were not *in the know* for help.

While the veterinarian owner, Isa, was human, it was clear there was something supernatural within her, and she too was aware of the mixed population of the Havenwood Falls community. Isa was slim and lovely, and just the tiniest bit terrifying, but she'd fallen into easy conversation with Circe once they'd taken a short tour around the animal hospital and the adjacent shelter. Isa had a few volunteers, but the shelter was woefully understaffed, so Circe hoped she'd be able to spend a few extra hours there as well.

She smiled at the memory of the petite redheaded volunteer—probably only a year or so younger than Circe—who had arrived wearing rubber boots and shorts, when Circe herself had been freezing.

She sprinkled her ingredients into the mortar and ground them into a fine dust as Chompers slurped huge gulps of water, spilling and sloshing it out of his bowl beside her.

"Good thing the kitchen floors are laminate in this place," she told the dog.

He smiled up at her with a row of crooked teeth, then ambled off to find his bed. She couldn't help but laugh whenever he walked away, knowing exactly how he would trot toward his padded cushion, circle three times, and then flop down, legs akimbo. If Circe was ever in danger of loving anything too much, it was that dog.

She returned to the front door, singing the required words as she dusted a few pinches of the concoction at its threshold. She did the same for the bedroom window, and then crossed to the living room to dust that sill as well.

When she leaned forward, mouth pursed to form the words, fingers outstretched with a pinch of powder, something launched through the glass.

Circe's back hit the hardwood floor of the living room, wind knocked out of her, and she had the faint realization that there had been no glass. The window had been open, not broken, and the high winds and cold mountain air hadn't moved through it to alert her. She had just checked it.

But she couldn't think of that. She could only struggle for

breath as the large form on top of her crushed her chest. He was reaching for her face, struggling against her to smear something sickly sweet on her skin while Chompers wrestled with his leg.

The large man was cursing, she thought, in some foreign language, and his magic felt *off.* The skin of his arm was cold and bristly beneath her hands as she tried to push him away. She'd left her potions on the counter, her knife right along with them. Such a stupid, stupid mistake. She'd only been here a matter of days, and they'd already found her. Had her pinned to the floor. Chompers growled and bit, but the man didn't let go to knock the dog back. He kept pressing down on her, trying to cover her face with that stinking rag. He clambered for a better grip on her, pressing knees and elbows hard into her limbs, and the weight of him was too much for Circe to push off or wiggle out of. The aunts had taught her self-defense, though, and they were not above fighting dirty.

Circe's full powers hadn't manifested, so she couldn't change a being's actual makeup, but she could create illusions. She pressed her palms to the floor beneath her, willing the wood to look like a chasm, like the sharp edge of a cliff, hundreds of feet down. Like the man was falling. She saw the moment he noticed, and even if he'd been warned she might fool him, it was the hesitation she needed. She called to the dust left on her fingers and used it to transform the shape of the bracelet wrapping her wrist into a crude knife. She didn't have the right ingredients, hadn't given it the proper time, but she didn't need the spell to stick long. She only needed a second to use it as a weapon before it fell back into the shape it truly was.

Circe gripped the lumpy blade in her fist and struck hard and fast at the man's ribs.

But the man had disappeared.

Suddenly, and quite unexpectedly, the hulking figure that had pinned her down was gone. Her makeshift blade stuck out of the side of someone else. Someone smaller and less beastly than her attacker.

Circe blinked, stunned, and the stabbed man stared back at her, just as shocked.

"You," she hissed.

And then the large man she'd intended to stab instead struck this new one in the face. Chompers leapt at the large man, tearing his dark pants to shreds, and Circe remembered herself. She picked up the lamp from the side table and smashed it into her attacker's head as he fought with the other man. The lamp cord jerked where it was attached to the wall, and Circe came off balance, holding the wire framework as shattered bits fell. The man she'd stabbed rammed into the bulky one, and both slammed into her newly repaired living room wall. The stabbed man reached into his jacket pocket, drew out a small square of cloth, and pressed it over the bulky man's mouth and nose. There was a short struggle as Circe looked on, bewildered, and then the bulky man seemed to fall asleep.

Circe's hands were trembling. She realized she was still holding parts of the busted lamp. The man she'd stabbed slumped against the wall beside his victim, blood dampening his side where her blade had been. It was on the floor now, once more a thick round bangle, sprinkled with blood.

The bracelet smelled strongly of magic and something earthy. And maybe some fur.

Circe stood there for far longer than she was proud of before she remembered to take some sort of action. She scrambled into the kitchen, grabbed her athame from the counter, and ran back to the living area. Chompers and the man she'd stabbed stared at her. She aimed the considerably more dangerous knife at the stabbed man, and Chompers took over watching the man who'd passed out. He was big on teamwork, that dog.

"What are you doing?" Circe hissed at the stabbed man.

He gaped at her, like maybe he had *no idea* what he was doing. And certainly that he'd not expected for it to end like this. His hand was pressed to his side, blood seeping slowly between his fingers. Circe cursed, then said sorry, because she didn't think it was polite to swear in front of guests, no matter what the witches who raised her said.

The man seemed to think she was apologizing for stabbing him, which she most definitely was not. He said, "It's not deep. I should be fine soon."

His voice said otherwise, though, and Circe could see he was in pain. She pursed her lips, considering her options.

"What are you going to do?" she asked the stabbed man.

"I'll stitch it up, I guess—"

The look she gave cut him off. "About me. About him."

She gestured toward the other man with the tip of her blade.

"No," the stabbed man said. "We aren't together. I was—I was trying to stop him. Didn't you see?"

She crossed her arms, keeping the knife securely in her fist. "I see all right. I see you every day, following me like I'm too slow to notice. I see you lurking around every corner and keeping track of everything I do. I see that you've got potions on you that were made by a skilled hand, and I know that hand wasn't yours." He opened his mouth to speak, and just to be sure he understood she'd meant he wasn't a witch, that she could sense the shifter on him, she snapped, "You smell like dog."

He looked hurt. Like, genuinely offended.

"So," she said. "What are you going to do?"

He closed his eyes, shook his head slowly. When he looked at her again, all the energy seemed to drain out of him. "I'm not going to do anything. I didn't lie—he's not with me. He's my replacement. If they've sent him, then it wouldn't matter if I handed you to them right now. I'm already a marked man."

She nodded. It was probably what he deserved.

"And what about him?" She gestured again toward the other man.

"What do you mean?"

"Well, *do* something with him."

His expression said, *like what?*

"I don't want him in here. This is my home. It's brand new,

and I prefer it without some random shifter passed out in the middle of my floor. Can you understand that?"

She was, admittedly, a little on edge after being attacked.

The stabbed man struggled to his feet. "I'm sorry, Circe. What would you have me do with him?"

She swallowed hard, staggered by his casual use of her name. Like they knew each other. Like they were friends. But he did know her, didn't he? The same way she'd gotten to know him. He'd been following her for weeks.

"Just get rid of him," she snapped. "Out the window."

The stabbed man stared at her.

She sighed. "He's got magic in his blood. It won't kill him. And if he gets a few broken bones, it's no more than he asked for."

"Are you not concerned what the neighbors might think?"

"You throw him out," she said. "I'll do the rest."

CHAPTER 4

*E*van watched as the woman he'd been following for weeks and weeks without doing magic turned a man into a shapeless lump of fur. She'd drawn a small vial of green powder out of her purse, spread it on her fingers, spat on each of her hands, and then pressed her palms to the man's skin. She was humming and singing something too low for him to make out the words, and the dirty brown fur morphed into a thing decidedly more solid.

"A coyote?"

She didn't look at him when she replied, because despite the fact that he'd just saved her, Circe wasn't as helpless and fragile as she'd seemed. She wasn't worried about turning her back on a man.

"Less suspicious if someone sees it outside," she said. "I might have used a dog, but I can't stand the sight of one looking hurt." She smiled at Chompers, who watched with something like approval in his dark eyes. "Okay." She stood, brushing her hands clean on her jeans. "He's still pretty heavy. I didn't change his true form; it's just a temporary illusion."

She gestured toward the window, and though he couldn't believe he was actually doing it, Evan picked up a man who was a coyote and threw him out the opening of the second-story apartment.

They both leaned over the sill to watch him land. They both winced when he did.

Evan pressed a hand to his side as he straightened up. Circe was right; the coyote had still been man-weight. He felt a little light-headed and leaned against the wall.

"Sit down," she said. "I'll make something for your side."

"I should go," he started, but Circe cut him off.

"What you should do is sit down. I have to call the Court of the Sun and the Moon to report this . . . coyote attack." She slid the window shut and moved to the kitchen to retrieve her stone mortar. "If someone has truly marked you, you'll have no chance to defend yourself in your condition." She sprinkled something from the bowl onto the window sill, whispering words beneath her breath. "I'll help you with that and then . . . we'll see."

And then she can use me as bait? Evan thought. *Dangle me out her window so she can catch her next attacker?* He swayed, and Circe grabbed Evan's arm to help him to a seat. He flopped hard onto a couch covered in throw pillows and overstuffed cushions, and Circe made him move his hand so she could see the wound. He didn't look at his side, but he saw her face.

He had the feeling she didn't like touching him.

He remembered he was her enemy.

He closed his eyes, knowing she could plant her knife in his exposed belly anytime she wanted. It would maybe be a better way to go than whatever the council of mages had planned.

"Hey," Circe snapped.

He blinked his eyes open, then wondered if he'd missed a moment or two. He'd lost time like that before, while the magic in his blood stitched him back together. Circe was wiping her hands on a white dish towel.

"Try to stay awake. I've got water on the boil. The remedy will take a few minutes to steep before I can use it." She pointed a thumb over her shoulder. "I'm going to take a quick shower. Don't answer the door. Don't try to leave."

Evan nodded, or at least thought he did, before his eyes were closed again. He heard shuffling noises, the muffled click of a door latch, and voices fading in and out. Circe, calling to report her attacker's body outside. What had she said? The Court of the Sun and the Moon? Evan wondered why she had waited, why she'd not immediately called for help. She'd had him at knifepoint, and the other man had been knocked out, so what was she planning?

And then he lost more time to sleep. When he finally came to, Circe was leaning over him, brows knit as she examined his wound. Her hair was damp, twisted into a knot over one shoulder. She wore a thin white T-shirt over black leggings. She was at ease enough to dress comfortably—that was something at least. Not that he could do much in the way of attacking her at the moment, even if he wanted to. His side ached, and his head felt as if he was in a fog.

Something cold pressed his skin, and he winced.

"There," Circe said. "That should do it."

She glanced up at him. Her eyes were cognac. He hadn't seen them this close before; he'd thought they were chestnut, like her hair.

"I put about five stitches in. It wasn't a wide cut, so you could have gotten by with less, but this will heal more cleanly."

She brushed a strand of hair away from her face. She had a set of stacked silver rings on her first finger, a small dark mark across her third. Her nails were short, cut clean, and polished shiny black. She usually wore pink, he thought.

Circe frowned at him, and he realized he'd said the thought out loud.

"Evan—" she started.

He pushed up from the couch. Or he intended to. He couldn't seem to get his limbs to work right. How did she know his name? It wasn't that she'd gone through his wallet. That ID said David Jackson, Casper, Wyoming. His throat was dry, his hands all itchy.

"What did you give me?"

His accusation fell flat, and Circe was not surprised. "Just something to help you let down your guard. It'll wear off soon."

"You drugged me to ask me questions?"

She crossed her arms over her chest. "Yes. And you broke into my apartment after stalking me for weeks."

She was so small, her face so soft and sweet. All he'd ever seen her be was kind. He couldn't believe she'd done this.

He couldn't believe after all this time, after wallowing in guilt over what he was going to have to do to her, that he actually felt betrayed.

"Give me the antidote."

Circe shrugged. "It doesn't matter now. You've told me what I needed to hear."

She walked toward the kitchen, and Evan watched her go. And he kept watching her. And he remembered something else about witches, something about how they could beguile and seduce. How the illusions were not just for changing men into beasts.

"What do you look like?" he asked her. "Really?" Under all that trickery, he meant. Beneath that face that couldn't be real.

She barked a laugh, returning to the living room with a mug in each hand.

"You think I'd turn myself into this? Evan, come on. I'd at least make myself tall." There was something in her tone that was off, though; something that said his question made her uncomfortable. She lifted a bare foot to press his legs over and sat on the edge of the couch next to him. "Besides, you're one to talk."

She handed him a mug of what appeared to be hot tea. It did not smell half so pleasant. "Here, drink this."

He narrowed his eyes on her.

"You wanted the antidote. You don't have to drink it." She started to take the glass away, but he brought it to his lips.

It was hot, and it smelled like road tar. He gulped it down anyway, desperate to be rid of whatever was fogging his head. It worked immediately, then he wanted to retch. She moved a plastic trash bin closer to him, then handed him the other mug.

"This one's tea. It will get rid of that terrible taste, but it's mostly just yarrow and peppermint to soothe your stomach."

She returned to the kitchen, humming something quietly as Evan leaned over the waste bin. He could hear her open the fridge, the click of a gas stove, and then a cast iron griddle sliding against its racks. He closed his eyes and breathed, catching the scent of peppermint and spice. It was soon replaced with seared steak, and at the sound of clattering dishes, Evan pushed himself to sitting. He didn't know if he could eat, but she'd gone to the trouble, and now that his head was clearing, he remembered he was technically in the wrong here. Although she *had* stabbed him, it had been an accident. The utter shock on her face couldn't have been faked, even by a woman he'd seen change a man into a canine.

She came back into the room, grinning a ridiculously out-of-place grin, and Evan was taken aback, again, at the change in her up close. There was something startling about her, something he couldn't seem to take his eyes off for long. He searched for what he might say to her when she'd bring him the plate, what words he could give her to reassure, or to say thanks. He wasn't certain what he owed her, but Evan wanted nothing more than to be in her good graces. He thought of the man outside the window. He did not want to be one of *them*. Not someone who worked for the mages who wanted her brought in.

He leaned forward to receive the plate, only to watch Circe walk right past him. She sat the plate on the floor and let out a long string of cooing, burbling *good boy*s. Her smile fell as Chompers took to the steak, and she glanced at Evan. His expression must have been something to behold. She laughed.

"Oh, you thought that was for you? Well, you can ask. Maybe he'll share."

Evan shook his head. "He deserves it."

Circe put her hands on her knees and pushed to standing. "He does. He's a good dog."

"Ugly but loyal?" Evan mused.

Circe narrowed her gaze on Evan, though he was pretty sure she knew the comment was only meant in jest. "Don't let him hear that. He has his heart set on something big. Maybe becoming a model one day." Her brow waggled. "Or a mascot."

"A mascot for what?"

She shrugged a shoulder. "A hotdog company, most likely. The boy likes to eat."

Evan laughed, even if it was half-hearted. And then he froze.

"What?" Circe asked.

"He is really a dog, though, isn't he?"

CHAPTER 5

*C*irce gave Evan her worst scowl. "Of course he's a dog. What is wrong with you?"

Evan raised one shoulder. "I don't know. I mean, there is a coyote on the ground outside who used to be something else. Maybe this bulldog used to be your mailman."

She looked at him for a minute, knowing her guilt over the coyote-man was stamped on her face, and said, "He's not there anymore. I called the Court of the Sun and the Moon. They came to get him." She sighed. "He was attacking me. It's not like I had much choice."

Evan was thoughtful for an equal measure of time. Circe wished she could read minds, but what he'd said when she'd drugged him to work on his side made things clear enough. She took a sip from her mug to hide her blush. She would *not* think of those things now, not with him inches away on her sofa.

"Why didn't you just call them then?" Evan asked. "He was incapacitated, and you had me under threat of your knife. Why wait?"

"I don't know," she answered. "I just . . . I wanted to be able to do this on my own."

She'd thought about that over and over when she'd locked

herself in her new bathroom to take a shower. What was she doing? Why was she keeping him safe? She didn't have a good answer. She'd been covered in dog slobber and the scent of that strange, horrible man. She'd just needed a shower. She'd just needed to think things through. And now it had been hours, and she'd spoken with the Court and not mentioned Evan. She'd made herself tea, and here she was, still not letting this man go. His wounds weren't that bad. They would heal. Besides, he'd been planning to kidnap her for some horrible council, so what if they did catch him? Circe had not meant to stab him. It had been an accident; it hadn't filled her with guilt. That was not what was eating at her. What really bothered her was that he'd been trying to save her.

It was not what bad men were supposed to do.

It was not what he'd been hired for. Not the thing he'd signed his life away over, risked it all with that thin scar at the base of his thumb.

Circe shivered, glancing at the closed curtains hiding the window the man had come through.

Evan noticed. "So you know you aren't safe here. What are you going to do?"

"I am safe here," she said stubbornly. "The town has wards. I have protections, my spells. There are people here to help me if I need it."

"They know how to get past the wards. And you're here alone. If you can't get to a phone or—"

She frowned. Obviously both Evan and the other man had somehow gotten past the town's wards. And she'd not set her own protections in place at that cursed window, even though she knew at the very least Evan had been out there. She'd gotten complacent. She'd trusted her stalker.

But he had come to her rescue. She hadn't been wrong.

"How can you act like you're so worried about it? You were going to kidnap me for some shady council of mages."

Evan looked like he'd been slapped. She'd gotten the

information dishonestly, but that didn't make it any less true. Even if he hadn't acted on it, Evan had known she was in danger. He'd not been watching her to keep her safe. He'd been watching her for them. He'd not acted himself until the last possible moment.

"I didn't have a choice," he said.

Circe believed him. He'd said as much when he'd been talking in his stupor. The magic in his blood was going to kill him. There was something she didn't know, though. "Why?"

His eyes met hers, soft and hazel, and Circe let herself really look at him. His hair was sandy, a shade darker at the roots. It was a little too long on top and looked like maybe he'd been cutting it himself. His jaw was square and a bit stubbly, and his lips . . . Circe drew a sharp breath, snapped her eyes back to his. Gods, why was she staring at his mouth? What was *wrong* with her?

Evan drew a breath of his own, long and deep. Full of hopelessness or regret, she couldn't be sure. "I was hexed. Years ago. I was hanging out with some friends—somewhere I shouldn't have been. One of them was mixed up with a supernatural—a fae, I think. I was so young. I didn't even understand the strangeness about him. Didn't know this other world existed. But I paid for it anyway. We all did. There were four of us, and only one of him. We didn't think it would be . . . well, we just didn't think. We stood up for our friend, puffed up our chests, and jumped in on his side. But there was some sort of payment, I guess, some debt owed, and when the witch came to collect from that fae, we were no more than flies as far as she was concerned. She snapped her fingers, and the friend beside me went down. I tried to help him, but I didn't know what she'd done. It took two more before I realized what was happening."

Evan shook his head. "When I leapt for her, she just looked at me, her eyes as black as pitch. The corner of her mouth went down, barely a grimace, and I slammed into the ground. The hex tore through me, like swords of ice."

Evan drew a shuddering breath, looked back to Circe. "She turned me. Used me to dispatch that fae. Guess she didn't want to get her hands dirty." At Circe's expression, Evan added, "She's gone now, killed by some fool she'd set another hex on. The guy thought he was going to fix her, that he was so cunning he could best a thousand-year-old sorceress. He had no idea he was dooming us to stay like this for eternity. No one has been able to help us. No one has figured out how to undo what she has done."

"You're a shifter?"

"Yes, but not like the ones you might have met. I wasn't born this way, Circe. My change is not tied to the moon. I don't have a pack. It's just me, and this hex, and whatever other poor souls like me that are out there trying to find a way to live."

Circe shivered each time Evan spoke her name. She curled her arms around a pillow, drew it in against her chest. He'd spoken some about that other man in his mutterings. About how the magic inside him would not let him die, even as it slowly ate at him. He had tried again and again to end the suffering, and it had driven him half insane. She understood why now. She hoped Evan had never been that desperate.

And then she realized he had.

"That's why you made a deal with the mages. To get out from under your hex."

Evan nodded. "They told me you were like her. That you were a witch who used men. Who turned them into beasts at your whim."

Circe's mouth went dry, and she felt a little sick. She was that woman. She was a horrible, horrible thing. What she did was transmogrification. The illusions came easier, yes, but only because she'd been doing that her entire life. Her true power would include the ability to change man into beast just as easily. It was brand new to her now—she was only just coming of age and developing that power—but if she were to live a thousand years, what sort of monstrous being would she become? The darkness was in her. Would she hex a man just to do it? Would she hurt someone for no valid reason?

Evan saw her expression, moved to touch her, then drew back as if in confusion.

"What will they do to you?" she asked him. He didn't answer. But Circe knew. They had taken his blood. His punishment would be worse than death. He'd only forfeited his life in that it now belonged to them. She swallowed hard and whispered, "What do they want with me?"

The aunts had told her she was in danger. Because of the curse. The curse that killed her mother. The curse that would be reborn the moment she fell in love. She didn't know why.

She'd been raised around magic, though. She understood that sometimes it truly was only a witch's whim. She knew there didn't need to be sound logic when the world was full of jealousy and spite.

Evan glanced down, and this time Circe knew it was shame. "I don't know. I made the agreement without even finding out why." He forced himself to look at her as he continued. "I thought you were like her. I thought it didn't matter why they needed you. I thought with one less witch, the world might be a better place."

His honesty cut her to the heart, but his words left open possibilities. His confession said that he was changed, that now he wasn't so sure. Circe wished she had the conviction to convince him she was worth saving. Or at least convince herself.

"Are you hungry?" she asked.

Evan might have been caught off guard by her sudden subject change, but he didn't let on. "No, I don't think I am." She wondered if his side was hurting him terribly, or if he had an ill feeling the way she did, thinking of hexes and curses and men shifting into beasts. He said, "I wouldn't mind another drink, though. Maybe something with just tea leaves and water this time?"

She managed a smile. "You'd be surprised what I can do with just leaves and water."

"I'm surprised by everything you do, Circe Alexander."

Circe felt her chest tighten, and she spun to make the short walk to the kitchen. She was in trouble, and she knew it. Evan didn't know about the terms of her curse, but she was one hundred percent aware. She could feel it in every bone of her body. She could feel him, too, like he was a lodestone. She was walking on dangerous ground.

The worst part was, it was maybe the most thrilling thing she'd ever done. The most *her* she'd ever felt.

She leaned behind a column to smack her forehead against the wall. "Circe," she muttered, "you are a bad, bad witch."

CHAPTER 6

$\mathcal{E}$van was in trouble. This girl was going to be the end of him, he just knew it. They'd sat on her sofa, talking as the lights outside faded and the moon rose. They were talking still. About everything, and nothing. What he'd wanted to be as a child, what his favorite foods were. Circe kept asking, and Evan kept making excuses to himself. Surely, she needed him there. She'd been attacked earlier in the afternoon; some strange man had been inside her home. A home that was new to her. She was scared. She was lonely. He was obligated for what he'd done. But those things were far from the truth.

Circe was strong.

Circe was determined.

Evan was there because he could not make himself want to leave.

She'd been telling him about the witches who'd raised her, and he could hear the wistfulness in her voice. She missed them, even though leaving to start her own life was what she wanted more than anything else. She'd been orphaned, and everything about her life had been someone else's choice. Now she was here and determined to make it work.

She didn't bring up Evan's family, and for that he was grateful.

He didn't like to think about the world he'd left behind. The memories he'd stored away. They were not sweet stories of bickering women and spells gone wrong. Not when a sorceress controlled your blood. Used you to kill.

Evan said, "And so the coven named you?"

She smirked. "Yes. After a mythological goddess who turned men into swine. 'Lest you forget men are pigs,' they like to remind me."

Evan remembered the goddess's story. It was a tale of isolation. "It's Greek, right?"

She nodded. "It means 'to secure with rings' or 'hoop around.' It's a reference to the binding power of magic." Her expression said, *Those witches, always thinking they're so clever.*

She sat her empty mug on the side table. "And Alexander is apparently from my mother's family. Since my father ran off and left me, the aunts refused to use his surname. They didn't like to talk about him at all. When I would finally wear them down with questions, I could tell they were filtering what they told me. It seemed like there were a lot of sidelong glances and clandestine conversations, and even though they are more than a little resourceful, they would only let on like they'd discovered a few small details."

She ran a thumb across the thin stacked bands on her finger as she considered. "I did some research once when I was younger, going through a bit of a rebellious phase. Breaking all the rules. I'd tried a tracking spell and a summoning spell and everything you can imagine, but what finally tipped me off with where to start was a scrap of paper in Anise's spellbook." She laughed, shook her head. "It was something like Hallewell. Lucius Hallewell, maybe." She waved it off. "I don't remember for sure. His name led to nothing but dead ends, and eventually I got some hobbies that didn't involve research or boys."

Evan froze. Every fiber of his being wanted to shout the name back at her, to be certain that was what she'd said. But it was. He knew it in his soul.

It explained everything.

And if the witches she was so fond of hadn't told her . . . Evan worked to school his features.

"Do you trust them?" he said. "The witches in the coven that raised you? The aunts. They're worthy of your trust?" He was stumbling over his words, but Circe didn't seem to notice.

"Yeah," she said. "I mean, they're witches. They like to meddle in my business, and they're constantly doing rituals to try to change the fates . . ." She shook her head. "I trust them. They're ridiculous and mostly insufferable, but they're good at heart."

She must have mistaken his expression. She said, "Let me take a look at your wound."

He might have argued, said it would heal on its own, that that wasn't what had him agitated. But he was a coward. He didn't want to tell her the women she loved, those she considered her family, had lied to her for her entire life.

He leaned back into the cushions to let her look at his side. She peeled away the layer of leaves and tonics she'd applied, made a clicking noise with her tongue. "It's a bit red around the edges, but the bleeding has stopped. How fast do you usually heal?"

"I've never been stabbed before," he told her.

She grimaced. Pressed her fingertips to his skin. Evan felt his stomach tighten at her touch.

"It isn't hot," she said. "I don't think there's infection. Does it hurt?"

It didn't. Having her hands on him was not that sort of torment. "No. I'm sure it's fine."

He started to pull his shirt back into place, but Circe laid her hand over his to stop him. "I want to put some more ointment over it before you sleep. Just to be safe."

Evan nodded. He couldn't look at her. She was too close. She smelled of citrus and mint, and something that reminded him of warm cider. He didn't know which were from the mixing she'd done, and which belonged to her. Gods help him, he wanted to sniff her hair. He cleared his throat.

Circe looked at him. There was a strange tilt to the corner of her mouth, like she was concentrating very hard.

"Ready?" she asked.

"Knock yourself out."

Circe dabbed her fingertips into a container from her side table and spread it carefully over his wound. She wiped her hands on a clean white towel, and then, instead of leaves and woven fabric, placed a square of sterile gauze over it with tape. Her fingertips lingered, tracing the edges of the bandage, and then farther out. Her thumb pressed against his abdomen, too low, and Evan thought he had never been tested so much.

"Circe," he said.

She stilled, seemingly startled, and pulled her hands free. She wiped them again on the dish towel, shaking her head a little before standing to clean up the mess. Evan took a steadying breath and lowered the hem of his shirt.

She tossed the trash into the waste bin, reaching beside him for the discarded gauze packaging. The black mark on her hand caught his eye.

"What is that?"

She blushed but folded a knee to sit on the couch beside him. "That is my official Resident of Havenwood Falls tattoo. All the cool kids get them." She narrowed her eyes. "I'm pretty sure you're breaking the law right now not having one, actually."

She held her hand forward so Evan could examine the tiny flowing script.

He took her fingers in his. "Jump?"

Her cheeks colored further, but maybe not from embarrassment. "It's from a Bradbury quote. 'Go to the edge of the cliff and jump off. Build your wings on the way down.'"

"Books," he said. "She likes to curl up alone with a good book." He didn't let go of her hand.

She quirked a brow. "You think because a girl likes books it means she's not daring? She's not trouble?"

"Actually," he said, "I'm sure it's quite the opposite."

Her skin was flush, her eyes glittering in the dim light. Loose strands of hair had pulled free of their knot, tickling the line of her jaw. Evan's fingers touched her palm, his thumb lay against the delicate tattoo. It was her ring finger. *Jump*, it said.

Jump.

Circe's jaw shifted behind her lips. She was biting the inside of her cheek. Evan let his thumb run from the base of her ring finger down, back up again. He was going to tug her to him. He knew he shouldn't, but there it was. He was powerless to stop himself.

Circe swallowed hard, then was suddenly on her feet. She clutched the wad of gauze in her other hand. "Evan, I think—I think we should get some sleep."

He let go of her.

She seemed relieved.

It felt like ice water. "I'm sorry, Circe. Thank you . . . for everything."

She pressed her lips together, nodded. And then she clicked off the room's only remaining lamp to put herself in shadow. Evan pulled the throw from the back of the couch over him, but his eyes remained slits as he watched her place their mugs in the sink and close her bedroom door. The lock clicked shut.

Trouble, he thought. *So much trouble.*

CHAPTER 7

*C*irce lay awake in her queen-size bed, staring at the darkened ceiling. There was a man in the next room. A man she'd convinced herself was no good for her. A man she had touched. A man who had laid bare the darkness of his life, and, somehow, had still been able to share his childhood wishes and dreams with her.

Circe hadn't admitted aloud that she had dreamed about him more than once, and not in the weird, creepy stalker sort of way.

She remembered that rebellious phase she'd talked so casually about. She remembered the terms of the curse, its edict that forming a bond with a man—falling for him—would bring her doom. Its warning of the dark things that would come.

The last thing Circe needed was Evan Grey in the room next to her. The last thing she could do was make herself stop thinking about him.

It had been hours and hours since the awful incident that had brought them together, and Circe had nearly forgotten about it. All they had done was sit together and talk. He'd told her everything. And what he hadn't told her then, he'd told her earlier —when he'd been under the influence of her potions.

Graceful, he'd said then. *Lovely.*

Circe had heard the words before. The witches who raised her had said it all the time. Morgan had told her she had eyes a man would drown in some day. Tia said that her smile could make the stars in the sky jealous. But they had a flair for the dramatic and only two speeds: everything was categorically the best or absolutely the worst. To hear the words from Evan was something else. To feel his touch was exactly *categorically the best* and *absolutely the worst* at once. Circe couldn't let this keep going. She had to stop. She had to make him leave.

She'd do it first thing in the morning.

Circe stared at the ceiling, the purpling light moving across in a thin strip. Morning was coming. Dawn was already here. Soon she'd have to face Evan again. She pressed her palms down on the blanket. She needed to just lie here and get some sleep. She would deal with it when she woke up. And then a terrible thought came to her: what if Evan woke before her? He'd be alone in her apartment. Had she left anything out? Anything potentially embarrassing or that he really shouldn't see? She'd barely had a chance to unpack, but she'd not brought much with her. She did a mental scan of the apartment and cringed when she thought of her sketchpad on the hall table. Gods, were there any drawings of him in it? She'd tried not to stare at him when he had followed her. She hadn't wanted to clue him in that she was on to him. The thing with being targeted, was that it was best to know where your attacker was coming from. She'd kept her eye on him the way he did her: covertly.

That didn't mean there weren't rough outlines of scruffy men in sunglasses and jackets with the collar drawn up all over those pages. Pages he could open to. Pages he could see. She cursed inwardly and flipped the comforter back.

She'd go get the sketchbook, and that was it. She wouldn't look at him. She wouldn't touch him. She'd only retrieve the incriminating evidence and then go to sleep.

She crept barefoot through the hallway, lights off despite the unfamiliar layout of her new apartment. She ran a hand over the bar that separated the kitchen from the living area and heard Chompers snoring in his bed across the room. She turned the corner to the short corridor between there and the doorway, and reached out blindly until she felt the edge of the hall table. She fumbled to right the small glass jar she knocked into, then touched the telltale metal spiral that bound her sketchbook. She sighed with relief.

Clutching it to her chest, she edged back toward the bedroom. At the end of the corridor, she looked in the darkness toward Evan's form.

In that moment, she couldn't help but think, What if the curse was right? What if Evan could cost her everything?

What if it wasn't?

What if this was all the life she'd ever live?

The lamp clicked on in the living room.

Circe caught her breath, thanking the gods she'd left on the black leggings instead of switching to her favorite bulldog-printed Christmas pajamas Louisa had gotten her as a joke.

"Don't you ever sleep?" Evan asked.

She nodded jerkily. "Just, uh, getting my notebook for some stuff I need to jot down."

Evan had been watching her for weeks. He surely knew the thing in her hand marked with "Sketch" in giant block letters was not a notebook.

"How's your side?"

"Fine," he said. "Doesn't really hurt at all now. You do great work."

She felt her bare toes drag across the hardwood, one foot curling behind the other. "It's nothing. Been doing those since I was a kid." She'd had harder spells, ones that had gone terribly wrong. Ointments were easy. No one lost a limb or turned an ugly hue if you mixed those a little too light or a little too strong.

"There's something I need to tell you," Evan admitted. "I should have said so before."

Suddenly, Circe was terrified whatever he said would be the

end. He was too stiff, determined. He was going to leave. He was going to say he'd changed his mind about whose side he was on.

Circe felt it like a knife in her chest. She'd just decided it was time to end this, hadn't she? So why, now, could she not recall the reasons? Words tumbled from her of their own accord. "What about you?"

His brow drew together. "What?"

"Sleeping," she said. "Don't you ever sleep?" Her quiet laugh echoed through the room. "I mean, following me around every day couldn't have left you much time. Do you not need sleep? Is it your . . . the . . ." She found herself waving a hand toward him to encompass his *condition*. She couldn't seem to say the word *curse*.

Evan stared at her.

She waited.

"Yeah," he said. "I guess I don't need as much. Circe, I—"

"What about food?" she said. "Do you need less food? Or more?"

Evan crossed the room, coming to rest an arm's length in front of her.

"I wonder how else it affects you. Do you know the words she used? Or maybe the ingredients—" She stopped short, realizing her nervous jabbering had gone too far. It was probably rude to ask the victim of a hex about his perpetrator.

Evan put a hand over hers to still the twitching. Over her sketchbook, its pages scattered with drawings of him. She swallowed hard.

When had she started watching him so closely? When had she decided he was something deserving of those attentions? Her gaze met his, and Circe knew she'd been lying to herself for weeks. She'd been interested in his presence since she'd first caught sight of him.

Evan seemed to notice he was reaching across the distance to touch her and dropped his hand.

"Circe," he said, his voice like a caress over her skin. She didn't want to hear what was coming.

She knew she had to.

She inched closer, entirely too aware of the space he was taking up in the room. His presence was a bonfire, and Circe's soul yearned for nothing more than heat. "What is it?"

She had a few thoughts of what she wanted his words to be. *I need to tell you how much I yearn to touch you, to taste your lips, to trace the lines of your face.* And she had a few thoughts of what she should do in response. Somewhere in the back of her mind, she understood the wisest would have been to lock herself in her room and call someone who'd slap some sense into her. She was pretty sure Morgan would happily do it.

At the thought, a loud *whack* echoed through the room. Circe's heart skipped, and Evan's posture went suddenly protective. They looked together toward the corridor, at the oak-handled broom that now lay across the wood-plank floor.

A portent.

Evan was beside her now, the warmth of his palm against her back. She looked at him, so close it was painful, and whispered, "Company's coming."

"Circe," he said again.

It was all he got out before the door to the apartment slammed open.

"Circe!" the witches shouted in a scattered harmony.

Morgan was through the door first, her raven hair slick against a thick wool cloak. "Darling, it's freezing here. You should really come home."

Tia pushed past her, elbowing briskly on the way. "Pshh. Do not listen to her. This weather is wonderful. But your wards are the absolute worst."

They swarmed the living room, six of them, and Louisa jerked her away from Evan to crush her in a hug.

"Oh, you look amazing," Anise cooed. "I just want to squeeze your little cheeks."

"Wait your turn," Louisa hissed.

Circe was being jostled, and shuffled, and moved farther from Evan with every single step.

"What are you all doing here?" she managed beneath the aunts' grip.

"Well, we're here to help you, of course," Morgan snapped.

Tia leaned in, craning her neck to see around Anise. "We heard you got attacked by a shifter. Did you use a hemlock for your elixir base? Nightshade?"

"I didn't poison him."

"What?" four of the witches said in unison. Tia pouted. "Why not?"

"He was incapacitated. I just put a minor illusion on him, and Evan threw him out the window until the Court could take care of it."

Six pair of eyes moved to the only man in the room. The *Evan.*

"Did someone from the Court call you?" Circe asked the aunts. "How did you even get here? How is everyone coming though the town wards?"

Anise patted Circe's hand. "You look lovely, dear. So happy to see you. We've missed you dreadfully. Why, Hazel has practically withered away."

"It's only been a few days."

She ran a hand over Circe's dark hair. "Time is strange that way, isn't it?"

Circe heard whispers over their conversation, three of the aunts hissing about shifters and windows, while Morgan said something to Evan. She had him by the corridor, walking toward him in a bid to remove him from the room.

"I know what you're hiding," Evan said in a harsh tone.

Morgan's reply was hushed, but Circe heard it anyway. "You know *nothing.*"

Circe pushed past Anise, trying to see beyond Tia's mop of fuzzy red curls.

"You have to tell her," Evan hissed.

Morgan smiled, and it was terrifying. "Say good day, Mr. Grey. It's time to go."

He was up against the door now, and his eyes met Circe's through the gathered chaos of a half dozen witches. Circe nodded. She didn't want Evan to go. But he couldn't be here. Not with them. Not when they found out who he was tied to. Circe didn't know how much the aunts already knew, but Morgan's use of his full name was not an accident. The aunts had their ways.

And just because they weren't a danger to her didn't mean they weren't dangerous.

Evan needed to go.

He frowned, but he did not argue. She wanted to call to him, to say . . . something. She just didn't know what. But he was gone, the door sealed behind him, and the aunts corralled her once again.

"You didn't have to bring everyone," she said.

"Oh." Tia waved a hand. "I know you're doing that sarcasm thing you're so fond of, but we actually did bring everyone. The others are down in their cars. *Someone*—and I won't say who, dear, even if you twist my arm—came into the parking area a little too hot and caught the side of a couple of light posts."

Circe cringed. "Are they hurt?"

"No, not at all. They're made of concrete, dear. I tell you, whoever built this complex did a wonderful job."

Circe blinked. She looked to Louisa, who only smiled.

In a matter of moments—at the drop of a broom—Circe's old world and new had collided spectacularly. She wanted to cry, but she wasn't certain if it was from happiness or despair. The echo of a car horn rose to her window from the lot below, and Circe could hear the catcalls being thrown at the man who'd just left her apartment. She slapped her palm to her face to cover the grimace.

"Seriously," she said to the room. "You all are not fit for public."

Tia swirled around her as Anise opened the pantry to examine each and every mug.

"Too bad," Tia sing-songed, "because we're going to a fes-ti-val."

"What?" Circe crossed her arms. "You can't be serious. I thought you said you were here to help me."

"Yes, dear. Of course we are," Anise said from the kitchen.

Louisa took Circe's hand. She felt a little like she was being passed around the room. It was dizzying to be in the presence of so many of the aunts at once.

It always had been.

Louisa said, "We weren't planning, of course, but on the way into town we saw the sign, and well, we took it as a sign, sign that it was. It will work perfectly."

Circe started to ask, "Perfectly for what?" but couldn't get a word in before Morgan took the conversation up. "The Into the Mystic New Age and Psychic Fair. Perfect indeed."

Louisa tugged Circe's hand to get her attention. "It is the spring equinox, dear. Did you forget?"

Circe had forgotten. She'd lost track of everything. All she could think of was Evan and this new life.

Every year on the equinox, the aunts had done a special ritual to bolster the protections they'd laid on Circe since she was a child. She assumed that would be over now, that she'd be responsible for setting those protections herself, since she was living on her own.

She sighed. So far she'd been doing a bang-up job.

Tia sprung up beside her, lavender mug of hot tea in hand. "You look ragged around the eyes, dear. Haven't been getting enough sleep?"

Had she not been so distracted, Circe would have noticed the hint of valerian and poppy in the air. But she took a sip out of habit, and by the time she realized, she was being dragged limply into her bed.

"No worries, sweetest. Have a nap and then we'll go to the fair."

She muttered something horrid in reply, but the women surrounding her bed only giggled.

"She's getting to be a grown-up, that one. My, my, how time does spend."

The click of a light switch sounded across the room, and the darkness behind Circe's eyelids intensified.

Damn it, she thought. *Drugged.*

CHAPTER 8

*E*van left the apartment, fuming and dealing with a building determination he knew was going to get him into even more trouble than he was already in. He'd promised himself he wouldn't do this again, but here he was, risking his own neck by sticking his fool self in the middle of someone else's business. He should have just told Circe who was after her and left.

He should have never stayed.

And now it was too late. He was involved. There was no stopping it.

He was going to help her.

It was early, the air cool and the rising sun throwing long shadows over the sidewalk when he walked past the Haven Saloon. It was probably a good thing it wasn't open yet with the mood he was in, but he would come back later to get some food. Right now, he needed a shower and a place to think. A large Victorian manor sat diagonally off the square, the sign proclaiming it Whisper Falls Inn. It was too far from Circe's apartment for Evan's liking, but he knew there was nothing to be done for her with a dozen witches at her ear. He'd parked his truck on a nearby side street when he first arrived, moving it occasionally so as not to draw attention. He stopped there first to get his backpack with a change of clothes.

He was given a second-floor room at the inn and a speculative look from the gray-eyed brunette who checked him in. He couldn't focus on why, though, because on the counter was a flyer for a local festival. A festival that celebrated the spring equinox.

An equinox when a mage might perform a ritual to increase its potency.

A deadline.

The deadline was today.

Evan cursed, dropped the key to his room in his pocket, and turned to go back outside. He had tried to speak with the witches and was ushered straight out of Circe's life. But there was someone else Circe trusted, and they knew enough about the supernatural world to remove a spelled coyote from outside her building without investigations, or the law. Evan would find this Court of the Sun and the Moon and warn them, even if the witches who raised Circe wouldn't.

He stepped again into the morning sun and realized the town square was already bustling with people starting their days, opening businesses, and preparing for the festival. He decided to cut around the foot traffic by going behind the shops. He crossed Main Street, following it east, and kept close to the building until he found the alley. His pace was brisk, and he'd formed a full resolve.

Nothing was going to stop Evan Grey from preventing the evil Circe's father was trying to bring onto them all.

Something struck his leg, like the sting of a wasp, and he smacked at it in instinct. His hand brushed the tip of a small dart, its fletch turkey feather tucked into lightweight metal. He yanked it free of his skin, eyes snapping up to find the dart's source. Heat spread up Evan's thigh, crossing his skin like fire. A shadow rushed toward him, and he dropped his backpack to shift. The cold of the hex shot through him, icy fingers that traced his bones.

It was always a shock, the pain when the hex pulled and snapped his skeleton, distorted his size and shaped his body into something other than what he was. It knocked him off balance, and he widened his stance, throwing his hands to the side as they broke into fur and claws, as his arms became too long for a man. Evan's neck wrenched, lifting his face to the sky as his jaw remade itself with fangs, then forward again as his neck took on the rigid spikes. His back widened, spreading his shoulders and ripping his shirt.

And then the frigid hex slammed into the heat of the poison in his leg.

Evan fell, grabbing his thigh as the hex and the toxin collided. His leg was flesh, his fingers fur, and his body felt like it was being crushed by the weight of that battle. A massive being slammed into him, and Evan knew right away it was a demon. The thing sank claws into his gut to drag Evan against the back of a building. He was trapped, unable to shift because of the poison and unable to stay partially transformed because the pain of it was stealing every bit of energy from him. He had no choice but to let the shift retreat, but before he did, he took one good swipe at the being's gnarled face.

Its skin was the color of rot, and its eyes were black. It wore a trench coat and jeans, but if the being thought it was fooling anyone, it was dead wrong. It pushed Evan up the wall, sliding his shifting form with long horrible claws.

"You're making a mistake," Evan told the thing when his mouth was once more that of a man. His voice was raspy, owing to the shift, the poison, and those cursed talons spearing his gut. "She's just a witch."

The thing smiled at him. "She has the blood of the gods. I can smell it on her."

"Lucius is no god," Evan spat.

The thing laughed. "Which is why he needs the girl."

Evan pressed his boots into the wall behind him, launching

himself forward to slam into the demon. They rolled across the alleyway, and the demon's claws tore free of Evan's gut. Blood soaked what was left of his shirtfront; he knew without the shift he wouldn't be able to properly heal the wound until he slept.

"Stay away from her," Evan warned.

"It is too late for that. The ceremony is near. The council waits."

The demon shoved a blast of power into Evan's chest, melting the patch of asphalt beneath him. At that close range, it was all he could do to withstand it. Flashes of his first shift, of the blood and claws and pain, and of every shift after crashed through Evan's mind. He could not allow himself to die; the moment this creature was done with him, it would be headed for Circe.

And if this beast was right, if Circe's line was that of a god, Lucius would bleed her out to feed the runes etched across his skin. Evan had spent enough time with the witch who'd hexed him to know that.

Evan curled in on himself, and the demon moved to make the final blow. Evan grabbed the vial from his boot and smashed it on the concrete. Lucius had given it to him—gods knew why. And now it crawled up the demon's leg like acid, burning through its flesh. Evan reached for his other boot, drawing out a thin blade, also a spelled gift from Circe's father. To protect Evan from her. From the dangerous, deadly witch.

Evan thrust the blade into the demon's chest and watched it turn to dust and ash.

He rolled onto his back, panting, and closed his eyes to the morning sun. Lucius was not a god. That meant Circe's mother must have had some trace of god's blood in her line. If she was of a goddess's bloodline, even heavily diluted, it would be potent enough to perform a dangerous rite. It would give Lucius the power he'd been craving. Too much power. Enough to destroy more than just a girl or a curse.

Lucius Hallewell was going to bleed out Circe for a ritual.

His own daughter.

Evan rolled to his side, retched onto the ground, then dragged himself to his pack. He couldn't pass out here. He needed sleep to heal, and he needed to cover this blood before someone discovered him.

He needed to find Circe.

CHAPTER 9

*C*irce woke refreshed and clearheaded, with a desire to wring those dirty witches' necks. It didn't happen, though, because the moment she opened her bedroom door, she was accosted with the overwhelming presence of thirteen women. Her tiny apartment living room was practically crawling with them. The aunts were draped over her sofa, her chair, making a circle of haphazard poses around her tiny coffee table, now littered with candles and cards. Chompers was panting happily on his bed, with what looked like a week's worth of steak in his bowl. Circe sighed, getting her first taste of the orange and lilac haze that filled the kitchen, then noticed all of the apartment's smoke detectors lay disassembled on the bar that divided the space.

"You could have just taken the batteries out," Circe said to the room.

The aunts shouted out greetings to her, and the room seemed to spin as they took to their feet, cloaks and tunics and scarves swirling as they dressed for the weather outdoors. "Get ready," they said. "We've been waiting *an eternity*."

Circe glared at them.

"How did you even get here? I thought the wards made this town nearly impossible for outsiders to locate."

Tia nodded. "They really do, dear. Those wards are perfectly stout. I can feel this town buzzing through my veins." Her hands came up to demonstrate, as if Circe could see the sense of magic Tia was feeling. She explained, "But Lyra invited us here and told us how to find our way. We couldn't miss the equinox."

Anise cleared her throat. "We may not be able to remember the town after time and the castings drag it into haze, so Lyra agreed to remind us." She smiled sweetly. "And we could never forget you, love."

Circe crossed her arms. "So the Beaumonts can know you're coming for a visit, but not me."

Morgan smirked, flipping a tarot card.

Hazel peeked around the corner to the corridor, giving Circe an unrepentant grin. "You must have slept for hours, dear. Hurry and dress, we want to get to the festival before the equinox."

Circe looked at the clock. "It's barely noon."

Hazel nodded emphatically. "Exactly. Now go!"

Circe pressed her fingers to the bridge of her nose, and then turned back toward her bedroom. A trail of leaves and jasmine crossed the threshold of her room.

"I can lay my own wards," she said over her shoulder.

"Let Louisa have her fun," someone called from the crowded kitchen. "She never gets to do anything for you anymore."

Circe closed the door behind her and went to the bathroom to splash cold water on her face. She was an adult. She could handle this. She would not let the aunts take over her new life. She should have already protected herself against sleeping concoctions.

She should have never taken that tea.

She reached into the vanity drawer, took out a bracelet, and wrapped it three times around her wrist. She hung the malachite pendant around her neck. The aunts had shown her their methods her entire life. They could only best her if she was willing to let them. She ran a brush through her tangled hair and put balm on her lips. She would enjoy them for their company, and as soon as this festival was over, she would send them on their way. She would have a talk with Addie about giving her a heads up when the aunts were making a plan.

Circe bit her lip, glancing in the mirror. Thoughts of Evan drifted up, but she pressed them back down. Whatever that was would have to wait.

The moment she exited the bedroom, wearing jeans and a thick-knit sweater, the witches ushered her out of the apartment and down the stairs. Louisa slipped a narrow bottle of dust into Circe's front jeans pocket, whispering, "just in case," as the others argued about how best to arrive. It was only a few blocks to the park, and with more than a dozen in their party, they decided not to drive. Though Circe knew from experience, when the aunts hit a festival, it was good to have a cargo van nearby.

"Who's going to buy the most today?" she asked.

"Hazel!" Three voices shouted in unison, while several more denied that they would spend one single cent. She could hear the music already, and as they walked toward the square, the sound of "Touch of Grey" grew. They found its source in a local food truck: Tacos for Daze. It was brightly painted and parked in front of the Haven Saloon, and Circe walked right up and asked for two tacos. There were groans of complaints from her party. "Are you seriously going to stop at the very first vendor?" And, "Tacos? Where's your sense of adventure?"

Circe smiled. "Tacos are their own adventure, Anise."

Then three of the witches ordered Sugar Magnolia Margaritas.

"So," Morgan said, "I see it's going to be one of *those* kind of days."

Tia twirled around her tauntingly, the margarita glass spinning along levelly and not spilling a drop. "The absolute best. I assure you."

They traipsed through melting patches of snow toward Town Square Park, and even Circe began to feel the excitement of the festival. They had been her favorite times as a child, one of the rare opportunities she'd had to run freely and act like a kid. The aunts had a terrible habit of getting distracted, and they'd always stuck

Hazel with the job of keeping an eye on her. It was not the woman's best skill.

The park was crowded with booths, each so colorful and enticing, the aunts could not agree on where to start.

"It's not yet one o'clock," Louisa said. "We have plenty of time to look around and still get back together before the big event."

Morgan gave her a fierce side-eye, but the group split into three smaller ones anyway, after much banter that unfamiliar onlookers might assume was near violent warfare.

Circe left them to it, walking with Anise down a table filled with crystals and candles. There were covered tents farther down, and booths displaying herbs and teas, books and jewelry.

A brunette dressed in jade, bejeweled and scarved, flashed them a smile. "Want to know your future?"

Tia jumped and squealed, her palms slapping together. "Oh, yes! Me, please."

The woman's gaze ran over the group, and Tia began the questioning. Who was she, what could she do, why had she chosen purple for the tent, how many moons crossed its surface.

"I'm Callie," she answered with a laugh. "And how about we start with a reading and go from there?"

Tia grabbed Anise's arm, but Anise shook her head. "You go ahead. I can tell you'll be in good hands with Callie."

Circe bit down a grin. Anise had never trusted other fortune tellers. If she wanted to know something, she read it in the leaves so she could do her own interpretations of the signs.

They kept walking, breathing it all in. Circe let the spring sun and the sound of the crowd fill her with that unmistakable festival atmosphere. Banners proclaimed *Past Life Readings*, *Find Your Spirit Guide*, and *Healing Massage*. Circe saw Addie among the crowd, casual in her jeans and a hoodie, its graphic a waxing crescent moon. Circe gave her a wave, but was tugged along by the witches as they followed the sound of "Brown Eyed Girl" farther into the festivities.

She couldn't keep herself from swaying to the rhythm and

humming along. She passed a few more familiar faces, startled to realize Havenwood Falls was already beginning to feel comfortable. Despite what had happened, despite the turmoil of the last twenty-four hours, it felt like *home*.

It was a good feeling.

Circe smiled and let herself sing about slipping and sliding along a waterfall. Her voice was echoed by a petite woman with graying auburn hair. She wore bright leggings under a long top, and though she looked less like a fortune teller than some of the others, she stood in front of a colorful tent proclaiming her Eloise Sinclair of Into the Mystic New Age Books and Gifts, the festival's namesake. The crowd steered Circe away from a psychic reading, and she was distracted once again by the sights and sounds.

A small girl was handing out honeyed candies for an herbal shop vendor, and Circe popped one into her mouth. She'd lost track of Anise, but she was sure they were all close by. She wasn't a little girl anymore, and you couldn't truly lose a pack of witches that big in a town this small.

Her eyes were drawn to a tall oaken cabinet, its top windowed on three sides to reveal a mannequin decked out with scarves and glittering beads. Circe grinned at the absurdity, knowing full well there were actual clairvoyants—women like Callie and Eloise— right here in Havenwood Falls. She came closer. The mannequin was draped in purple, her lips too red, her eyeshadow too blue. Her face was turned down, her plastic hands spangled with rings two to a finger where they hovered over a glowing crystal ball. Her nails were lacquered that same purple as the ball, and Circe found herself mesmerized by the color, the light of it.

She was standing in front of the machine now, a strange yearning in her heart that she did not understand. The mannequin's hands moved, its arms shifting in that jerky, mechanical way, the music-box melody clashing with the Van Morrison coming out of the festival's speakers. Color swirled inside the globe of the crystal ball, there was a strange *click*, and the mannequin's hands lurched to a sudden stop.

A ticket came out of the machine. Circe glanced around, but no one was paying her any mind. She leaned forward, tugging the card from the delivery slot. It had come out upside down, displaying the familiar tarot image of the Tower. Circe flipped the card over and read the message on her fortune.

The curse does not lie within you. It was borne of the coven.

Circe stared at the message, feeling like her bones had turned to ash.

The curse does not lie within you.

It was borne of the coven.

Her coven.

CHAPTER 10

*E*van woke in a darkened room, his face plastered to the tile floor. The smell of cleaning supplies and bleached cotton towels clued him in, brought back the memory of checking in. The gray-eyed attendant. The Victorian manor.

Whisper Falls Inn.

He wasn't sure how he'd made it back there, but he was glad he had. He rolled over, staring at the ceiling in the spare light that came through the bathroom door. His backpack was on the floor beside him, contents strewn across the tile. He was pretty sure he'd forgotten to get his phone out of his ruined jacket in the alley, though he couldn't think of anyone he would actually call. He needed to find Circe. He stumbled to his feet, finding the clock on the nightstand beside the ornate headboard. It was nearly one o'clock. He was dangerously short on time.

He flicked on the light switch and saw the mess of his clothes, the dried blood covering his healing flesh. He knew he'd never make it across the square like that, so he peeled off the ragged material to shower off the blood.

He wasted precious time checking her apartment, and then following the trail of witches who had taken her to the festival in the park. When he finally found her, she was surrounded by them, and Evan had to hide behind the tents and banners until she moved out on her own. She'd been arm-in-arm with the blonde he'd thought was named Anise, Hazel close on their heels. Morgan was speaking with some locals three booths down—the tattoo artist and two silver-haired women wearing business attire. He'd watched Circe meander through the crowds, laughing and singing as if she wasn't in imminent danger from her murderous father.

Then Circe had walked away from the others, seemingly in a trance as she headed for an old-fashioned fortune machine the likes of which Evan had only seen in movies. "Madame Mystic" was painted in purple script on the thin metal signs nailed above the box's windows. Circe was smiling, and then she wasn't. She leaned forward, drew a card from the ticket slot.

Evan watched in horror as Circe turned to ash.

He stepped forward, torn between fear and action, but he realized what appeared to be ash was only a cloud of smoke—the way he'd seen Circe hide the small bird so many weeks ago. Evan could feel something horrible crawl over his skin. It was a premonition, or maybe the feeling of it from Circe, but she was scared or hurt or something else that was very, very wrong. He rushed to her—to the hazy fog that was Circe—and tried to take her in his arms. He whispered her name, but if the witches noticed they did not look his way. Circe came into form, at least he thought she had—but it was he who turned to ash. His hands where they touched her were gray now, the same smoke that disguised her figure. She was hiding him. Hiding them both. *From what?*

"Evan," she whispered, and the pain in her voice was more than he could bear. He pulled her against him and turned to walk away from whatever it was that had upset her so badly. They stepped over a pile of cards like the one she'd held in her hands only a moment before, but Evan only saw the same image on all: two naked forms, a tree behind each form.

Circe was crying.

Evan took her to the inn, her cloaking spell allowing them to get to his room unnoticed. The space was small, holding only a queen-size bed, a wooden dresser, a narrow desk, and a chair. They sat on the edge of the bed, and Evan slid his arm around her. The smoke covering them dissipated.

He let her sit there, let her think through whatever it was she was concentrating on so hard, and kept his hand against her so that she knew he was there should she need him. It was painful to see her hurting, and the idea that he had gotten so attached to her was terrifying. Everything about her scared the hell out of Evan in the most satisfying way. Like her tattoo. Like jumping from a cliff and hoping for wings on the way down. Being near Circe had opened something inside Evan without his realization, and now, it was as if he could finally breathe free.

She hadn't been crying hard, but eventually she wiped her cheek with the back of her hand to look up at him. Her lashes were damp, the tip of her nose just a little pink.

"They lied to me, Evan."

Her hands were folded tightly in her lap; he reached to take one in his. "I'm sorry. I should have told you."

"My whole life." She let out a harsh breath. "I'm so mad at them. And there's nothing I can do. It's over, already done. Anything I did now would just be revenge."

Evan slid his hand slowly up her back, down again. He did not know what to say. She was right. She knew she was.

"I don't want to be that person. I don't ever want anyone to make me that person. I just—I just want them to have not done this to me."

She was breathing more easily now, the shock of it gone, only the hurt and disappointment left. She leaned into Evan's side.

Her fingers twisted to twine with his where they lay in her lap. She traced a thumb over his knuckles one by one methodically in between her slow breaths.

An onyx charm lay against her wrist, the rest of the bracelet hidden beneath her sleeve.

After a moment, she smiled up at him with chagrin. "I'm

sorry," she said. "I just broke into your room and cried all over your stuff." She ran her fingers over her hair. "I must look a mess."

Evan pulled her hand down. "You look lovely."

She blushed. "Do you mind if I . . ." She gestured toward the restroom, and Evan drew his embrace free to let her go.

He heard her splashing water, then silence as he imagined she was drying her face. Then there was a lighter sound, and between the aged insulation in the inn's walls and his sensitive hearing, Evan realized she was whispering. He tried not to listen, he really did. But words snuck through, broken only by the thunder of his heart.

"It's okay . . . don't let them take this from you . . . let yourself be with him . . . take your life back . . . live for you . . . let yourself *feel* for once . . ."

He searched frantically for the television remote—anything to create noise. He wanted badly to clear his throat so that she'd understand how thin the walls were, but he couldn't seem to get enough air. What was she doing? Giving herself a pep talk? Gods, why had he brought her into his hotel room? This wasn't what he'd meant to do. He was hexed; she was a witch. This was a terrible, terrible idea. He caught sight of himself in the mirror over the dresser, all damp hair and flushed skin. The latch to the bathroom door clicked, and Evan jumped, turning to face her, television remote finally in hand. She saw his expression.

"It's okay," she told him. "I'm angry at them, but this isn't revenge. I feel safe with you, Evan. We don't have to worry about the curse."

He felt himself deflate. She'd been worried about his hex. Had she thought he might shift on her? Had she thought he might actually hurt her? Turn into a beast and tear through her tender flesh? The idea of it made him ill.

"Circe," he started, then had to stop. He swallowed hard. "I would never hurt you. I know why I came here, what I am, and why I followed you, but I swear to you, even as a beast, I would never—could not hurt you."

She gave a surprised half laugh. "Oh, Evan, I never thought for a moment you could. Not in that way."

He opened his mouth to say, "What?" but she was moving toward him, and all thought ceased.

The remote fell to the floor.

Circe crossed the space between them, her face bright and open, her eyes only for him. She stopped barely a few inches from him, waited. He let his hand raise to her cheek, let his fingers sink into her chestnut hair. She smelled of spring and of the festival, of the oils and fragrances that had been on display. Her sweater was soft and black and only made her skin more luminous, her cheeks more pink. She looked up at him, no rush or anger in her gaze. True to her word, she had placed her hurt out of mind. She was letting herself be free.

He was more grateful for this moment than he had ever been for any of his life. He wanted to confess to her, to tell her all the things he had done, but she already knew. She knew about the hex, she knew what was in his blood. She had accepted him despite those things.

There would be no debts here. She was not offering herself in exchange for anything; she was giving them both the gift of freedom, for however long that might be.

The pad of his thumb crossed her lips, trailing down as he let his fingertips trace her flesh. She watched him, and it dragged out the moment, letting it feel like an eternity of exploration. He leaned down, tasting her. Her mouth parted beneath his, and it was sweetened honey. She was warm and soft, and she rose into his kiss just the slightest bit. Like the patience she'd given him was ebbing, like her warmth was pressing slowly to heat.

Her hands rose to his sides, sliding beneath the hem of his shirt to find his skin. Evan sucked in a breath at her touch and realized he too was becoming unduly eager. He wanted to touch every part of her, wanted to feel her bare skin. Gods, he wanted to see her naked and sprawled across his bed. Their kiss deepened, and she was pressed against him, and still it wasn't enough.

Evan's hands slid up her back beneath that sweater, pulled her closer. She stood on tiptoe, climbing on top of his boots. They were both breathing too fast, their pulses pounding in a rhythm he should not have been able to feel.

Circe drew back from their kiss, sighing deeply. She bit her lip, watching him through her lashes as she toed off the heel of one boot. The bit lip turned to a wicked smile as she kicked off the other. Evan clumsily followed suit as she pulled him toward the bed.

She fell before him on a flat white comforter, her hair spilling over it, her arms stretching beside her to brush the fabric.

"I've never slept in a hotel," she confessed.

Evan's smirk answered she would not be getting that sleep right now.

She threw her head back and laughed, full and genuine. It exposed her neck and the line of her jaw. Evan climbed onto the bed beside her, carefully sliding his hand up her thigh and over her hip. He squeezed and drew her to face him, so they were side by side on the bed. A green pendant on a chain around her neck slid sideways; Circe saw him looking.

"I took precautions," she said, "after my apartment was busted into."

"Do you think they'll be able to find you here?"

She shrugged one shoulder, let her hand climb to his waist. "Not if I've done my castings well."

It made him feel a little better. He would be at her side, and he'd left his cell phone—the only means to track him—in the alley behind those shops.

"And what if they do?" he asked.

She smiled. "Let them come. I am not afraid of them."

He leaned forward to brush his lips over hers. "And what of me? What if I never let you go?"

A shiver ran through him, and he had the oddest sensation it was not his own. Circe breathed her reply against his lips. "What if you don't?"

What if you don't?

Evan thought in that moment there was nothing more likely in the world.

He took her mouth with his, pressing her to her back as he held himself over her, and Circe arched into him, curling her knees around his waist as quick as a cat. He broke their kiss to grin at her, and she drew her sweater over her head, throwing it off the edge of the bed. Evan felt the crush in his chest when he saw her there, hair loose over the white linens, skin as soft and sweet as he'd imagined. He drew back further, running his hands over the sides of her lace-trimmed bra, down the curve of her waist, across the plane above her pants. Her stomach trembled, and when his fingers reached the fastener of her jeans, he looked up at her.

Her expression said it was agony, but only the best kind. He slid back and leaned over to kiss her above that waistband. Her breath hitched before being released in a sigh. He undid the button and zipper, and she lifted her hips for him. He kissed her again, trailing his mouth over her flesh as he pulled the jeans free. He repeated the process as he moved once more up her form, lingering longer this time at the delicate skin of her hips, her thighs, her stomach. Her panties were soft black satin, and Evan ran his kiss over those as well. Circe groaned, rose into him, and he kicked off his own jeans. He raised up to pull his shirt off, but he was only halfway out of it before Circe tugged him down. She yanked it over his head and took his mouth with hers.

"Evan," she whispered, and the sound of it said so much more. She couldn't wait any longer, and gods help him, even if he'd wanted to tease her, he couldn't wait either. They shuffled bedding and pillows, colliding as they went, unable to draw away from each other long enough to properly remove their clothes. But then they were bare, by sheer determination, and Evan had an instant of wild disbelief as he held himself over her, seeing her expression clouded by lust, her body entirely open to him. He let the naked desire show on his face as he touched her, running a hand over the slickness at the junction of her thighs. He had to close his eyes for a moment, to catch his breath at the unbearable heat, at how much she wanted him.

He leaned down once more to kiss her deeply, felt the press of her against him. He kept his hands on her hips as he straightened and slid, excruciatingly slowly, into her. She was so wet, so soft. Her arms slipped above her to the headboard, her body bowing upward as Evan thrust into her with building speed.

"Circe," he murmured, unable to form any other word. She pressed harder into him in reply, breathing out a throaty moan. It did not take long until they were both breathless, until their pleasure hit that plateau and was released with a low animal groan, and then Evan was beside her, holding her to him, kissing her face and touching her skin and never, never wanting to let her go.

Circe was naked except for the tangle of sheets and the jewels wrapped at her wrist and neck. She held her hand over her chest, as if she couldn't quite catch her breath. Evan's breathing became more regular, and he sensed something else, some strange scent in the air, metallic and sharp. He leaned up to look at Circe, her expression stricken.

"What is it?"

She stared at him, closed her eyes, and shook her head. "Oh, Evan. I've done it. I'm so sorry." Her eyes came open again, bright but crumpled at the edges in her distress. "I thought I was safe. I thought—I thought it would be okay."

He rose further, glanced around the room. "What are you talking about? Circe, what is it?"

She looked as if she was on the verge of tears.

"The curse," she said.

Evan jerked to sitting, turned his arms and hands. He was not shifting; no part of him felt the icy hex crawling through his blood. "You are safe. It's okay. You don't have to worry about the hex. I won't turn, not with you this close."

Her brow drew down. "What are you talking about?" And then she saw his stomach, with the pink healing lines and marks from that demon's claws. "What happened to you?" She spoke the words with surprise, raising up to sitting, same as him. She reached automatically toward his wounds, and her hand came free of her chest.

The pendant had exploded. She'd held her hand there to cover it.

"What was that?" Evan asked. "Circe, was that malachite?"

She met his gaze, expression unknowable, and nodded. "Bad things are coming. I thought I was safe. I thought I could do this one thing." She swallowed hard. "I triggered the curse."

"Stop staying that. I told you I'm not shifting."

"Would you quit talking about shifting for one second? This is serious, Evan. What happened to your stomach?"

He ran a hand through his hair. "I was attacked, earlier this afternoon. The council sent a demon after me." *After you.*

Her eyes went wide.

"It's all right," he told her. "I took care of him. But there will be more." He laid his hand over hers. "You set protections, right? You're safe. You said they couldn't find you." He looked at the clock. "And once the equinox has passed, you should be safe for a while until we can figure out how to deal with this."

"The aunts," she said in a small voice. "Evan, I said the aunts couldn't find me." She clutched the sheet to her chest. "They lied to me, told me someone else had set my curse. It was them all along. I thought, I thought you said you knew . . ."

He stared at her, his heart cold. "I knew they were keeping a secret from you. A secret about the council and why they wanted your blood." Her words were seeping slowly through the confusion, falling into place in all the wrong order. "What you do you mean *your* curse?"

"You didn't know. About my curse." She was moving from the bed, gathering her clothes.

Evan wanted to stop her, but he found himself doing the same thing. There was a danger building in the air, and it wasn't just this revelation.

She looked up at him as she slid on her jeans. "You thought I meant your . . . thing." She gestured toward him, as if to encompass the hex that caused him to turn into a horrid beast with one mild flick of her wrist. As if this other curse was so much larger that the two could not even compare. "And I thought you meant—What is it? What did you think I already knew?"

Evan straightened, pulling his shirt down to cover the damage to his skin. "The council is coming for you. Today, for a ritual that must be done at the equinox."

She looked at the clock, back to him.

"Circe," he said. "There's something more."

The man who wants to kill you is your father.

She waited, eyes bright, for Evan to destroy her world.

There was a sudden vibration beneath them, the room's floor shifting as if from an earthquake. Circe turned from Evan, and both of them ran for the single door.

CHAPTER 11

$\mathcal{C}$ irce and Evan reached the end of the corridor before they realized the quaking had stopped. Or rather, they realized the rest of the hotel had never moved.

"They're trying to force us," Evan said. "He wants you on the run."

She glanced at the stairwell, wishing they weren't on the second floor. "They can't do it here. The inn is full of supernaturals. They'll want us outside." The idea of the equinox, of a blood rite on the same day the aunts had always protected her, niggled at the back of her mind. What would this council want to do that was tied to the same day? Circe's gaze, suddenly sharp, cut to Evan. "What do you mean *he*? I thought this was a whole council of mages."

Evan placed a hand on her elbow. His voice was full of regret. "Lucius," he said. "The council is headed by Lucius Hallewell."

Circe felt a strange chill run through her, settling in the pit of her gut. It made her a little queasy. "What?"

"I'm sorry. That was what I'd meant to tell you. The secret I thought the witches were keeping from you."

Circe remembered speaking the words, words she'd not told anyone else in the world but Evan.

Because she'd known better than to discuss her findings with the aunts. Knew any talk of her father would only hurt or annoy them, and cause a flurry of new restrictions on her free time and ability to do such research. They had kept it from her on purpose.

Her father.

She felt numb, the words falling from her mouth as she stared blankly down the empty corridor. "My father wants to use me in a ritual." She rolled the idea around for a moment, let it fall into place with everything she'd learned. Everything that was fact and everything the aunts had told her. Their utter disgust for even the idea of him. Evan waited, but Circe knew they needed to go. She had to make a decision. "Why would he leave me?" she asked. "If he wanted me, if he had some use for me and was going to try so hard to recover me—why not just keep me?"

She knew in her heart the answer, but she had to say it aloud. She needed Evan's confirmation of her fears.

"Your powers would not have manifested until this year." Evan's reply was careful. Circe heard what he did not say anyway. Circe knew the truth in her broken heart.

"They stole me. They knew what he'd been planning, and they took me when I was a child." That fit so much easier in her memory, fell into each tiny crack left by the things her aunts had never said. They'd done their ritual when they knew he'd need to do his. Had they been in league all along? Had they known Circe's mother? Had they loved her as one of their own?

Had she once been their thirteenth?

A rumble started at the opposite end of the hallway, crawling slowly toward them. Circe was not sure at first if the sound was coming from inside of her, from the building emotion that felt as if she might explode. It wasn't, though. It was her father, calling her, forcing her out so that he could take her blood.

"Circe," Evan insisted.

Her eyes met his. Her feet did not move. "Why does he want me? What is it that I have—what is in my magic that is so much stronger than the others?"

Evan turned her to face him full on. "Your mother was a descendant of the gods. The demon sent to find you could smell it in your blood."

Circe nodded. It made sense. Horrible as it was, this was the sort of thing that called for a curse. This was the sort of magic the aunts would do anything to protect.

The sort of power a mage would kill for.

"Okay," she said to the stairwell door. "I'm ready."

Evan's hand pressed briefly to her back, promising he'd be there for her. She felt his concern, though, as he moved past her to open the door. He did not know the true strength inside her, but he was willing to risk himself anyway.

She followed him down the back stairwell—a covert passage for employees—and beyond her new resolve, she could sense Evan's fear turning to something else. The hex in his blood was colder, the magic not boiling to the surface the way she might have expected but rising nonetheless.

"Evan," she said. "Please don't shift. I will protect you."

He stopped on the landing between the first and second floor, looked up at her where she stood the few steps above him. Circe understood now how Evan's curse was hurting him. How the desire to shift brought it on, and how each shift was slowly draining him. Whatever time Evan had left, she did not want him to waste on her behalf.

She felt the cold settle in him once more, saw his eyes go soft even as his mouth flattened into a grimace. Circe walked past him to the stairwell door.

"I promise," she said. "Just trust in me."

They silently walked into the first-floor lobby, finding the quickest exit from the inn. The moment they were outside, Evan sensed the shifters lingering near the edge of the building. They moved toward Circe and Evan, and Circe could feel the change in him. She put a hand on his arm, felt the hairs raised on his skin. She didn't have to say it again. She had asked him not to shift, and he'd resist it if he could. If the magic would let him.

Circe glared at the approaching men.

"Don't lay a hand on either of us," she said levelly. The men hesitated, but she knew they'd be under orders. "I will go with you, but touch me once and it will be the last thing you ever touch as a man."

Her words were effective. The shifters must have been warned. Circe wondered why all the men her father had sent her were shifters, given her ability. Did he assume she could not transform a man who already shifted? That her power would be less potent? Or was that power a talent she'd been given by him? She wanted to know what he knew about her gift, but she would have to think about that later. She could not let him get inside her head.

Evan put his hand on the small of Circe's back, leading her toward the street. He must have been able to sense more than just the shifters, or somehow the mages had a way to call him to them using his blood. She hoped that wasn't the case. Being tied to one hex was bad enough.

She wanted to ask Evan how powerful her father was, but she knew the answer already. Powerful enough an entire coven of witches was determined to stop him from doing a blood rite. Powerful enough he was able to call her from their room at the inn despite her protections. They walked the few blocks to where the street ended, and Evan kept moving through the low vegetation that led into trees.

They were going to the forest.

The late afternoon sun threw shadows across the ground, but the shadows were not long enough. The equinox had not passed. She tried to remember the words the aunts had used in her yearly rituals, how they might have been trying to protect her. To delay this.

They walked on, the trees tall and thin, leaving Circe feeling exposed and vulnerable. She wrapped her arms around herself, wishing she had worn a coat. Wishing she had filled her pockets with more concoctions than her meager supply. The ground was covered with snow, unlike the areas that had been cleared in town.

Circe stepped carefully over the hidden roots and vines. She saw figures moving behind the trees, shapes of men and cloaks and beings that were not the locals of Havenwood Falls.

These were her father's men.

Eventually, they reached a clearing, patches of snow and fallen pine needles over barren ground. Seven mages stood in a semicircle at the far edge of it, hooded cloaks covering their forms. At least ten more figures moved through the trees behind them, but Circe did not know which were mages and which were their hired hands. At their entrance into the clearing, the mages shifted, and Circe saw the stone platform beyond.

She felt the figures moving behind her and Evan, knew they were trying to cage her in.

"I came of my own accord," she announced. Her eyes were on the central figure—not taller or broader than any other man but positioned in the center of power. "I will not be threatened in my own home."

There was no response from the waiting mages. Circe could feel Evan's tension beside her, his need to shift causing him physical pain.

"I demand that you release the bond on Evan Grey. That you remove yourself from Havenwood Falls and never return."

There. They didn't care, but she'd said it. It made her feel a little better that they'd been warned.

"Evan," Circe said. "Stand behind me."

His gaze snapped to her, disbelief shaping his expression in an almost comical way. Still, she did not remove her attention from her father.

Evan stepped behind her, eyes on the men who inched nearer every second that passed. One of the figures lit two candles on the stone altar, another began to burn smudge sticks, filling the clearing with spice and smoke. The mages began to speak, reciting a low, rhythmic chant in a language unfamiliar to her. She'd waited long enough. They had no intention of hearing her out.

Circe unwound the bracelet at her wrist, crushing its beads in the palm of her hand. She let the dust fall around them, singing the words of the spell loud and clear.

The mages stopped chanting, their cloaked forms going still. A precise wind drove through the clearing, knocking out the candle flames and eating the smoke, pulling the hems of the mages' cloaks to snap in the gust.

Evan murmured his approval behind her, but Circe was frozen. "That wasn't me."

A cackle cut through the now still air, and Circe had to bite down a crazed laugh of her own. *Tia.* It was Tia. Thirteen witches came into the clearing at a full run, and by the sound of things behind her, Circe counted at least three of the shifters down and out.

That still left a few too many for her liking.

The aunts lined the trees behind Circe, fanning out on either side. She could feel Evan's breath on her neck behind her. He'd no longer need to watch her back. Her coven had done that.

More cloaked figures moved from behind the trees, the sounds beyond Circe's and Evan's backs indicating they'd grown to quite a crowd. Circe couldn't look away from her target.

She could not give him even a breath to take advantage.

He had no such concern. His gaze left hers to scan the clearing, to take in those who stood around her.

"She knows, Lucius." The voice came from beside her, unmistakably Morgan's, but the tone chilling in a way Circe had never heard, even counting the time one of Anise's cats had shredded Morgan's favorite black strappy dress.

The man Circe stared at lifted a hand, his flesh covered in black symbols and lines. He drew down his hood. His hair was short and dark, his skin olive, his eyes green. He looked familiar, but not because he was anyone Circe had ever seen. The likeness was in the tilt of his eyes, the shape of his nose. That of a father and daughter. That of the woman in Circe's own mirror.

She hated that they shared anything in common, let alone blood.

He held his hands forward and said in a conversational tone, "Daughter."

Circe felt the bile rise in her throat. She had tried to talk to him, she had stood right before him, and he'd never flinched. And now, ritual candles burned out and smoke cleared away, he would assume she had forgotten. That she would run to his open arms.

She stepped forward, as if to do exactly that.

She felt Evan try to move with her, but one of the aunts must have bade him to stay. She was glad of it. She didn't want him in reach of this man who would sacrifice his own kin.

"I thought you left me," Circe said. "All these years."

His expression did not change, but as she moved closer, she could see the toll his spells had placed on him. The reason he craved the power so bad.

"I would never leave you," he told her. "You were stolen from my very arms."

There was a rumble of mutters and growls from the witches behind her, but Circe did not turn around. She kept placing one foot in front of the other, moving closer to this man who wanted her dead. "And now," she answered, "here I am."

He took on an air of uncertainty then, sudden and probably something rarely seen.

Circe liked that.

His hands came down, palms facing her. "That's close enough."

She smiled. "Yes," she said. "I believe it is."

Lucius threw his arms wide, and power burst through the clearing. It hurt, nearly knocking her from her feet, but Circe felt the bottle Louisa had dropped in her pocket earlier explode, and she understood that was why she'd been able to withstand the hit. Palms fisted, Circe stared up at this man, no feelings of love for him in her heart. She'd been hurt by them, truly, but the coven behind her was her real family. Her only family.

This man was a monster.

Lucius's fingers drew in, and he used the power to call to Evan.

He had Evan's blood; Circe couldn't do anything about that. Still, she stood her ground.

There was a cry behind her, Evan shifting unwillingly into a beast. Circe could not help him. She could not turn around. It sounded as if his bones were breaking, as if his body was being torn to shreds. But the magic would put him back together. The hex inside of him would keep him alive. Moments passed, and then she could feel him, moving toward her until his ragged breath whispered up the back of her neck and the fur of his muzzle brushed her skin.

"You would have him eat me, then?"

Her father stared at her. All he needed was her blood on that altar by 3:58 p.m. He did not care how it got there.

She felt the tear trickle over the curve of her cheek. She did not need to fake that, but the sentiment was not for her father. It was for Evan. Circe couldn't imagine the pain he must be in—being forced into his beast form by first a witch's hex, and now by this mage. She used the grief anyway, as if she might raise her hand to wipe those tears. When her fisted hands reached high enough, she turned them open, palm up, and blew the remaining dust into her father's face.

The line of mages sprang forward, shouting words of power and throwing castings of their own. But it was too late. Circe spat, leapt forward to brace her hands on her father—on the exposed flesh of his neck and face. Cloaked figures filled the clearing, throwing the mages to the ground with their powers and their bare hands. A chorus of howls echoed through the trees, both animal and man, but Circe could not focus on anything but the task before her, this one thing that was the hardest spell she'd ever cast.

She could feel Lucius's energy fighting her, and it only made her push back harder. She thrust her magic into him. Circe did not need his blood. She had power of her own, the very thing he'd wanted to steal, and she could feel it growing every moment closer to the equinox. The aunts' ritual had not been performed. Circe's power had never been stronger.

Lucius writhed and struggled beneath her, snapping his jaws and digging his clawed fingers into the earth. Darkness shot through his veins, crossing the tattoos in hectic patterns. His hands began to lengthen, his skin turning ashen before sprouting coarse black fur. She had never done an animal she was unfamiliar with, and her lack of remembered details and anger were turning him more monstrous than she might have intended. She yanked the cord of his cloak free of the material and bound him where he lay, this once-deadly mage now panting and hopeless and utterly beaten by a single measly witch.

Circe smiled, standing to dust her palms off on her pant legs. Morgan came beside her, staring down at the dark, mangled form. She shook her head. "Oh, Circe."

Circe looked up at her, for Morgan was quite tall when she wanted to be. "What?" she said. "Isn't that what you wanted?"

Tia popped up on her other side, snorted a laugh. "Men are pigs and all?"

She was trying out that sarcasm thing; Circe thought she liked it.

"Technically a boar, I think." She shrugged, turned to survey the clearing. Six cloaked mages scattered the ground, beaten and bloodied to various degrees, all bound with spelled twine or leathers, all gagged with their own cloaks to prevent spellcasting. Three cloaked figures neared, dropping their hoods.

"Addie," Circe breathed.

Addie gave Circe a nod and kicked her black boots against a stone to knock the snow loose. "Nice job, C."

"Circe," Morgan said, gesturing to the silver-haired woman beside Addie and a tall man with slick black hair farther out. "This is Saundra Beaumont and Roman Bishop."

Saundra nodded, but instead of a *hey* gesture like Addie's, this one clearly meant business. The man glanced at her, his blue eyes interested but his demeanor leaning more toward bored or annoyed, which one Circe couldn't be sure.

Circe looked to Morgan.

"Both sit on the Court of the Sun and the Moon and on the High Council of the Luna Coven," Morgan explained. "Saundra is Lyra's mother. She and Roman agreed to assist with your situation in exchange for a bit of help from us. Lucius, you see, was more than a danger to only you. He worked for an exceptionally nasty entity known as the Collector. They will take custody of Lucius, and he will no longer be a threat to us."

"The Collector?" Circe asked.

"That's not for you to worry about," Morgan assured her. "The important thing is that Lucius has been handled, and what he planned to do to you and, eventually, other residents of Havenwood Falls, will never come to pass."

Circe blinked, glancing around the clearing again. The cloaked figures were dissipating. Roman gestured loosely to Lucius's body, bound as it was. "Take him to the cell."

There was more movement as cloaked figures heeded his order, and Saundra gave Morgan a significant look. Circe paid the ordeal no attention—she had no interest in where they took that man who had been nothing like a father. Instead, she reached into her back pocket, drawing free the tarot card she'd received at the festival.

She presented it to Morgan, letting the printed accusation speak for itself.

Morgan cleared her throat. "Yes, dear. Perhaps we should discuss this later, privately."

Circe crossed her arms, stood her ground. She was done with this, and even if she didn't know much about who this Saundra and Roman were to Morgan, she was done waiting. "How about now?"

Morgan sighed, sliding the card into the folds of her cloak. "The protections we laid on you—your curse, as you have come to know it—was never the true cause of your doom. Your future had been foretold long before you came to us, and as such, we had no choice but to take action. It is true that your mother faced her own end due to a curse, but only after she fell into Lucius's hands. That was when the darkness took her."

At Circe's flinch, Morgan placed a hand over hers. "We saved you, Circe. Protected you in the only way we knew how."

Circe nodded for her to go on.

Morgan pressed her lips together, and Circe could tell she avoided glancing at Saundra and Roman, who watched on. She said, "Prophecy said your fate would come when you created a bond with a shifter, someone with dirty blood that Lucius would be able to track back to you. So we did what we could to delay that end. To keep them from finding you. Unfortunately, Lucius did what he could as well."

"And the rituals?" Circe asked.

Morgan's hand went to Circe's cheek. "We fell in love with you the moment we laid eyes on you, child. We could have done nothing else but everything in our power to save you."

Circe drew a breath, trying to keep the pain in her chest from showing. She stepped back from Morgan so that her aunt might not see. She didn't want to relive those memories now, not in front of everyone.

Not in front of anyone.

She watched as Roman drew up the hood of his cloak and turned, Saundra following after. Addie gave Circe a small smile. Circe had a feeling none of this was as new to them as it was to her.

She took in the clearing again. She did not see the shifters Lucius had had control of. She did not know how much of this battle she had missed, but as she scanned the forest, she could not focus on the rest any longer.

She could only see Evan.

Anise and Louisa squatted over him, Hazel standing behind them with her hands bent into unnatural shapes. Like a puppet master.

"Let him go," Circe said.

"We're only keeping him safe. We didn't want him to harm you."

Circe moved toward the group. "He can't hurt me now. Lucius is no longer a man—he can only use Evan's blood when he's in human form."

Anise raised a speculative brow.

"I just know," Circe told her. She waved her hands to shoo them away.

The aunts watched her watch Evan, muttering and whispering amongst themselves.

"I thought this curse was supposed to keep her away from men . . . looks like he got his hooks in her anyway, doesn't it? I told you he'd follow her here . . . that's how those prophecies work, you can't trust them . . . every single time. You just can't win . . . maybe we should have used nightsbane . . . would you stop with the drugging everyone all the time, did you ever consider maybe that's not the answer . . ."

Evan was bleeding through large patches of matted fur. He was gray all over, dark streaked with ash. His arms were long, nearly the length of his back legs. His feet were like a jungle cat's, but the rest of him resembled something large and canine. He was still his full size, only stretched into something terrible and lethal and covered with hair. She knelt beside him, placed a hand on his fur where his shoulder might be. He did not move, but his eyes opened, black and depthless, to look at her.

"I'm here, Evan."

He blinked, the sound that came out of him half whine, half growl. The shift on its own would have been bad enough. At Lucius's hand, it must have been a thousand times worse.

Circe looked up at the aunts. "Did Lucius give this power to me? Is that man the reason I can do what I do?"

Louisa's eyes were soft, but her voice rang strong and true. "No. Nothing that is good in you came from that man. Your mother gave you this gift, and that's what it is. That thief could not do it on his own. He was only obsessed with those who could."

"And the lies, they're done now?"

Anise winced. "It was only to help you, dear. Only to keep you safe."

Circe thought of the rituals she'd grown up with. The fears they'd instilled in her.

The curse they'd warned her was to bring her end.

She stroked the suffering beast with a trembling hand, so sorry that she'd ever been such a fool.

"I'll help you, Evan." She glanced over his wounded form and felt the cold hex beneath his skin. "I don't know how, but I'll help you."

EPILOGUE

*C*irce sat at her studio desk, staring at the calendar pinned above it on her apartment wall. She'd been painting, working on a watercolor sketch of the shops on Main Street, some of her favorite places to be. The washed-out figures of locals walked in front of Shelf Indulgence's imaginative window display and sat on a bench outside Madame Tahini's Potions, Lotions, Palm Readings, and Other Extra-Sensory Services. They made their way into Coffee Haven for tea and art, two of Circe's favorite things of all.

She smiled as she dropped her brush into the glass jar she'd picked up at Howe's Herbal Shoppe, thinking of how she might approach Willow Fairchild—the empath she'd since discovered was fae and the owner of Coffee Haven—with her newly finished watercolor in hand. Havenwood Falls was full of artists, and Circe felt the peculiar nervous excitement of sharing her art with peers. She had been nothing but happy the last few months, and more often than ever in her life she forgot to watch the time go by. Without a countdown to the day her curse would commence, dates escaped her notice, slipped by as if they were nothing at all.

But now she'd noticed. Today was June twenty-first, the summer solstice, and it could not help but bring to mind that first day of spring. The aunts had told her more truths after all, that Tia had been warned in prophecy, that Anise had read it in her leaves, that Louisa had thrown the prediction in bones. Some terrible and epic thing was bound to happen, and the only way to save Circe was to hide her from her own goddess blood. To create a curse that would bind her, that would bring her up and direct her here, where a slim few survivable outcomes awaited her instead of the thousand other nasty ends. Her blood had been so powerful, they'd been forced to rebind the magic every spring.

To hide her from the mages. From her father.

They hadn't counted on Evan, though. The hex in his blood was not what they'd expected from a shifter, and they'd had enough trouble getting rid of him that they knew they were running out of time. Circe's fate was coming.

When the Court had discovered Lucius had a connection to the Collector, Saundra had sent Lyra right away. She'd known that Lucius was Circe's father, and so they removed the aunts' memory blocks and together made a plan to bring Circe to the safety of Havenwood Falls. To trap Lucius before he could gain the power he needed to continue the Collector's schemes.

The aunts explained they had made arrangements with the Luna Coven and the Court of the Sun and the Moon for the day of the ritual, that each had been there in case Circe had needed them, but that the aunts had had faith she would do the right thing. That she could take care of herself. They'd insisted she go to the festival that day so that she might be under the protection of the locals during Lucius's planned ritual. And so that she could face her father before the Court took custody of him. Plus, Anise had said, they just really loved festivals.

Circe had finally forgiven the aunts, but she'd refused to follow them back to the church where she'd been raised. Havenwood Falls was her home now, and despite what they thought of its weather and Evan's presence here, Havenwood Falls was where she intended to stay. Hazel had hugged her and whispered that the cold was certainly worth it in exchange for the view. Circe was still not sure if Hazel had meant the view of the mountains or the view that was Evan, but she'd wished them well and sent them on their way, with permission to arrange visits only when invited by Circe.

You had to be strict with witches.

She'd also discovered that not only had the Court of the Sun and the Moon known of the aunts' plot all along, they were the reason Lucius and his mages had made it past the town wards. Lucius had a history that Circe knew little about, but apparently he'd done enough to warrant letting him believe he'd found a way to circumvent their protections so they could be done with him once and for all.

Who the Collector was, Circe didn't think she'd ever know. The Court went above and beyond to protect its borders, and no matter what their own stake in it, Circe would be forever grateful for what they'd done for her. She didn't care how they'd dealt with Lucius once he'd been taken from that clearing, and she wasn't sure she ever wanted to find out. But she hoped someday she could be more like the members of the Court, that she might learn how to better use her power to help the Havenwood Falls residents the way she'd been helping Evan.

It was a beautiful possibility, the idea of turning something that had been a curse into good. What she'd done for Evan, maybe she could do for others. She had a satisfying job at the animal hospital, and she was meeting so many locals and supernaturals, she had more than just hope.

Circe was discovering that maybe she wasn't such an introvert after all. Maybe she just hadn't found her people before.

There was still the issue of figuring out how to remove Evan's hex, to clean his blood from both its ties to that sorceress and to Circe's father, but her magic could at least give him a reprieve. She could at least slow the process until something more could be done.

She could give him a chance at life.

Circe glanced at the *jump* tattooed on her ring finger, remembering the quote. *Go to the edge of the cliff and jump off.*

Build your wings on the way down. Evan had received his Court-issued tattoo from Addie days after Circe had returned him to his human form. It was small and clean, covering the scar the mages had left at the base of his thumb. *Wings*, it read. Evan had gotten a tattoo of wings. She recalled the first time she'd seen it, the blush on his skin and the thrill in her heart.

It gave her butterflies even now.

Circe glanced at the clock, remembering the date was important for something else. Evan was at work until five, finally able to hold a steady job now that he could mostly contain his shifting. McCabe & Sons Construction had hired him as a trial for the summer, as soon as business had picked up after the spring thaw. The McCabes were shifters, and they understood Evan's condition. If he were to have a slip, Circe knew they would have his back—even if Evan hadn't seemed to take to the cat shifters as quickly as he had some of the other locals.

They had both found their footing here. They had begun to make friends, to feel anchored.

To look forward without fear.

Evan had an apartment of his own now in Havenwood Village, and he would be knocking on her door by six sharp. The summer solstice brought another festival on the square: Midsummer's Night. Circe had never been so eager for a fair, but this one would be especially remarkable. The human residents of Havenwood Falls would be put into a deep sleep, so that the supernatural beings who filled the town could have a night free to be their true selves. Evan's curse would allow him to attend, and the night would be filled with games and dancing, and the mayhem that only supernaturals were capable of. She smiled at the thought of it, at the anticipation of spending it with Evan, and some part of her, far in the back of her mind, knew that if it went well, she might even someday invite the aunts.

~

Song of the Witches
by
William Shakespeare
From Macbeth, Act IV, Scene 1

Round about the cauldron go:
In the poisoned entrails throw.
Toad, that under cold stone
Days and nights has thirty-one
Sweated venom sleeping got,
Boil thou first i' the charmed pot.

Double, double toil and trouble;
Fire burn and cauldron bubble.

Fillet of a fenny snake,
In the cauldron boil and bake;
Eye of newt and toe of frog,
Wool of bat and tongue of dog,
Adder's fork and blind-worm's sting,
Lizard's leg and owlet's wing.
For a charm of powerful trouble,
Like a hell-broth boil and bubble.

Double, double toil and trouble;
Fire burn and cauldron bubble.

Scale of dragon, tooth of wolf,
Witch's mummy, maw and gulf
Of the ravin'd salt-sea shark,
Root of hemlock digg'd i' the dark,
Liver of blaspheming Jew;
Gall of goat; and slips of yew
Sliver'd in the moon's eclipse;
Nose of Turk, and Tartar's lips;

Finger of birth-strangled babe
Ditch-deliver'd by a drab,
Make the gruel thick and slab:
Add thereto a tiger's chaudron,
For the ingredients of our cauldron.

Double, double toil and trouble,
Fire burn and cauldron bubble.
Cool it with a baboon's blood,
Then the charm is firm and good.

ABOUT THE AUTHOR

Melissa is the author of ten YA and fantasy novels, and countless to-do lists. She is currently working on the next book, but when not writing can generally be found talking (about books), painting (things she's read in books), or hiding between her headphones (listening to books). Check out her Instagram for art and book love or follow via one of the many links at www.melissa-wright.com

For info on contests and new releases, sign up for the newsletter here: http://eepurl.com/zbisj

ACKNOWLEDGMENTS

Thank you Kristie Cook for allowing me to have some small part in the Havenwood Falls world and its community of amazing authors. This has been an adventure of the best kind. Thanks to each of the Havenwood Falls authors for welcoming me, and for sharing your creations so graciously. Special thanks to author E.J. Fechenda for the use of her characters at Coffee Haven and McCabe & Sons Construction (and for giving poor Evan a job), Kristie Cook for a room at Whisper Falls Inn, and for Addie and the Court, to Lila Felix for serving the tacos, Randi Cooley Wilson for Callie, and R.K. Ryals for fortunes and music with Eloise at the Into the Mystic New Age and Psychic Fair, and for Isa Hilton and Cressida Manos at the Havenwood Falls Animal Hospital and shelter. Thank you to all the Havenwood Falls authors who've dreamed up a world so wonderful and allowed me to play in it. Thanks to my crit partner Jennifer Silverwood for keeping me in line. Thank you to the incredible Ang'dora Productions team, the amazing beta readers and editors, and to designer Regina Wamba for the beautiful cover art.

OF SALT AND STARS

SEVEN JANE

A Havenwood Falls New Adult Novella

HAVENWOOD FALLS

OF SALT AND STARS

SEVEN JANE

ALSO BY SEVEN JANE

The Isle of Gold

The Drowning Bride (A Legends of Havenwood Falls Novella)

To everyone who's ever fallen in love with the water.

And to MR, the brightest star in my sky.

The darkest hour is just before the dawn.
—Proverb

CHAPTER 1

MANY YEARS AGO

*A*t the edge of the lush green forests that surround Havenwood Falls, where the sweet-smelling junipers and majestic pines tickle the walls of the silver snowcapped mountains that border the town, in a place seldom traveled and even less often remembered, there once stood a well.

It was a well of the wishing sort, with a peaked cedar canopy that hovered above a yawning mouth of gray stone rendered soft by the breath of innumerable years. The well was one of those rare structures that during the day appeared carved of sunlight, its golden shine so blinding that the only way to look upon it was to shield one's eyes and sip it in quick glances lest it steal your vision completely. At night, however, the well was perhaps even more beautiful, when under the glow of a silver moon it seemed as soft and elusive as the stuff of dreams, formed into being by the twinkling of a thousand stars. Regardless of the time of day, the air always seemed more fragrant near the well—scented by day with a pomander of wildflowers and by night with the heady flora of thistle and night-blooming jasmine. So tangible, too, was the

magic in this place that the air was always just a little cooler here—
a wrap was necessary even during the hottest parts of the year—
and it was so quiet that the whisper of the clear water that swelled
nearly to the well's lips could even be heard above the rustling of
the forest itself.

The animals that lived in the surrounding wood did not drink
from the well, nor was its water harvested as drinking water for the
town. Indeed, no bucket was ever hung from the awning from
which to draw, for those few who knew of the well also knew that
it was enchanted, and its waters imbued with a very special sort of
magic. See, the well was not merely the fount of a spring. Far
below the water's surface, in a hidden lake in a cavern below the
earth, dwelled a creature as temporal and beautiful as the structure
itself—a naiad by the name Noelani.

The naiad's well was a carefully guarded secret in Havenwood
Falls, and only a few knew of its location, but those that were
lucky enough to know the well's secret—most often women but
occasionally men and children as well—would visit. There they
would cut their hair and cast hushed wishes to Noelani, the Lady
of the Water, and dip long wooden spoons into the well for a sip
of her water's magic.

Most of the well's patrons—both human and supernatural
alike—wished for love, for like other naiads, Noelani was a spirit
of such things. Young girls were keen to look for their beloved's
reflection hovering under the wildflower petals that floated on the
well's surface. Older—but no less lovestruck—young brides garbed
in their wedding dresses came to collect vials of Noelani's water,
which brought them fertility. And when their bones began to ache,
elderly women in their widow's habits sipped spoonsful of the
well's water for vitality. If one was lucky, they might even catch a
glimpse of the naiad herself, alight on the well's brim under the
glow of the sun or the full moon, her long red hair swirling in the
water beneath her as she sang songs more beautiful than those of
the sirens at the banks of the waterfalls on the other side of
Havenwood Falls. If this were the case, then the person would

have been even more richly blessed, for it was said that whoever's eyes met Noelani's would be granted the gift of her magic, and some of her love would remain in their hearts forever, making all of their days blessed and sweet.

For many years, the naiad's well was a place of good fortune for all who visited. Noelani was happy, and her water was pure. But that was long ago, and such lovely places rarely endure for long—even those so consumed with love, for love is the most fickle of all beasts.

THE OPPOSITE of love is not hate but jealousy, and it was this that caused the well to ferment and the magic of Noelani to become diseased. It was jealousy of the ugliest kind—that which bleeds from the eyes and can sour milk just by the look of it—that led to the death of a young bride by the name of Stella Malley, who, on the very eve of her wedding, had come to ask the naiad's blessing and instead found herself drowned by the man who'd promised to marry her.

The manner in which he killed her—some say he held her head below the water until her lungs filled all the way to her throat, others that he strangled her with the train of her veil and sank her body with stones—is less important than his reason for doing so. The root of his this man's darkness was jealousy, not of what he couldn't have—for Stella had promised to be his—but of what he couldn't *control*. With her long black hair, creamed honey skin, and black eyes that sparkled like stars, Stella was as lovely as the midnight sky. But even more charming than her face was her heart, which drew others to her in droves and caused her to outshine the man who would have been her husband, and—had such a thing been possible—her shadow.

The man—his name important only because it is on the list of those that have been banished from Havenwood Falls, and such things are sparingly done—was a Mister Peter Heilen. And when

Heilen forced his betrothed's face into the naiad's well, Noelani watched, helpless from below as Stella thrashed, the poor girl's lungs filling with water she could not breathe. As precious moments passed, Noelani saw the light inside Stella's eyes grow dim and faint until it burnt out altogether, and when the richness of her skin had been replaced with the gray tinge of death, her face relaxed and her mouth fell open.

Only Noelani heard Stella's final scream, and the sound was so anguished that when it infused the water, it also filled the naiad's heart with rage. With Stella's scream in her stomach, the naiad shrieked, her beautiful voice so racked with pain that when it broke forth from the water, the drops pierced Heilen's skin like shards of glass, causing him to stumble and look into the well. When he did, his eyes met Noelani's. He saw her red hair pooled like blood around her and her pearly white teeth grown long with fury, and he was afraid. And as the jealous are also often cowards, he ran, leaving Stella's body to topple into the well and sink, lost forever.

By the time Stella's corpse had made its way to the bottom of the well, it had turned the blue water black, and along with it, Noelani's heart. Death is a sorrowful thing, but murder is bitter, and crimes of passion are tinged with powerful dark magic that can snuff out even the brightest candle. Noelani's warmth turned cold as stone within her, and the love inside her drowned in a pool of darkness much in the same way that Stella Malley had been drowned in Heilen's.

Still, Noelani had seen the face of the man who'd murdered his bride, and so when he left the naiad's well, a part of her had been forced to go with him, trapped inside his eyes. The love held within Noelani's magic soon soured within him, turning every drop of love he encountered into something vapid and impenetrable until, one night many years later, he drowned in his bed where he slept—as dry and far from the water as he had been able to go to escape what he'd seen that night in the well. Heilen's death was a mystery, for how could a man as dry as a dead leaf choke on water that had risen up his throat from his own insides? But the doctors said he had drowned, and so he had. And because of the curse Heilen had brought upon himself and Noelani, there had been no one left behind to mourn his death, for he had never again had the chance for love.

TIME HAS CHANGED THE WELL. What was once a place of love and light has fallen largely to the ruin of legend. Years have passed since any girl or young bride or even a widow has dared visit its part of the forest, for they know there is no love left for the naiad to give. The well's once clear and flowing water has sunk lower and lower until all that remains at the bottom is salt from Noelani's tears. The cool air around the well has iced over, the remnants of Noelani's sobs still on the air in the form of ice and frost, and the forest has crept in around the well until the meadow has been overcome completely by a rambling snarl of thorn and root. The scent of wildflowers has been overrun by the stench of death, and in the absence of Noelani's light, the forest had grown thick with loveless creatures both cruel and vile.

None has seen the naiad Noelani, but those who tell tales of such things insist that Stella's bitter death consumed the once lovely creature, her beautiful red hair turned black, and her skin grew gaunt and pallid like a corpse left too long underwater. Those who might wander too far into the woods are warned to avoid the wrath of the well, for even if one were to survive the dangers of the forest, the creature that would crawl forth from her prison would not be the naiad, but a miserable and cursed thing. A rusalka they called Noelani now—a monster, dark and sinister, with a heart consumed with spiteful evil. And if she saw you, it would not be blessing that she'd give. Instead, she would pass on her curse and drag you down into the depths of darkness with her.

THE TIME of the well has passed, and the love of Noelani is lost. What remained of her magic passed to Heilen, and when he died, it faded with him—or so those who remember were inclined to believe. Noelani's story has faded largely to legend, and whatever remains of her—whether naiad or rusalka—is left to wallow in her well, guarded by the Court of the Sun and the Moon, who leave Noelani in peace so long as she brings no harm to the residents of Havenwood Falls. Some once whispered of a cure, a return of Noelani's love that could only be brought about from the seeds of her deepest hate, but it has been many years, and none have come forward that might break her curse and heal her broken heart.

And so Noelani waits, trapped in her own darkness, for a star to save her.

CHAPTER 2

*M*aris's eyes snapped open in the midnight darkness of her bedroom. She'd been having that dream again—the same one she'd been having her whole life. Okay, well, maybe not her *whole* life, but certainly for as many of her twenty-four years as she could remember. For the most part, they'd been the passing kind of nighttime fancies, the type that you woke up still feeling but only barely able to remember, and even those last little tendrils had faded completely by the time her feet touched the morning floor. But lately, the dreams had begun to linger, growing more and more insistent, as if they were trying to tell her something—to carve the memory of them into her heart with ghostly fingers and bedtime secrets. And they had begun to hurt, as if the longing in her dreams was enough to wound her heart, so that Maris sometimes woke with a dull ache in her chest.

Lately, her awakenings had grown even stranger. Sometimes she woke with her mouth full of warm, salty water. Other times she'd find strands of hair much darker than her own wound in the crevices of her body—around the backs of knees, her wrists, her throat—but when she'd go to remove them the strands would be gone. At first it had baffled and confused her, and lately it began to frighten her, although it was impossible to say why because it was impossible to understand in the first place.

This bramble stuck in Maris's daytime thoughts, invading her dreams night after night in a pattern that had become as regular as her heartbeat. After Maris's father passed away a little more than a month ago—dried up and dead broke in some pitiful little hostel somewhere in the desert while she'd been buried under snow in Denver—the dreams had taken on an air of urgency, and the strange incidents had increased. Still, even though she often woke up sweat-drenched and panting, Maris could barely remember the dream by the time her eyes opened, and certainly couldn't recall enough to decipher any hidden message.

Insofar as she could tell, there was nothing truly remarkable about the dream itself. There was no grand inspiration or message that could be decoded with a dream dictionary, and she'd never once experienced any of that waking form of déjà vu that might connect the dream to her real life. The strange events aside, the dream wasn't scary or suspenseful—at least not enough that she would remember it being so. It wasn't even particularly thrilling. In fact, it was much the opposite. The scraps she could remember were beautiful—maybe *the* most beautiful she'd ever had, like something out of a fairy tale.

In the dream, it was always light out, but only just barely, with wisps of sunset coloring the sky in pastel shades of pink and orange. There was a forest she'd never set foot in and a small pool of water she'd never swum in, and both of these were more lush and vibrant than any parcel of land she'd ever seen—even in Colorado, where beautiful landscapes were a dime a dozen. But even more breathtaking than the scenery, there was *her*.

The woman in the dream.

The woman *of* her dreams.

The woman in Maris's dream was always constant, even if the scenery changed—which it did, but only with the weather, which followed the seasonal cycle of Maris's waking life. The woman—if she was that, because there was something distinctly magical about her that marked her as not completely human but certainly feminine—swam in a large stone well. Sometimes the water that rippled atop the edges of the stones was frosted over with a layer of glittering ice; other times Maris could tell by its look that it was as warm as bathwater. Throughout all of these, however, the woman never changed. She always appeared, rising out of the water so that it spilled off her milk-white skin like rain and weighed down hair that was the color of liquid scarlet but might have been strawberry blond when dry. She had the most dazzling emerald-green eyes and a curve to her lips that was simultaneously taunting and coy, and she never wore anything more than a thin white slip of a dress, which gave her an air of innocence that was almost certainly misleading if one judged the way it clung, damp and revealing, against her flesh. She seemed always covered in dew and softness, and there was a small mark on the inside of one of her wrists: a tattoo of a star with four lines that stretched to create eight points —the one called the North Star.

"Maris," the woman would whisper, her lips shiny and wet with water and a voice that sounded like the ocean and deeper things and had a way of pulling Maris's heart into her throat.

"Yes," Maris would hear herself responding, as in her peripheral vision she watched her own hand reach for the water— for the woman in the water.

"Come away with me," the woman would say then, and the words were nectar on Maris's tongue when at last she closed the distance between the two of them and could taste the words on the woman's waiting lips. There was something that changed in Maris each time she kissed the woman in the well—a blossoming inside of her that grew and became more solid and real every time she touched the woman's lips with hers, until the dream had ceased to be a fantasy and began to feel like home.

If Maris had her way, she'd wrap every bit of herself—every strand of her dishwater blond hair, every square inch of the freckled, sun-kissed skin she'd inherited from the mother she'd never known, each of her ten long fingers and ten agile toes—around the woman in her dream. She'd hold her close, touch her lips against her sweet, glistening flesh, and slide with her beneath the water and never let her go. But then, just as this seemed like it might be a possibility, the dream would end, and Maris's eyes would open somewhere grim and dry and far away, the ethereal image of the woman's eyes tinting her vision emerald until she blinked it away. Darkness would creep in on the edges of the dream, and all would be lost—until the next night.

The woman in the dream had a way of undoing Maris, and not the least of it was because she was a *woman*.

Though she'd often been accused of being insatiable when it came to matters of the heart—a trait she'd had since puberty and had long since quit being ashamed of—Maris Heilen had never been terribly choosy about her lovers' genders. That wasn't to say she'd been particularly inclusive in her bedroom either, though whether that was by default or decision she wasn't sure. Honestly, the sex of her lovers had always paled in comparison to the actual act itself. Although her tastes had been diverse and far-ranging, her lovers had always and consistently been men. She'd bedded men with blond hair and with dark, men lean and bulky, those fair-skinned and those carved from ebony, tattooed and pierced and unadorned, smooth-faced and bearded, a decade older or a handful of years younger, and every possible combination in between. None had ever held her fancy for very long, though one summer she'd very nearly accidentally fallen for a Frenchman who'd had *chocolat* brown eyes and curling chestnut hair and who didn't speak a lick of English—something that had never been a problem for Maris when weighed against his gentle caresses and endlessly generous lovemaking.

In any case, no matter how many or how different the men that passed through Maris's bed, she was inevitably left unsatisfied, as if there was a hole deep inside of her that could never be filled, though she'd tried like hell to address that in the most literal of ways—not that she'd bothered herself to keep a tally of her conquests. A man wouldn't have done so, so why should she?

And through all of these men, Maris stayed empty, longing for something more that she could never quite articulate, let alone hold in her hands, until at last she'd come to believe it would never be a man who claimed her heart. Even so, Maris had never considered herself to be particularly attracted to women. But, if that was true, then so was the fact that she wasn't *not* attracted to women, either. They were beautiful and so lovely in ways that men just couldn't be, with their long smooth limbs and shapely curves, their soft blushing skin. It had simply never occurred to Maris to take one to bed, and she wasn't sure whether that was disinterest or some sort of deep insecurity—like if she finally opened herself up to someone she might fall into them, never to resurface. Lust, Maris was comfortable with. Lust she could control; she could embrace or let go and it wouldn't hurt her. Love was something else entirely. It was deep and bottomless, consuming.

To love someone, Maris feared, was to drown, and in that sea of emotions, she had never even learned how to swim.

Still, Maris couldn't deny that she felt something stirring within her whenever she caught herself looking at other women in the manner that she often caught men looking at her—all hungry-eyed and wet-lipped, like they were starving creatures just presented with a savory meal. Whatever it was that she felt, Maris had never done more than look, though no woman who had ever crossed Maris's line of sight could have compared to the woman in her dreams, including her *boyfriend*—a word Maris still wasn't entirely comfortable with two years into their relationship—who was currently asleep and snoring softly in the bed beside her.

Barely three months ago Maris had done something she thought she never would, not that she'd ever planned to find herself landlocked in Colorado to begin with. She'd agreed to relieve herself of her private little sanctuary in Lower Highland—a recent addition to Denver's neighborhoods known as one of *the* hippest new neighborhoods in the country—and shack up with a tech nerd from Capitol Hill. Not just any man, but Graham, her current long-term boyfriend who seemed to be becoming a little bit more serious about their relationship than Maris was totally equipped to deal with. Graham, with his unruly jet-black hair and rugged jawline. Graham, who knew how to wear a starched white dress shirt like it was lingerie, and often did, accessorizing his look with the top three buttons left undone under a shadow of dark stubble that had as much of a strange, weakening effect on Maris's knees now as it had on the first night they'd met. It had been the first thing she'd noticed about him when they crossed glances across the bar where she'd been slinging drinks for some extra cash: his unkempt hair and unshaven face juxtaposed against the stark white crispness of his shirt, a brooding counterfeit of a budding businessman. And Graham had not disappointed when Maris had given the last call and the pair had stumbled their way back between the sheets at her place.

Once upon a time, Maris would have taken Graham for a night, maybe two—three if the days bled together, which they often did—and then set him free to float away on the current of her spent desire. Such days, Maris reflected, seemed a lifetime ago now. Two years had a way of feeling like an eternity, and Maris wasn't entirely sure how she felt about anything so endlessly *long* and boringly predictable. She'd always been a free spirit, as restless as the tide itself, and now she felt stuck, like someone had built a dam around her heart and refused to set her free.

Maris's friends said she was settling for Graham, not because he wasn't handsome or stable or all the right things a man approaching thirty should be, but because he *was* handsome and stable and all the right things a man approaching thirty should be. And Maris would never admit it, but she knew she'd only settled for Graham. From his dark hair to his maddening tendency to root his feet in the ground and gather mud around them, Graham was unyielding and inflexible and aggravatingly *planted*. It was what had caused her to give Graham the nickname Grim, though she rarely called him that to his face. What Maris wanted—what she longed for—was the woman she'd been falling in love with in her dreams for the better part of two decades. She wanted to be *free*, as free as she felt in her dreams, where her ladylove waited for her.

Free like the water itself—fluid, flowing, and wavering.

"Come away with me," the woman in her dreams called, and Maris was desperate to go. This desire was bizarre and engrossing and endlessly frustrating, and the need to find this woman was so strong that it kept her constantly on her toes, afraid to settle and ever unsure of where to go. Maris was haunted by it.

But then, Maris had always been haunted, she reflected, her eyes staring at the expanse of ceiling above her head as she waited patiently to fall back asleep. Her father had, too, though he'd never spoken a word of it to his daughter. He hadn't had to. Maris could see it behind his eyes, a constant shadow of some unseen thing that waited for him just beyond the edges of his vision. She'd been able to assemble bits and pieces of his past, but much of the information was confusing and contradictory, like he himself was an unreliable witness. He spoke of a woman, whose face he couldn't remember, lost in a place he wasn't sure existed on any map, and he had insisted more than once these images followed him throughout his dreams in a series of nightmares that always ended with his own death. The last time they spoke, Maris confided her dreams to her father. In turn, he had warned her not to engage with the woman in the well, for it would only bring suffering on her, too. A week later, he died.

Maris's body must have reacted to the tense thoughts invading her mind, because next to her Graham's heavy arm slid reassuringly over her stomach, folding securely between her flesh and the mattress as he brought her body against his. It was an automatic gesture, and Maris allowed herself to be pulled into his gravity on the other side of the bed. She felt the tickle of his dark hair against her skin as he tucked his face into her neck and gently kissed her throat.

"Hey, babe," Graham murmured in a voice thick with sleep.

Something inside her stirred—a need to feel wanted, to feel loved—and the force of it only served to amplify the echoing hollowness in her chest.

"Go back to sleep," Maris whispered as softly as she could, smoothing away his hair.

Part of her wanted to wake Graham up, to pull the sheet away from his body so that the moonlight striped his bare chest and call him into her, but she didn't. With the woman's face still floating up in her memory, such a thing felt cheap and unfair. Instead, Maris let her body melt in the warmth Graham's kiss had left on her neck, hoping it would draw her back to sleep. She put her hand on top of his where it rested heavily against her stomach, forcing herself to reflect on the solidness of Graham's hard body around hers, his skin warm and inviting. It was too dark in the bedroom to see his arm where it lay across her body, but she knew from memory what it would look like—taut, tanned flesh against the stark white of the bed sheets. Graham was comfortable, and safe, but he was also an anchor, and the weight of him made it hard for Maris to breathe. She'd been with him for two years— longer than she'd been with anyone—and every day that passed had only made her sure of one thing.

It's time. The thought bubbled up from the bottom of Maris's thoughts and hung unspoken in the dark bedroom. Behind it came two more words, but these last were not Maris's. They belonged to the woman in the well, and they were sweet and sad and so full of longing that Maris felt a tear slip down her cheek as sleep finally reclaimed her.

"Find me," the woman was calling, and Maris was ready to go.

CHAPTER 3

*CW*hen Maris next opened her eyes, the bedroom had filled with golden-yellow sunlight and Graham's side of the bed was empty. He had always been an early riser, usually up before the sun itself. This never bothered Maris. She enjoyed waking up alone—and as late as possible. Something about the night called to her, and she'd always found it difficult to sleep when the starlight was so bright overhead.

The condo was filled with the smell of freshly brewed coffee wafting in from the kitchen, and if Maris listened hard enough, she could hear the faint sounds of Graham flipping through the crisp pages of the *Denver Post* that was still delivered hot off the presses to their doorstep every morning, even though the world was already abuzz with digital news. A digital version of a daily paper simply did not meet Graham's standards. "Anything worth being considered news is worth being put into print," he was fond of saying, and she enjoyed chiding him for his antiquated ways, especially since he was a tech guru. But since Maris never bothered to read the news, it didn't really matter to her one way or another.

Maris slid out of the sheets and into the silk kimono robe that waited at the foot of her bed. She stepped lightly on the pads of her toes, trying not to make a sound as she glided across the hardwood floors toward the kitchen. As she'd expected, Graham sat at the breakfast table, shirtless with his back to her, the paper held in the air in front of him. Even while he was seated, Maris loved the way Graham looked from behind. Years spent in the gym had developed muscles in his shoulders and back she hadn't even known existed, and they bunched together and rippled apart as he brought the pages together and then reopened them. Somehow over the past two years, Maris had persuaded Graham to let his hair grow just a little bit longer, just enough so that his dark locks twisted into curls and she could tug at them between her fingers. On weekend mornings, if she could catch him before he'd combed them back, she could see the curls unkempt and tumbling down the back of his head to rest softly against the nape of his neck. This was how she found him now—his skin slipping smoothly into black drawstring pajama pants, his legs outstretched casually under the wooden dining table with his bare feet resting on the cold hardwood floor.

When she was near enough to touch him, Maris curled her arms around Graham's neck. Even with her doubts, it was impossible not to touch him.

"Good morning," she cooed, kissing his earlobe as she reached for his coffee. She liked hers with copious amounts of cream and at least two heaps of sugar, but Graham took his black. Maris held her breath and took a sip, ignoring the bitter sludge as a surge of caffeine sped through her veins.

Graham waited until she set the mug back down, then curled his fingers around Maris's hip and drew her into his lap with one arm behind her, fashioning a sort of hammock with his body so that she could lie easily in his arms. He tossed the paper on the table and brushed away a bit of hair that covered her face. "And good morning to you. How did you sleep?"

A quick image of her dream flashed in Maris's thoughts, and she answered around the blush that crept up her cheeks. "I always sleep well."

Graham smiled above her. It was patient if unconvincing. "Are you sure?"

"Of course I'm sure."

"Then I must have dreamed you woke up in the middle of the night again."

Maris didn't want to talk to Graham about her dreams. They were private. She'd only recently admitted that she'd been having more of them since her father's death, which Graham insisted was probably grief and a guilty conscience for not attending his funeral. Maris had told him plainly that her father hadn't left anyone but her behind to mourn him, and she could do that just fine from home, but although Graham listened and assured her he understood, she knew he didn't. She'd rather let him believe it was grief interrupting her sleep than have him know she was busy dreaming of another woman, waiting for her in a place that felt like home.

Realizing she'd not answered, Maris attempted to cover up her delay with a yawn. "I don't remember waking up, but maybe I did. No big deal either way, babe."

Maris had a long history with dishonesty, but she still hated to lie outright, especially to Graham. It didn't help that he seemed to have some sort of built-in lie detector—it had been one of the qualities that made his parents urge him to go to law school, a calling he'd rebuked, much to his family's dismay. He narrowed his eyes at her, but all he said was, "Well, good then. I'm glad you aren't bothered by those dreams anymore."

"Sleeping like a baby," she fibbed again, softening her lie with a shrug she knew would make the silk robe slip from her shoulder. When all else failed, distraction was an easy alternative—and Maris was something of a master at it.

Graham's dark eyes bored into hers and said quite plainly he didn't believe her. Then they flicked to the exposed bit of flesh that ran from her shoulder down to the curve of her left breast. Maris could feel her cheeks flush under the weight of his gaze as Graham's eyes softened and took on an entirely different emotion.

"I do believe you're blushing, Maris Heilen," Graham said, his voice dropping dangerously low and blossoming with heat. His jaw slackened, and his face took on the expression it always wore when he caught her coming out of the shower or undressing before bed, or singing in the kitchen while she prepared dinner, or working in the glow of her laptop late at night. Graham had a habit of having hungry eyes for her, no matter what she was doing, but then, so a lot of men had, over the years, and Maris had an equally large appetite. A thought crept into her mind—a remembered image of the woman in the well's shining wet lips—and the pink in Maris's cheeks deepened to red.

Maris was blushing, only not for the reasons Graham might have thought. But she bit her lower lip and played along, slipping into a fantasy that was much easier to wear than her true thoughts.

"Blushing? Oh no, I'm not blushing." She pretended to fan herself with her hand, waving it back and forth dramatically in front of her face. "It's just warm in here is all."

The sharp curve in Graham's raised eyebrow matched the smirk on his mouth. "It must be all the silk you're wearing," he said matter-of-factly, running his palm heavily down the front of her chest to let his fingers play at the folds of silk where they were belted across her waist. "Traps the body heat."

"This little old thing?" she teased, tickling his fingertips with the edges of hers. "Oh, I don't think it could be this little old thing causing this kind of *heat*."

As Maris purred the last word she could virtually see the thirst on Graham's lips as he bent his head back against the chair and inhaled deeply, the air shuddering around the lump in his throat. If she didn't know better, Maris would think he was a man trying to talk himself out of doing something impulsive, something he knew better than to do. But she did know better, and she knew he was just gathering himself to do exactly what he wanted.

With one arm still around her back, Graham laced his free arm under Maris's thighs and stood up abruptly, the chair clattering to the floor noisily behind him. He turned with her in his arms and began to walk solidly back to the bedroom, his eyes never leaving her face.

"Do you know what you do to me?" he asked in a thick voice. His hands were hot where they touched her skin.

"Yes," she answered, because she knew exactly what she was doing—not talking about her dreams, or how desperately she needed to get away from her suffocatingly perfect life—and using Graham's desire for her to buy her some time.

"THERE'S something I've been meaning to ask you," Graham said, rolling over on his side to face her when they had finished their lovemaking. His hair was disheveled, and there were little beads of sweat running down the glistening perfection of his chest. Maris felt smug with satisfaction, and strangely empty too.

"What's that?" she asked, though she wasn't really listening. She was too busy idly tracing the tip of her finger down the sharp angle of his collarbone and feeling like she could answer any question he could dream up this time around. Maris never felt quite so powerful as she did after a nice romp in bed.

Graham pulled her wandering hand to his lips, brushed a quick kiss on her palm, and kept the tips of her fingers clasped in his hand as he rolled away. With his back momentarily to her, he produced a small jewelry box from the drawer of his bedside table. He returned, sliding closer, and gingerly placed the box down unopened on the sheets between them.

Maris immediately recognized the black velvet square, and an uncomfortable sensation coiled in the pit of her stomach. She'd noticed the box before, wedged in Graham's nightstand behind a stack of papers and other oddities men kept in their personal drawers, when she'd been looking for his spare keys a week before. Her sense of power deserted her, leaving her suddenly very aware of the lump that had risen in her throat, and very cold uncovered on the bed. Whatever question he'd planned to ask, Maris definitely hadn't been expecting this one. Worse, she knew the only answer she'd be able to give wasn't the one he'd be looking for, because no matter how she tried to sugarcoat it to save his feelings, it wasn't going be a *yes*.

Graham's pending question hung unspoken in the air between them while the box sat importantly on the bed. Maris stared at it and tried not to choke on her own breath. Beside her, Graham took a deep breath and stayed silent, tracing his thumb along the side of Maris's arm.

Under any other circumstance, Graham Parker was a man of bold gestures. He had doted on her unhesitatingly and lavishly, doing his damnedest to spoil her—to tame her with lavish gifts and promises of security, two things she'd never had, even when she'd asked him not to.

"Graham, we've talked about"—Maris waved her hand in the box's general direction—"this."

They *had* talked. Maris had made her feelings clear in a series of uncomfortable conversations, rebuttals of invitations to wedding showers, and complete aversion to anything that even smacked of marriage or babies or retirement planning. If Graham had listened at all, he'd have known this.

"I know it's a big step, Maris," Graham started at last, his words sounding tight and slightly stunted. He drew in another breath and held it until his body visibly relaxed. Then he opened the box's lid as he brought it and his body closer to her. Gently, he placed the box on top of Maris's chest, where it sat heavily atop her heart. The ring winked at her in the light of the bedroom, and in Maris's opinion, it had a distinctly mischievous look to it, like it knew what trouble it was stirring. It was beautiful, large, and faceted, and she hated it with every ounce of her being.

"It doesn't have to happen right away," Graham continued, and Maris realized she'd stopped listening and probably missed something—maybe missed *it*, the actual question. "But it's been two years, and I've never felt this way for another woman before.

You've bespelled me, Maris, and I want to spend the rest of my life with you."

It was a sweet proposal, really, and as Maris finally dared her eyes to meet Graham's, she saw that it was also genuine. He truly loved her.

The poor dear. She never should have let it go this far. She should have walked away a long time ago—done what she always did best and take off long before things could get too serious and anyone could get hurt. No, that wasn't fair. They'd done this to each other, both her and Grim Graham. She'd stuck around when she knew she should have gone, and he'd tried to keep her when he should've known to let her go. Sure, the sex was great, but they could never make each other happy.

Graham opened his mouth, and Maris saw that dreaded question hanging on his lips, probably for the second time. She smiled at him as she closed the box and touched the back of her hand against the softness of his face.

"I'm sorry, Graham," she said, and she was, even though the vision of the woman's face was already floating up in her thoughts over his, filling her with the resolution that the time she had been waiting for had arrived—the very thing she'd been thinking since her eyes had opened in the darkness of their bedroom the night before. It was time to find the woman in the well. "I'm sorry, but I can't."

CHAPTER 4

*I*t took Maris longer to figure out where she was going than it did to pack up her belongings into the backseat of her midnight blue Toyota Rav4 and start trying to get there. By the time she'd loaded everything up, slid into the beige leather seat, pressed the button to start the engine, and thumbed through her Spotify playlists, Maris still wasn't sure exactly where she was headed, only that it was as far away from here—and from Graham —as possible.

To be fair, the whole process of leaving hadn't taken her long. Most of what she owned—namely, a few mismatched pieces of furniture she'd never liked anyway—she'd sold off when she moved in with Graham a few months back. The rest was mostly just clothes and other personal items, and even those were few. Now, even with all her worldly possessions piled in the back, her small SUV was full, but not overcrowded. Maris liked to travel light. Besides, she'd never been the sentimental type, not that she'd had much of that sort of thing to worry about holding on to—a side benefit of always being somewhere you were already planning on leaving eventually. A few carefully packed duffel bags and it was like she'd never been there. Now you see me . . .

Poof.

The biggest bump in her exit strategy had been Graham.

Honestly, the poor guy had taken Maris's refusal better than she'd imagined he would, not that he'd been particularly thrilled about it—not that she'd expected him to be. He hadn't yelled or raised his voice, and he hadn't broken down into tears, either. He'd just looked at her, confused and faintly disappointed, and—in a series of increasingly frustrated tones while he watched her pack up her things—asked her the one question she couldn't answer: *why*. He'd done his best to convince her to stay—he'd been working on that for their entire relationship, even though she'd told him not to and really should have seen this coming. Maris had thought up a litany of excuses—It's not you, it's me; I love you but I'm not *in* love with you; there's this woman I keep dreaming about—but eventually she just settled on *I'm sorry*. An apology wasn't worth much more than an excuse, but at least she hadn't had to lie to him. Again.

And so now she was sitting in her car, suddenly single and very much alone for the first time in more than two years, trying to figure out what the hell to do next. She didn't have a lot of prospects, but then she didn't have anything holding her back. The world was her oyster. She'd made it from Denver to Boulder, just far enough away from Graham's condo that she could breathe deeply again, and was idling in a Whole Foods parking lot at the intersection of the Denver Boulder Turnpike and Northwest Parkway, staring at the Flatirons in the distance and dreaming of water half a country away. Graham had called half a dozen times, each of the little incoming beeps grating on Maris's nerves until her lips had thinned to razor wire and she blocked his number— temporarily—just long enough for her to get far enough away that she couldn't feel guilty about not answering or going back. That was a lesson she'd learned the hard way: never turn around.

Keep going. Head for the water.

Maris thumbed open the navigator app, turned on location services, and slid her finger across the map on the screen of her iPhone. Colorado wasn't exactly a short distance from anything, but it was a central point to just about everything and all the water she could ever want—the Great Lakes, the coasts, the Gulf. East would take her—eventually—to the Atlantic. She could go south to Florida, or maybe north to New England, wind her way up the eastern seaboard. She'd always loved the leaves there in fall, though the Atlantic Ocean was browner than the Pacific and not clear enough for her taste. South would take her down toward the Gulf of Mexico, to New Orleans or Galveston Island, neither of which boasted particularly lovely waters. West was desert—her father's final resting place somewhere amongst those barren sands and saguaro cactus—but beyond that waited California and the Pacific Northwest and their white sands and craggy cliffs. North . . . no, she wouldn't go north. The only thing north was more land in every direction. She needed water, to be near the sea. She felt its call so strongly, it was almost as if her life depended on it, like she'd dry up and turn to dust like her father if she didn't go. She'd been landlocked for far too long.

And the woman, if she were waiting, would be near water. Even though she'd only seen the woman in the well, Maris knew this with a certainty that she couldn't question. If she could find the right water, she could find the well. She considered the compass rose on her map—a decoration on a digital interface—and considered the direction its needle pointed.

Despite her worries about finding herself in the desert, Maris turned her car west. Then she pulled back onto the turnpike as she twisted the volume knob on her radio to max and tried to remember the scent of saltwater.

FOUR HOURS LATER, Maris pulled into a truck stop on the outer edges of Grand Junction to refill and reset as she watched the sky melt into a lovely shade of blushing strawberry orange that wasn't too different than the hair of the woman in her dream. Maris hadn't really thought farther than Grand Junction, and now that she was here she felt stuck, like she couldn't go any farther. She considered her map again and then, with a frustrated sigh, turned her phone off and tossed it in her backpack.

When Maris had packed up at Graham's, she'd done so the way she'd practiced and perfected over a lifetime of rootlessness: the majority of her stuff was situated in the larger suitcases hidden under the privacy screen of her hatchback, and the important stuff and a few changes of clothes were neatly organized in her backpack in the passenger seat. This arrangement, Maris had learned, gave her endless options. Once, she'd done the same and ditched all of her stuff at a consignment shop on the side of the highway, sold her car at a used car lot, and hitchhiked all the way to Miami, where she'd gotten a gig aboard a cruise ship headed to the Caribbean. Another time, she'd left her car in an airport garage and sat on standby until she got a seat on a plane headed to Nevada just to see the Hoover Dam. As long as she had her backpack, she was golden.

It was the closest she'd ever come to feeling free, except for when she found a chance to swim, which, ironically, she rarely did. When she'd been little, her father had insisted the water would swallow her up whole like it had done her mother, who had drowned shortly after Maris had been born, in a swimming accident at the lake near where she'd grown up. Maris had often wondered if that's why her father had moved to the desert—to escape the water. She thought again of the simultaneous pull to water and fear of drowning, and wondered if she would share her mother's fate.

Feeling restless from her dark thoughts, Maris grabbed a bottle of water and a vegetarian cheese and pimento sandwich from the truck stop —she wasn't vegetarian per se, but had never been able to bring herself to eat meat from a gas station—and returned to her car, sitting inside the open hatch as she stared west. It was warm out, the sun was shining, and for the first time in a long time, there was a stirring in her heart. Part excitement and part anticipation, Maris felt as if she was waiting for something to happen. She had no idea what that might be, but she hoped it would be just the thing she was looking for. There was a small voice niggling in her innermost thoughts that teased her with the possibility that her dreams might soon be coming true in a very literal way—assuming such a thing was even possible.

Maris had just finished the first half of her cheese sandwich when she was ripped from her reverie by the noisy drumming of a shuttle pulling into the other end of the truck stop parking lot. Slowly, as if making its way directly toward her, it moved across the lot and headed in her direction. It was one of those big, fancy oversized buses, the kind that made road trips far more comfortable than they had any right to be. As it came to a stop a few feet away from her car, Maris saw the shuttle was wrapped in a banner that boasted stunning picturesque landscapes of a town she'd never heard of. Her eyes wandered through the scenes as she lifted the other half of her sandwich to her mouth. There were beautiful snowcapped mountains—something she'd frankly had her fill of, living in Colorado—rich, vibrant forests, and then, as the shuttle wheezed to a stop, Maris caught a glimpse of water.

It wasn't an ocean, and it wasn't the well in her dreams. It wasn't even a well, but a waterfall—the titular Havenwood Falls, Maris assumed—pouring down what must have been hundreds of feet to decant itself into a large pond that was surrounded by boulders at the base of the mountain. Still, there was something strikingly familiar about the water—the shape of it, which Maris could almost hear, cascading down the mountain, its waters clear and reflective even in photography. She'd never seen the falls, but it felt like the image of them was burned in her memory nonetheless, like an heirloom passed down through generations of Heilens before her. Through the picture Maris could hear the rushing sound it made; she could feel the gentle spray of the water as it splashed against the rocks that surrounded its base. Inside of these images, Maris smelled the water of her own dreams, floral and scented as if flower petals had bled out their fragrance within it. She could feel the cool dampness of it on her skin.

And the vision of the woman's face, fresh and wet and succulent, billowed up in Maris's thoughts. The woman smiled the distinctively coy smile that could only belong to her, and one of her fingers stretched out toward Maris, bending and beckoning as it played upon her heartstrings in the broad daylight of waking hours.

Maris forgot immediately about heading west.

She reached the bus before she even realized she'd started walking in its direction. The rest of her sandwich wasn't in her hand, and she had no idea what she'd done with it. She wiped her hands on her jeans, only half caring that it might leave a stain, and stared at the image on the shuttle's side. There wasn't much copy on the banner, just two words.

The name was inviting and mysterious at once. "Havenwood Falls," Maris read aloud, murmuring more to herself than to the driver, who saw fit to answer anyway.

"That's the place." He beamed as he stepped down from his seat and steadied himself on the pavement beside her. His eyes mirrored hers as they admired the waterfall on the banner together. There was an inflection in his voice Maris recognized but couldn't place, and for the first time in a long time, the telltale tingle of déjà vu pimpled her skin with goose flesh.

The driver was an older man, not quite elderly but well beyond the age that might be considered young, and the evidence of it showed in gray whiskers that decorated his face like Christmas tree tinsel. He had deep-set dark brown eyes and a complexion that might have been Hispanic or possibly Native American, and he was dressed head to toe in denim in a way that gave Maris the impression he'd be uncomfortable in anything else. He smiled at her, and it wasn't a stranger's smile but something much closer to one an old friend might give another that they hadn't seen in a while. "No other place quite like it."

Maris thought for a moment, reflecting on the various town names she'd seen on the app on her phone, and then said, "I've never heard of anywhere around here called Havenwood Falls. It wasn't on my map."

"Most haven't," the driver confirmed with a flick of his hand. A mischievous smile teased across his jowls as if he knew this fact and was proud of it—an odd thing for someone who drove a tourist shuttle. A curious thought moved through his eyes, and he studied Maris as she studied the image of the falls, his dark eyes turning shiny with interest as they flicked to her parked car and back. "Where you headed to, miss?"

Maris tore her eyes from the shuttle's wrapper and shrugged. "West. Toward the ocean, I think. Just someplace . . . someplace else. Not here."

That was about the least specific answer—and the most accurate one—she could give, but the man nodded as if he understood exactly what she meant.

"Maybe Havenwood Falls is the place you've been looking for," he suggested. "Seems like you see something you like."

She wanted to object, but couldn't.

"The place is beautiful," she admitted, examining the banner again. "It looks . . . familiar." She wanted to add, "Like somewhere I've seen in my dreams," but didn't. That wasn't something a sane person said. Besides, Maris was positive she'd never heard of a place called Havenwood Falls before—not unless it was indeed the place she'd been visiting in her dreams, a thought that didn't do much to reassure her of her sanity.

This road trip was suddenly becoming complicated. Maris weighed her options. She could keep driving, ditch the car and hitchhike, or find an airport and an open seat on a plane to somewhere. The strawberry sky was quickly running to hues of deepening purple, even though it was barely six o'clock—an early night for early spring. Whatever she did, it would be night soon, and she'd need a place to camp out. A rude little thought reminded her that it would be the first night she hadn't sleep beside Graham in more nights than she could count. She didn't care about that so much, but she wasn't particularly looking forward to sleeping alone. An empty bed was a cold bed. Maybe she'd meet someone in Havenwood Falls.

"How far is it?" Maris asked, dismissing the thought almost as quickly as she had time to think it. To hell with Grim Graham and his proposal and his boring life, and to hell with feeling lonely, too. "I've been driving for a while. Maybe if it's close, I'll stay a night before I keep going."

The driver sucked his teeth thoughtfully, eyeing Maris's well-packed SUV a few steps away. "Well," he said, "it's not that far. Just up the mountains a ways."

Maris nodded as if she'd made up her mind. She *had*, but she hadn't exactly meant to. She'd meant to go west, toward the ocean, not up, higher into the Colorado mountains and some strange little town she'd never heard of—but what good was fleeing a perfectly boring life if you didn't recolor it with adventure?

"Perfect," she decided. "I'll follow you whenever you're ready to head out. I just need to fill up."

The man smiled, but it was shallow. "Roads are tricky up that way. If you don't know where you're going, it's real easy to get turned around—maybe miss a turn and end up on the other side of nowhere up in the mountains. Why don't you climb aboard? I'd be happy to give you a lift. No charge."

Maris considered this. She'd never liked driving up those windy mountain roads.

"If you're worried about leaving your car here, don't be," her would-be driver added, as if reading her thoughts. "The town's got an agreement with this stop, knows visitors up to Havenwood Falls leave their cars here and take the shuttle up. Town's not that big anyway, easy enough to get around on foot. If you decide to stay, there's a service that'll tow it up for cheap."

Maris didn't need any more convincing. The violet sky was quickly darkening into eggplant, and the thought of a secluded little getaway was relieving anxiety she hadn't known she had. "Okay," she agreed. "I'll grab my bag. Are you waiting on any other passengers?"

"Looks like you're it. All aboard."

Under normal circumstances, Maris might have been skeptical —hopping onto a bus to a place she'd never heard of with no other passengers and a driver who seemed keen on being mysterious. Today, she just felt lucky. As she retrieved her backpack from her car and locked everything up, her eyes found their way back to the wrapper on the shuttle, to the falls flowing freely down the side of a sparkling mountain, and she closed her eyes and thought about the woman in the water.

West could wait. Tonight she was going to find the water in Havenwood Falls—and whatever waited for her there.

CHAPTER 5

*P*urple had bled to black and the stars were in full view when Maris opened her eyes again in her seat at the back of the shuttle. She hadn't felt tired when she'd boarded the bus in Grand Junction, but that was kind of beside the point now, since she was peeling her face from the fabric of her backpack, which had been repurposed as a makeshift pillow. She hadn't slept much last night and so must have been lulled to sleep by the steady turning of the tires on sparingly traveled roads under a darkening sky. The last thing Maris remembered was rolling across the truck stop parking lot back in Grand Junction, watching her SUV shrinking to a small dot as the bus rumbled onto the road that led up into the mountains. Either she'd fallen asleep before they'd ever made it fully back onto the highway, or they'd made their journey up the mountain in the space of a single blink.

It didn't much matter now—not that Maris cared. Sometimes part of the adventure was the journey there, and following her heart and hopping on board a shuttle on a whim at a truck stop certainly counted as adventurous, spontaneous, and impulsive—all things her father and her newly *ex*-boyfriend had never appreciated about her. Even though she was half asleep, the thought managed to lift Maris's lips into the closest thing she could manage to a smirk. She loved moving about life like a piece of wreckage caught in a storm, taken wherever the tide fancied carrying her. At the moment, however, she was anxious to get off the shuttle and stretch her legs—and her neck. The backpack had left an unpleasant twinge in her shoulder. They had to be nearly there anyway; the driver had said it wasn't a long way.

She was just about to ask, when, sensing she was awake, her driver called out to her over his shoulder. As his voice carried, his eyes met hers in the rearview mirror. "Well, hello again," he said cheerfully—a mite too cheerfully to the ears of someone still stuck in the cloud of half-sleep. Still, the sound of his voice gave life to the quiet of the bus and Maris along with it. "We're just about to our destination. Not much longer than a few minutes now and you'll be getting the best view in Havenwood Falls. Taking you right to the top." He emphasized this last with a good-natured wink in the rearview mirror and a haughtily pointed index finger raised to the underside of the shuttle's roof.

Maris nodded and stretched, trying not to groan as she worked the kinks from her sleepy limbs, which were more sluggish than normal. When she yawned, her breath caught in her throat. Everything felt dry. Her breath was shallow, and her stomach was uneasy. Altitude sickness was kicking in. She had no idea how high they'd climbed, but it was enough that she was feeling the impact of it. Peering out the window, all Maris could make out in the darkness were the fuzzy, shadowed shapes of rocks and trees and other such things you'd expect to see in the Colorado mountains.

"Sorry to fall asleep on you," Maris said, when her brain fog had cleared enough to allow speech. The words came out slurred on parched lips. She cleared her throat and tried again as she dug around in her bag for the bottle of water she'd brought with her. "Doesn't make for a fun passenger."

"Oh, not a problem. It's a nice ride to relax. I'd probably take myself a nap too if I weren't the one driving." He followed this with a chuckle that made Maris laugh despite the fact that he hadn't really said anything funny.

Maris was still struggling to wake up. Her nap had been that heavy kind that daytime dozes often were—heavy and lingering, the kind that left one feeling groggy and far more tired than they had been before they ever fell asleep. Blinking the sleep from her eyes, she extracted a tube of lip balm from her pocket and rubbed it against her mouth, enjoying the minty sensation that hydrated the desert that had formed on her lips. She rubbed at her cheeks to bring some sensation back to her skin and then attempted to smooth her hair, which the dry mountain air had spun into a static spider web. She was technically awake, but not quite awake enough for her body to realize it yet. Numbness clung to her bones and everything had a hazy quality to it, as if she were stuck in that place between sleep and waking. It wasn't a bad feeling, particularly after the events of that morning. A few hours ago, she'd woken up in a life she had never felt comfortable in, and now she was half a state away, on a shuttle at night in the middle of nowhere with nothing but a backpack and—Maris checked her pockets—a mostly dead cell phone that currently had no signal.

Most people might have been unnerved, but to Maris, it was invigorating. She was loving every minute of her new adventure. Briefly, she considered unblocking Graham's number, but then decided against it.

A few minutes later, feeling had finally returned to Maris's limbs as the shuttle crept up a long gravel driveway and bumped to a stop. As the driver slid the door open Maris could hear the roaring sound of rushing water in the distance, and she let the noise play in her ears as he came around the side of the shuttle, opened the door, and extended his hand. Maris accepted the driver's outstretched hand, and the scent of fresh water rose around her as she stepped down onto the pavement. Even in the dark, she could just make out the fine mist rising over the edge of the falls. She didn't know anything about Havenwood Falls, but she knew where he had brought her.

"It's the falls," she mused to no one in particular, slinging her backpack over her shoulder in preparation to make her way to see them.

Her driver released his grip on her hand and, steering her away from the falls, gestured grandly toward a large building that waited at its top. "Figured you might be hungry when you woke up, and I noticed the way you were looking at the falls, so I thought this was the first place you should see."

As he said it, Maris's stomach rumbled. "Definitely," she agreed. "Thanks."

The driver clamped a fatherly hand on her shoulder. Normally Maris would have hated such a gesture, but this one felt kind of nice. Warm and reassuring. Friendly.

"Enjoy your time at the falls," he said by way of goodbye, and Maris could hear the capital letter, marking the import of the statement.

Maris took a deep breath and inhaled as much of the scent of water she could. It wasn't exactly the scent she'd been craving, but it was close enough.

"I plan to," she said.

Fallview Tavern & Grille presided over the crashing water with all the dignity one would expect from what was clearly a landmark building of obvious significance. It was either authentically old or the architect who had designed it had done a spectacular job of emulating a nineteenth-century log-sided tavern with all the proper trimmings. There were some modern twists as well, designed to embellish the natural beauty of the falls, which were spectacular on their own. Just around the back of the tavern, illuminated by the glow of fairy lights, a multilevel patio was webbed with staircases. The lights' eager twinkling gave the impression that the tavern was a live, moving thing and not a simple building.

As much as she wanted to explore the widow's walk that

overlooked where the falls slid off the mountain, Maris's stomach was calling. Obeying the demands of her appetite, Maris made her way to the wide entry doors and stepped inside the tavern, allowing the beautiful rustic behemoth to swallow her whole.

As impressive as the outside was, the tavern's inside was even grander, and when Maris's breath caught in her throat again, it had nothing to do with dryness. The interior was large and spacious, with high ceilings held aloft by wooden support beams that wore a large iron chandelier like an earring. A large stone fireplace rose above hardwood floors that may have been original, and the walls were lined with iron sconces. Each was situated with thick candles that added flickering glows that danced along the edges of the space, reflecting from skylights that undoubtedly flooded the room with sunshine during daylight hours. Tables and chairs were scattered about the large dining area, giving the space the sort of carefully orchestrated haphazard look that people paid a lot of money to fake. All of the tables were currently empty, and many had their chairs overturned on their tops, a sure sign that closing time was drawing near. Tasteful and artistic with a rugged-meets-modern sort of vibe, the tavern was the perfect blend of the old world and new that was so smooth and seamless, it seemed almost crafted by magic, and Maris—who had always held an appreciation for architecture—instantly fell in love with the place.

"Hello there," called a man's voice from the bar at the back of the room. Maris had long ago learned how to assign faces to names purely from the sound of their voice, and she had an uncannily accurate knack for it. The owner of this voice sounded young, masculine, and decidedly handsome—not that Maris was interested; it was just the sort of thing she noticed. Swiveling toward the bar, Maris approached the black marble surface and the man who stood behind it. A dishrag in hand, he wiped dry a glass with the expert flourish of someone who knew his way around a restaurant and was proud of it.

Maris had been right in her assessment of his voice. The man behind the bar was probably not much older than she was. He was of lean build—the kind people called a swimmer's body—with curly brown hair and blue eyes that added the only real dash of color to the room. He was dressed simply in blue jeans and a black V-neck T-shirt, and she could see the edges of a tattoo that climbed up the expanse of what appeared to be a rather hairless chest. It was hard to tell what it was, but it looked tribal—maybe a dragon, or some other type of winged animal.

As Maris approached the bar, the man set down the glass on the counter and extended a hand. She expected him to tell her that the place was closing, but this was before she noticed the way he looked at her—more or less that same double-take most men did when they first saw her, but his glance was a little more knowing, like he thought he'd seen her somewhere before, though of course he hadn't.

Rather than updating her on closing time as she'd expected, he said instead, "Welcome to Havenwood Falls and Fallview Tavern. You must be new in town." It didn't sound like a question, but Maris nodded anyway. "Name's Simon," he continued. "What's yours?"

Maris accepted his hand and returned what she hoped was a confident shake.

"Maris. Maris Heilen," she said. She thought she saw something shimmer in Simon's eyes when he heard her name—some confirmation of that recognizing look from before—but she assumed it was a trick of the flickering candlelight. It was impossible that anyone here would recognize her name, so she ignored it. "How did you know I was new in town?"

Simon flipped the towel over his shoulder and shrugged. "It's a small town. New faces stand out, and only folks riding in on a shuttle show up this time of night."

"Yeah, right. It dropped me off right outside." She looked around at the empty restaurant. "You own this place?"

"Nah," he said. "Just the cook. Speaking of which, what can I get you? On the house."

Maris felt her eyebrows pull upward in suspicion, and she

softened this with a coy smile and a tilt of her head that showed off the smooth curve of her cheekbone. She leaned forward on the counter so that her breasts pressed beneath her thin camisole. This were largely automatic, a posture she'd practiced often when preening for tips on the other side of the bar. "On the house?"

His smile matched hers. "Sure. First night in town deserves a welcome meal."

"How about a first night drink?" Maris wasn't trying to flirt, but Simon was too cute to resist, and she enjoyed having people in her gravity too much to ignore the opportunity.

Simon laughed and might have blushed a little. "I'm happy to grab you a beer, but I'm afraid I'm not much of a bartender. Anything I mix up is likely to taste like bilge water."

It was Maris's turn to laugh. "Well, we're in luck. That's my specialty."

"Bilge water?" Simon winked.

Maris laughed again, feeling strangely happy for the first time that day. Like the shuttle driver, Simon felt more like an old friend than a shiny new stranger. "No, not *bilge water*—bartending. I'm a bartender by trade"—a brief glimpse of the life she'd left behind passed before her eyes—"or at least I used to be, in my last life."

"Last life?" Simon was humoring her. There was that shimmer again in his pale blue eyes as he pulled a glass from under the counter and pushed it toward her, then motioned she should come around the bar. She did, trying to name the color of his eyes as she moved. Blue—they were definitely blue—but there was an interesting sort of iridescence about them, as if they were scales instead of eyes, refracting the light in little prisms. Reptilian, but not cold. When she looked closely, Maris half expected a second inner lid to slide over and wet the eye. Whatever it was that made them sparkle like that, it wasn't scary—but it was damned sexy. She'd never seen eyes like his before.

Again, not that Maris was interested. It was just hard not to appreciate.

"I reincarnated today." Maris grinned over her shoulder at

Mr. Sexy Eyes as she plucked a few choice bottles from the liquor rack behind the bar, selected some juices from the mini-fridge beneath the bar top, and scooped three ice cubes into a cocktail shaker. "Left my old life and decided to start a new one. Happened across a shuttle here while I was taking a rest in Grand Junction, and, well"—she made a motion with her hands like a stage magician might before a particularly stunning trick —"surprise. Here I am."

Turning her eyes to her work, she began mixing various liquors together in the shaker without bothering to measure amounts, then poured the mixture into a wide-rimmed martini glass. Finished, she grabbed a peeling knife lying nearby and curled off a piece of lemon zest for garnish. Then she lifted the glass and, with a flourish, handed it to Simon.

"Deep blue sea martini. Family recipe." She beamed. "And my signature cocktail."

He sipped, and the pleasure in his mouth rippled across his features. "This is delicious."

"I know."

Simon took another long swallow, licked his lips appreciatively, and settled the mostly empty martini glass on the bar top as Maris mixed one for herself. "So, how long do you plan on staying in Havenwood Falls?"

Maris considered. Timelines were never her specialty, and she was a horrible planner. She hadn't meant to get here, but now that she was, there was nothing inside of her that compelled her to make a hasty exit. Quite the opposite, in fact: she'd barely seen anything of this quiet little town, but it felt like . . . like she belonged here. It felt like she was meant to find this place. And somehow it was all connected to the woman in the water—the woman in her dreams. Maybe it was destiny, or some weird trick of fate.

Of course, that was not something she was going to share with her handsome new friend, who was currently letting his sexy blue eyes wander all over her body. She shrugged. "Might stick around for a while, assuming I can find a place to stay and a way to earn my keep."

"Well, the best place to shack up around here is Whisper Falls Inn. Right down in the heart of the town square, but if you listen real hard, you can still hear the falls. I can call a Luber for you—it'll take you right down there and get you settled in. I hear the rooms are . . . cozy."

As he talked, Simon moved closer to her, until Maris could feel the heat pulsing off his body and reflecting back against hers. She inhaled, and his scent was musky and intoxicating—primal, animalistic even. When Maris lifted her head to look at him, it was through half-lidded eyes. "Well, I'm halfway to staying a little longer then."

She was tempted to reach out to stroke the side of his face, but his fingers were already on her hand. She inhaled sharply as he took the glass she'd forgotten she'd been holding and lifted it to his lips, smiling. Maris laughed breathily and tucked a stray strand of her dishwater blond hair behind her ear, trying to recalibrate.

She was about to say something—probably some innuendo about the cozy cottages at Whisper Falls Inn—when he spoke again. "In regards to earning your keep," Simon went on, his voice dropping to a throaty sort of teasing tenor that toed the line between business and pleasure, "if this is how you mix drinks, I think we can find a place for you behind our bar."

Maris forgot all about flirting and swallowed back her witty repartee. "Really? You'd give me a job?"

There was a sharp noise behind them, and Simon spoke without tearing his strange iridescent eyes from Maris. His voice was normal again, but his body heat was still on high. "Isn't that right, Odette? We've been looking for a new bartender. Seems one might have found her way to us."

Maris spun on her heel to see a handsome woman standing behind them, positioned almost perfectly beneath the large iron chandelier that hung in the center of the room as if she'd walked in through the patio doors from the falls outside and been pinned there beneath a giant magnet. She was tall and shapely and could only be described as elegant, possessed of a beauty that made her seem somehow ageless, and possibly too beautiful to be completely of good intentions. There was a waiting dark lurking behind her pale skin and delicate yet severe jaw structure.

Something in Maris quickened as she stared at the woman who walked toward the bar, her eyes never leaving where they had speared into Maris's. She watched Odette approach, and Maris had the distinct feeling that air was being sucked from the room. Still, there was something alluring and recognizable about the woman, and Maris saw the woman in the well in the way the other woman's limbs moved, as if she were swimming rather than walking, treading water with her footsteps.

When she was a few feet from the bar, Odette's eyes left Maris and moved to Simon, who introduced everyone in a voice straining to sound casual. "Odette, this is Maris Heilen." A flash of recognition moved in Odette's eyes, a similar flicker to the one Maris had first seen in Simon's when she'd given him her name. "She's just arrived in Havenwood Falls. Maris, this is Odette Alverson, owner of Fallview."

"Nice to meet you," Maris managed to say, but Odette's expression remained unchanged.

For a moment, the tavern's proprietress said nothing, but then she smiled, and it had the effect of changing her face completely, reshaping it from something mildly terrifying and spectral to a warmer, softer, much more human expression.

"Nice to meet you, Maris Heilen. Yes, I do believe you'll be an excellent addition to our little family here at Fallview Tavern." She cast a meaningful look at Simon and then back at Maris, who knew a dismissal when she saw it. "At the moment, though, we're just about to close. I've sent for a car to take you over to Whisper Falls Inn. You can start tomorrow," Odette finished. Maris shot a look at Simon before retrieving her backpack from the patron side of the bar.

The temperature in the room had gone from warm to cold,

chilled but not unwelcoming. It was a little enticing actually, like slipping your toes into pool water for the first time.

"Great," Maris smiled, biting her lips to stymie the excitement she felt bubbling in her veins. "Thank you both. I really appreciate it. See you tomorrow."

With a wave goodbye, Maris made her way out of the tavern to the single car that was sitting outside, engine running. She did a double take. She'd expected Uber—assuming she'd misheard Simon earlier—or even the traditional yellow cab. Maybe some local car service if the main ride-sharing service hadn't made it out this far. Whatever this ride was, what was waiting for her wasn't anything she might have expected. The car was orange and old, and Maris was pretty sure it was a hearse and not a town car. It flashed its headlights at her, and she walked toward it.

Taking a last look over her shoulder at the tavern, Maris watched as Simon and Odette moved together and stood side by side in the large picture window. Simon lifted his arm in a friendly wave goodbye as Odette's sharp eyes stared out across the darkness, her expression haunted and far away.

Maris's eyes must have been playing tricks on her, but as she stared at the figures watching her, she thought she could read the words moving across Simon's lips.

"You know who she is," he seemed to say to the woman beside him, and to this Odette's lips moved in a statement equally as odd.

"Worse," Maris thought she read Odette Alverson say, "I know *what* she is."

CHAPTER 6

$\mathcal{M}$aris was starting to believe everything in Havenwood Falls, people included, must have belonged to another time, or another place, or otherwise be made of a substance slightly different—and much more interesting—than what passed for normal in the rest of the world. Everything here seemed vaguely surreal and just a little abnormal—not anything that anyone who wasn't looking for it would notice, but enough that Maris, who had always enjoyed people-watching, was starting to pick up on. The people she'd met so far, including the fatherly shuttle driver (whose name she never caught), Simon with his iridescent blue eyes, Odette Alverson and her strange beauty, and now her Luber driver—a funny little man called Jakeel who sported a thick mustache and a disco shirt and was so small he'd added a child's booster seat to help him see over the steering wheel of his car—were all just a little more colorful than your average person, and even in the dark, Havenwood Falls was just a little too picturesque to be real. It was a postcard come to life, and there was a constant tinge of enigma in the air that tickled along Maris's desire to know more.

Whisper Falls Inn, Maris soon came to find as she rolled her window down to get a better look, was no different. She watched as the large, three-story Victorian appeared in the headlights of Jakeel's bright orange Luber née hearse. Positioned diagonally on the corner of two streets, right in the southeast corner of the town square, as Simon had said it would be, the place was larger than life. It sat somewhat haughtily, sandwiched between parking lots and surrounded by a privacy tree line. And, even though it already amassed more than half of a city block, it still seemed hungry for more.

True to its architectural heritage, the inn had all the trimmings of a proper Victorian: a wraparound porch, turrets, bay windows, and a swirling gingerbread trim. It was hard to guess how many guest rooms might be in the home, but Maris had to assume they were numerous. There was an expanse of lawn that connected the main house to a line of cottages, and although the property had the authentic look of one that might have dated back to the previous century, it was obviously well cared for.

"Here we are," Jakeel announced, though it really wasn't necessary, as the car crunched to a stop in front of the main entrance. "Whisper Falls Inn. Family run and operated for just about as long as the town's been around. Michaela Petran runs it now—nice girl, probably close to your age—you'll probably find her waiting for you inside."

Maris slung her backpack over her shoulder and leaned forward to pay her driver. He waved her hand away and wriggled his mustache at her instead. "No way, honey," he said, eyes sparkling mischievously. "Your new friends over at Fallview already paid the tab."

Maris blinked. Well, that was a first. "Seriously? Well . . . that was really nice of them."

"Most people here in Havenwood Falls are nice enough, unless you find yourself on their bad side." He winked to soften a statement that Maris suspected had a lot of truth hidden in it. Then he gave her a look that bordered on dangerous, but not particularly unpleasant—a totally weird combo. "Plus, it's good to have fresh blood in town."

It wasn't very often that Maris found herself lost for words, but right now was one of those moments. The vibe she felt—the one that suggested there was more to Havenwood Falls than might meet the eye—was so strong it was strumming her insides like a bass violin. "Okay," she finally managed as she opened the door and swung one leg into the night air. "See ya."

Jakeel's eyes were already back on the steering wheel. "Yep, see you tomorrow."

"Tomorrow?"

She could see a smile creep up the side of his face, pushing his thick mustache upward like a caterpillar moving up a branch. "I'm the only driver in town, honey, and you ain't got no wheels."

Oh, right. Maris hadn't really thought about that, not that she ever worried about moving around, car or no car. "That's true," she agreed as she shut the door behind her, having no idea *when* she'd actually see the odd little man again but figuring she very likely would. "See you tomorrow then, Jakeel."

"Night, Ms. Heilen," Jakeel returned, sending a wink over his shoulder with one eye before both made their way to the house waiting at Maris's back through the still-open backseat window. "And don't let the bedbugs bite."

With a little bit more acceleration than was entirely necessary, Jakeel sped away before Maris could remember ever telling the odd little man her last name.

The woman named Michaela Petran—who did indeed appear to be around the same age as Maris—was, as Jakeel had suggested she'd be, waiting for Maris behind the front counter of Whisper Falls Inn. She was a few inches shorter than Maris, with dark brown hair and the most beautiful gray-green eyes that Maris had ever seen. Or perhaps they were the *only* eyes that shade of gray-green that Maris had ever seen. The folks in this town either had some wicked eye pigment genes or one hell of a contact lens supplier.

"Hey," Maris said as she dropped her bag at the counter and began rummaging around in its pockets for her wallet. Finding it, she handed Michaela her credit card and ID. "I'm looking for a room, or maybe more than a room, I guess. Don't know exactly how long I'll be in town."

"You're Maris Heilen?" Michaela confirmed in a friendly but decidedly no-bullshit kind of way without actually looking at the cards in her hand. When Maris didn't answer immediately, Michaela added an explanation. "Got a call from Simon up at Fallview that he was sending a visitor down by way of Jakeel. We get a lot of late-night arrivals."

"Oh," Maris breathed out, pulling her phone automatically from her pocket to check the time on the screen. It had died, its poor little twelve percent of battery life apparently not enough to keep it ticking till she could find a place to recharge. Then, worried that Michaela's hesitation might be the result of a space issue—it had never occurred to her that maybe there'd be no room at the inn—Maris leaned forward, biting on her lower lip as was her habit when she was nervous. "Please tell me you have a room? I don't get the feeling there's a Marriott around the corner for visitor overflow."

Michaela laughed and returned Maris's cards to her in addition to a large brass key. "Yes, we have room. Believe it or not, it's the slow season." Maris took the key as Michaela explained how to get to her room. "The cottages are mostly full, though, primarily with family, and it can be a bit noisy at times with all the coming and going. I'm putting you upstairs, in one of the luxury suites in the third-floor turret. Figured it might be nice for you to be in the main house, and it's one of the only places in the house to catch a glimpse of the falls—that okay?"

It was Maris's turn to laugh. "A suite in a turret? I'll take it. Sounds like something out of a fairy tale"—Maris considered—"or a dream."

The smile Michaela gave Maris now reminded her distinctly of similar ones she'd seen on Simon's face, on Odette Alverson's, and even on Jakeel's. "You look like the kind of girl who likes to dream."

Maris didn't know what that meant, but she couldn't quite bring herself to disagree. Suddenly, she was terribly tired. No, not tired exactly—she just couldn't wait to get to sleep and see the lady in the water. If there was a link between her dreams and this place, then the best place to figure it out was in her sleep.

~

UPSTAIRS, Maris tossed her backpack into a chair, took a warm shower, and fell promptly into a fitful and unpleasant sleep.

She had hoped she'd dream of the well, and the lady in the water, and she did. But this dream was unlike any she could remember ever having before—and it was not one she hoped she would ever repeat. It was twisted and frightening, and not at all the lovely meeting that had been teasing from the back of her thoughts ever since she'd arrived in Havenwood Falls.

In the dream, it was dark. Not nighttime exactly, but even darker than that, as if the sun had forgotten how to shine and darkness had eclipsed the world so completely that even a memory of sunlight didn't dare to peep through. And it was cold—terribly, terribly cold. So cold that even the fog of sleep couldn't shield Maris from feeling the icy breath of the air around her. Her bones ached with the sting of it, and paired with the unending blackness, she could have just as easily been standing in the absence of space rather than the middle of a frozen forest. Nothing grew. There was no scent of flowers in the air—there was no scent of anything, really, but the cold itself. It was so cold that the evidence of the lush plant life that had previously been in this place wasn't even white, but gray. Frozen and sullen and dull.

The well was there, as it always was, but it, too, was changed. Like the world around it, the well was dark and cold, but it was these things in a way that had little to do with light or temperature. The water was not frozen, but it was slick and cold. It was a hard thing to explain, but it was as if all the warmth—not just the physical kind but the sort suffused with the love and allure that had always made the well's water thick and comforting in Maris's dreams—had been drained from it, so that she could see without touching that the water had become startlingly thin, its life sucked away both in terms of its substance and its contents, becoming so low that even when Maris leaned over the side of it, her fingertips could not graze the water's surface. Slivers of ice floated menacingly on the water's surface, sharp and pointed like little frozen daggers awaiting something to cut. Something else glittered atop the water, decorating the edges of the stones where the water lapped against them. Maris touched one of the sparkling crystals and brought it to her lips. Salt. It was as if the well was full of tears.

"Where are you?" Maris called out in her dream, the wet words sticking to her lips like ice chips as they tumbled down into the bottomless darkness of the well. Her eyes scanned the shadows for the woman, watching the water for movement—for a sign of her milk-white skin or flaming red hair that might bring color into the black void. "What has happened to you? I'm here. I'm trying to find you. Please come to me."

Maris hadn't realized it at first, but she was crying. Most of the tears froze on her cheeks before they could fall, but one escaped, tumbling down the side of her face and lighting upon the top of the semi-frozen water with an audible clink. Its arrival stirred the first movement since Maris had arrived in her dream.

She stared into the dark as a darker shadow filled the belly of the well. Blacker and denser than the water, it swelled upward, bringing along with it a tangle of a thousand swirling shadowy tentacles, each winding their way around the mass, reaching for the water's surface. As the figure rose, so did a heavy, sickly feeling in the pit of Maris's stomach, and she put her palm over her mouth to keep a scream from finding its way out. She shouldn't be scared, but she was—she was terrified, but couldn't force herself to look away. Something was wrong. Horribly, horribly wrong. Whatever was coming was not the beauty she'd become infatuated with, the woman who had captured her heart in a series of nighttime moments she could only imagine were real. In her heart, Maris knew that this figure coming had something to do with her beloved, but it carried nothing of her light or her spirit. Whatever had become of her, she was now darkness incarnate, and Maris finally found enough energy to stumble backward. As she did, her heel caught on a snarl of hard gray bramble, and she tumbled to the ground, unable to do anything but watch as the darkness rose above the outer rim of the well.

The scream that Maris had kept hushed behind her palm stalled in her throat as she saw what emerged above the well's surface. It had the same face of her love—the same bone structure, the same taunting lips—but it belonged now to something else entirely. Like the world around, the color had drained from the woman, replacing her beauty with the pallid mark of a corpse. Her skin was deathly white, a gray so deep it was almost blue, and her lips had shriveled into tight, wet black smudges. Eyes that had once been vibrant green had lost their hue so that it was impossible to tell the iris from the pupil as they scanned the area in an unseeing, sweeping gaze. Her body had shriveled beneath her white gown so that her once curvaceous form was reduced to a collection of skeletal knobs and angles, and her hair, her beautiful long curling strawberry hair, was now knotted and tangled, writhing like a mass of black snakes around the place where her sharp, talon-like hands clawed at the base of the well.

The woman that Maris had loved lifted her face upward, as if scenting Maris's presence, and when her unseeing eyes landed on Maris, she could feel them, cold and sharp and hateful, on her skin. Then, before Maris could so much as react, the woman opened her mouth, wide and black, and screamed.

"Come away with me," the figure screamed.

Her—whatever she had become—voice was so sharp and

piercing that it shattered the dream. Maris's eyes snapped open in the pale darkness of her bedroom in the turret, which by comparison was not very dark at all and very, very warm. She gasped, panting and shaking, trying to shake off her terror as her eyes adjusted to the room around her. Her hands ran the length of her body as if trying to reassure her that what she had dreamt had been nothing but a nightmare—a stressful reaction, perhaps, to her sudden departure from Denver, and Graham, and all she had left behind—but even as she was on her way to believing this lie, Maris's hands found that the truth of the dream might be much stranger.

A shudder of panic punctuated her breath as Maris's fingertips ran across a patch of ice on her bed sheets, the same salty coldness as the frost she found lingering on the skin of her face. She opened her lips to cry out, but her throat was choked, filled with a tangled clump of wet black hair.

CHAPTER 7

*W*hen Maris awoke several hours later, she could only vaguely remember her nightmare. The most she could recall was a sense of being frightened, and cold, and possibly wet (and not in the enjoyable way), but she didn't have the foggiest recollection of why. She did, however, clearly remember the ice, and the hair, although both seemed to have vanished. Now it was early—the small clock on her bedside table said it was nine in the morning, which was several hours earlier than Maris normally woke—and the sun was shining brightly outside, but there was a weird darkness that clung to Maris's bones despite the beautiful morning waiting on the other side of her bedroom window. She could have rolled over and gone back to sleep, and maybe even caught another hour to two, but she was ready to get up.

Despite the fact that she knew it would be a warm waning spring day, Maris was uncommonly cold when she wriggled her way out from beneath the pile of blankets on her bed. Luckily, she'd tossed a light jacket in her backpack—the kind that could be zipped up into its own little pouch—and so she pulled on her jeans and a fresh T-shirt and added the jacket over the top. Her hair had been wet when she'd gone to bed, so it was a lively tangle of unruly curls, but that was an easy fix, too. She swept the stray curls up into a messy bun, gave her face and teeth a quick scrub, and applied a quick slick of lip gloss as she descended the stairs without bothering to check her phone. It had been much too late yesterday when she'd arrived in Havenwood Falls—a town she'd already decided kept an early bedtime—to do much exploring, but with the day young, she figured she could cover a lot of ground before making her way back to Fallview Tavern and Grille and finding out if she really had a job or if Simon had just been flirting with her.

About halfway down the stairs, Maris decided that her obvious first visit should be to the falls themselves—the ones she'd seen in the banner on the shuttle that had lured her to Havenwood Falls yesterday. Sure, that was literally *right* at the tavern, but whatever. It'd be a nice round trip. Maybe there was a map of the area at the front desk, some kind of basic layout of the town they might give the tourists or something that would show her where all the best places to visit might be. She was especially interested in checking out the scenery, particularly the water. She'd start at the falls and maybe see what else she could find. The chill in her bones got just a little bit cooler when she thought this, as if encouraging her.

Arriving in the lobby area, the first thing Maris saw was a familiar face. Without meaning to, a wide smile spread across her face—the kind that had the tendency to draw people to her like moth to a flame whether she wanted it or not—and the coldness in Maris's bones heated into something much warmer.

Simon.

Sitting with him were Michaela Petran—who smiled and rose as Maris approached, then returned to her station behind the front desk—and another girl who wore librarian's glasses and a diamond stud piercing in her nose, both of these offset by a colorful jumble of tattoos that marched up and down her arms like a circus parade. She looked at Maris anxiously as she approached, but Simon's face wore the same calm expression he'd had last night.

Maris's smile faltered as Simon waved her over, gesturing to a plate of pastries and a steaming coffee carafe set upon the table.

The chick sitting with him looked friendly enough, but there was something about her that suggested this wasn't an accidental meeting, and Maris wondered what she was in for. Curiosity flared in her.

Maris would have died a long time ago if she'd been born a cat.

"Morning," Simon said, as Maris reached the table and settled herself into Michaela's vacated chair. As Maris surveyed the food, her stomach growled. Then she remembered she'd skipped dinner, and that the last food she'd had was the truck stop cheese sandwich she wasn't even sure she'd finished. Usually, she couldn't sleep on an empty stomach, but this morning she could barely even remember her head hitting the pillow.

Maris returned the greeting, and then a thought struck her. "I'm not late, am I? I thought I wasn't supposed to be at the Grille until tonight?"

Simon smiled. "Not late. I'm early. Found myself out this way and thought I'd swing by. Glad to see you made it to the inn all right."

Maris shrugged, grabbing what looked like a cinnamon scone from the platter on the table. "This looks great. I didn't know they served breakfast here, but I'm starving."

Simon laughed and ran a hand through his curls in a way that looked automatic as Maris dove into the pastry, groaning audibly as the sweet bread filled her mouth with notes of cinnamon and cardamom. "Well, then, tuck in. All these goodies aren't going to eat themselves. Baked fresh this morning down at the Daily Knead. Great sandwiches and stuff for lunch, too, if you're interested."

Nodding, she reached for the carafe, but the girl with the tattoos had her fingers around its grip first and had already begun to fill Maris's cup, then top off her own and Simon's. Setting it back on the little paper doily on the table, she pushed the little pots of cream and sugar in Maris's direction.

"I guess I'll introduce myself." She winked, smiling brightly as she gave her head a little tip in Simon's general direction. "My name's Adelaide Beaumont, but my friends call me Addie. Welcome to Havenwood Falls."

Maris wiped the crumbs from her fingers and accepted Addie's handshake, only barely glancing at Simon. Simon may have been the mutual friend, but this was very clearly girl time.

"I'm Maris—just Maris. Maris Heilen. Nice to meet you, too." Then, selecting another, smaller piece of what might have been a sectioned Danish, she asked, "So what brings you to the inn first thing in the morning? Are you Simon's girlfriend or friends with Michaela?"

Simon looked as if he was about to say something, but Addie interrupted, a small laugh lifting her words. "No, and yes. Simon says you just arrived last night, on the shuttle from Grand Junction. How are you settling in?"

"Great, thanks. I'd thought I'd just stay the night, but looks like I might hang around a while. Simon even offered to let me bartend at Fallview. Michaela set me up with a sweet room here. Already feels like home."

"That's Havenwood Falls for you," Addie agreed, and Maris wondered if there was another meaning hiding out in her words.

"It's been less than twenty-four hours, and everyone has been so nice. Seriously, I've shown up in a lot of places without a plan, and this has been the nicest greeting I think I've ever had. Most folks don't care at all when a stranger shows up, but it's like you all having some kind of welcoming committee or something. It's a little like I've stumbled into an episode of *The Twilight Zone*—just a really, really nice one." Maris winked when she said it so the comment didn't get misinterpreted as rudeness or arrogance. Still, there was some truth in her words. Michaela and Jakeel had also seemed to know too much about her for someone who'd just walked into town, and they'd gone out of their way to help. Simon had given her a job based on a flirt. And there'd been that strange way that Odette Alverson looked at her and then agreed to hire her, skills unseen. Maris got that it was a small town and good news traveled fast, but this seemed *really* fast.

For a split second, Addie looked taken aback, but then she smiled and tapped her fingertip to her temple. "Got a sense about these things," she joked.

Having polished off her first mug of stout black coffee, Maris laughed as she refilled her cup. She took a closer look at Addie, with her light brown hair tucked under a black beanie, her skin decorated with more tattoos and piercings and pieces of jewelry than Maris could count. She was wearing a black tank top with a pentagram on it, black ripped jeans, and black combat boots, but for all her rough edges, Maris could see herself becoming fast friends with Addie Beaumont.

"What are you, some kind of witch?" she teased.

Addie grinned a particularly mischievous-looking grin and elbowed Simon, who Maris had almost forgotten was there. "Exactly."

By the time the trio had finished the coffee—including a second pot, which Michaela had delivered before joining in the conversation until another guest called away her attention—and eaten their fill of breakfast pastries, Maris was quickly starting to fall in love with this little town and its quirky inhabitants. And so, when Addie pulled out the traveling tattoo kit she "always carried with her" and offered her a free tattoo right there on the spot, Maris had a really hard time thinking of a reason to say no.

She did hesitate, though. Tattoos were permanent, and Maris had never been one to say yes to anything forever, even ink. She'd managed to go her whole life without a single tattoo, and she relayed this to Addie, who waved away her objection as she assembled pieces of her kit and set out some ink on the tabletop. Simon cleared away the dishes to give them more room, and, perhaps, some privacy.

"We can totally do a temporary one," Addie reassured her. "If it fits, after a while, we can always make it permanent, or not. Up to you."

Options. Maris liked options. A temporary tattoo was just the thing: fun to wear for now, and she could decide what to do with it when she felt ready. "Okay," she said, "I'm in."

Addie buzzed the tattoo gun and wriggled her eyebrows encouragingly while Maris bit her lip in excitement. "What's it gonna be, Maris?" Addie asked. "You pick, or it's dealer's choice."

It took Maris less than three seconds to decide, which wasn't so much as a decision, really, as an image that flashed instantly across her thoughts. She unzipped the jacket and pulled her left arm out, offering her upturned wrist to Addie.

"A North Star," she said, touching the fingers of her right hand to the area of skin right above the folds in her skin from her wrist.

With the steadfast attention of a true artist, Addie held Maris's wrist with one hand and rubbed an ointment on her skin at the selected spot. For several moments, she didn't say anything, then, as she began to etch the design on Maris's skin in a shade of ink that was not the traditional black Maris had expected, she said something that made Maris's heart skip a beat.

"You know, there's an old legend in Havenwood Falls about a woman with a tattoo just like this one—a North Star on her inner wrist," she said.

Maris's hand clenched and unclenched of its own accord, and the chill she'd felt that morning breathed coolly over her skin. She slipped her free arm back into her jacket. "Really?"

Addie, her eyes still on the tattoo that was taking shape on Maris's wrist, nodded. "Yes. Well, not a woman exactly. A naiad, actually—a water spirit that granted blessings to those who sought her out in the well where she lived, somewhere deep in the forest. They said if you saw the naiad, she'd give you some of her magic and you would keep it with you, blessed in love for the rest of your years."

Maris's heart was racing, and she hoped Addie wouldn't notice her pulse beating wildly in her wrist.

"What was her name?" she asked, her voice breathy and uneven.

This time, Addie met her eyes, shining from behind her black-rimmed glasses. "Her name was Noelani, but she isn't called that anymore."

Noelani. Now that Maris heard the name, she remembered it. She'd whispered it a million times in her dreams to the woman in the well.

"Why?" Something in Addie's eyes made the breath that was stuck in Maris's throat turn hard, uncomfortable. She gulped, jerking as the needle in Addie's tattoo gun pierced her wrist in a sensitive spot.

"Well," Addie continued, "legend has it that Noelani was once a beautiful creature, full of love and blessings, until one day many years ago—in the seventies, I heard—a woman was drowned in Noelani's well by her fiancé. It is said that as Noelani watched the woman die, all of the love inside her died out. She was, like, made sick by the rage and betrayal of it all, and she became something dark and evil."

The chill in Maris was so strong that her skin had grown pale. Remnants of last night's dream—no, last night's *nightmare*—crept back into her thoughts, and for the first time since she'd opened her eyes that morning, she remembered the monstrous wraith that had crawled out of the well. She remembered the sense of emptiness, too, and the feeling that all life and light had been sucked away.

"Where is Noelani now? Can she ever return to the way she was?"

Addie didn't answer at first. She was busy putting the finishing touches on Maris's tattoo, which looked so similar to the one Maris had seen in her dreams that it might have been copied from a picture rather than sketched from an idea.

"I don't honestly know," she admitted finally, with a shrug. "That's where the legend more or less ended. Naiads can't survive without water, even when they've turned into something else, and

OF SALT AND STARS

that's what she is now—something else. The name we use for Noelani now is rusalka. It means a malicious spirit that lives in the water, because that's what she is, Maris. She's no longer the beautiful thing she once was, but something full of anger and hate."

The story had ceased to be mere legend, and now it sounded as if Addie was warning her about something—someone—very real here in Havenwood Falls. "But she wasn't always that way. Couldn't she go back to the way she was before?"

Addie shrugged again. "Some say a pure enough love could bring her back to herself, but others say that she's lost forever. No one has ever dared to find out."

"What do you mean, 'dared to find out'?"

Addie screwed up her face and shook her head, as if she was clearing her thoughts like an Etch-A-Sketch. "Oh, I don't know. It's just an old story, after all."

Maris wasn't letting it go. "But still, what does the story say would happen if someone tried, you know, tried to bring Noelani back?"

Addie pursed her lips like she didn't want to answer. When she didn't, Maris tapped her fingers against the other woman's knee in a gentle prod. "Oh, all right. Two things could happen. One, if the person who tries to save Noelani is pure of heart, she'll return to how she once was. That's the best case scenario. Worst case is that the rusalka pulls the person down into the well with her—forever."

Maris had gone from chilled to freezing. She attempted to pour a fresh cup of coffee to warm her up, but the carafe was empty. She decided against any further line of questioning in that direction and changed course.

"And what happened to the fiancé?" Maris asked. "The man who drowned the woman he was supposed to marry—what happened to him?"

Since she'd finished the tattoo, Addie had turned to clean her tattoo gun. At this question, she shrugged again. "Well, that's the saddest part, I think . . . and the most fitting. Remember I told you that those who saw Noelani would take some of her magic with them?"

Maris nodded.

"Well, he saw her—or rather, she saw him. No one really knows what happened, but it's said that he left Havenwood Falls with some of Noelani's darkness inside him. He would have spent the rest of his days cursed and eventually the darkness would have swallowed him up as much as it swallowed up Noelani."

As the story of Noelani and her well and her consuming darkness unwound itself in Maris's mind, she began to feel that somehow, her dreams of Noelani were more than just dreams. Somehow, the fate of the woman in the well was tied to her own.

"What was his name?" she asked, her voice barely more than a whisper.

"Who?" Addie asked, refusing to make eye contact.

"The man who drowned his bride," Maris clarified, "who cursed the naiad—what was his name?"

"Oh, I don't think—"

Maris found her voice again, and her words were firm. "What was his name?"

With a deep sigh, Addie put the tattoo gun down in its case and finally met Maris's eyes. She took Maris's hand in hers, examining her work. "Well," she said, sliding her fingers over the fresh tattoo before turning Maris's hand over and letting her fingers continue their journey on the life lines of Maris's palm. "That's the strange thing, isn't it? According to the story, the man's name was Heilen. Peter Heilen."

CHAPTER 8

*U*ntil now, Maris had only fainted once in her life, and that was when she'd first heard her father had died. Even then she wasn't entirely convinced it was the shock of the news of his death that had caused her to faint, mostly because she'd done so hours before she got the official call. The time that she'd fainted matched almost exactly the time the coroner would eventually determine the man had passed. It was several hours later when someone from the police department had phoned to check for next of kin and invite her, hesitantly, to identify the body in the morgue—a request she'd politely declined to do in person and, instead, conducted over the sterile safety of a video call. Maris hadn't been close to her father in years—or, really, ever—but his death had hit her nonetheless, stinging somewhere deep within her core in a place she seldom visited. She'd dropped on the spot, right behind the bar where she'd been slinging drinks and chatting up a full panel of tipsy men who were just drunk enough to tip her well without harassing her. Even though she hadn't spoken to her father in nearly a year, Maris had felt like something within her had been ripped away when Peter Heilen died. That—the loss, not his death —was what Maris long believed had made her faint, as if his sudden vacancy had affected her and was trying to pull a piece of her along with him. Like something inside of her was bound to something inside of him.

Now, reopening her eyes in her bedroom in the turret at Whisper Falls Inn in the surreal little town of Havenwood Falls, Maris again wondered if it had been her father's death that tore away a piece of her when he'd died, or if his departure from the mortal timeline had caused something else entirely to begin a long-awaited unraveling within her, a slow undoing that had been initiated, somehow, by his passing. Her dreams had taken on a different sort of urgency then, and this had all coincided with the time Maris had first started thinking about leaving Graham, and Denver, behind. Since then it had all festered, some deep yearning pulling her away from the life she had known and toward something else. She'd fallen in love with the woman in the dream as if she'd been a real person, crying out to her. Now, Maris wasn't typically the sort of girl that kept her feet on the ground, but even for her, the possibility that she could be a part of something so magical and mysterious was almost completely inconceivable. What was the saying, truth is stranger than fiction? It was simply all too bizarre to be real.

Whether dream or fiction or something else, this was all just a bit much, Maris decided, harrumphing disagreeably as she rolled onto her side. She had always had a suspicion that her dreams were more than what they seemed, but this . . . this was unbelievable—that the woman she'd been dreaming of her was tied to her, by what? A magical curse? Because her father had murdered a woman he had promised to marry, sometime before Maris herself had been born? It was impossible, preposterous. In the stunning brightness of the midday sun, Maris wasn't even sure the events of this morning had happened at all. They felt far away and only vaguely believable, and maybe as if they'd been nothing more than another one of her strange, too-real dreams. It was hard to rationalize a legend lurking within your real life under the best of circumstances, but it was another thing altogether to find yourself right in the middle of living out a full-on twisted fairy tale.

No, that couldn't be true. This wasn't a fairy tale, and Maris's dreams were just dreams—events of her overstimulated imagination, as Grim Graham had once suggested. Clearly, she'd gone off the deep end—no pun intended. Either that, or her new "friends" in Havenwood Falls were having a hell of a time hazing her. She'd have to reconsider her recent infatuation with this strange little town. Maybe what she needed to do was to get out of this inn, find the shuttle back to Grand Junction, get right back in her car, and keep going west toward . . .

Toward what? She'd been letting the current take her west. Toward water. Toward the woman that may or may not really exist that she'd managed to somehow fall in love with through a series of recurring dreams that felt too real. If they *were* real—and if Havenwood Falls was truly linked to her, the woman called Noelani—then Maris had no choice but to stay and find her. That is, unless she'd gotten food poisoning or something from that gross gas station food and had been sleeping off the sickness through a series of weird hallucinations and crazy thoughts. A whole lot less mystical, that possibility was distinctly more rational. Logic had never been her best friend, but right now she couldn't let her emotions get the best of her, either.

Maris lay in bed silently for a few moments considering this strange turn of fate and arguing with herself. She had almost resolved that the events of the past two days—particularly, the weirdness of this morning—had been just another odd dream before she realized that this wasn't her first time to wake up this morning. She was fully dressed, wearing the same jeans and shirt she'd put on in her "dream." Something itched on her wrist, and Maris pulled at the sleeve of her jacket to reveal the tattoo Addie

Beaumont had given her: a North Star, which matched exactly to the woman in her dream. As if these things weren't evidence enough that the morning's events had not been fantasy, Maris discovered, much to her surprise, that she was not alone.

Simon was in her room, although Maris suspected that he was only pretending to be asleep from his position in the sitting chair that was placed, incidentally, at the lip of the turret window. This provided the room a breathtaking view of the town, and beyond it, the thick forest that hugged the falls. The high sun indicated it must have been around noon, and Maris was less surprised about finding a man in her bedroom (that had happened on more than one occasion, though her guest was typically in her bed beside her and not fully clothed on the other side of the room) than she was at the fact that she had failed to lose herself staring at the view outside her window before.

Sitting up in her bed and listening over the sounds of Simon's steady breathing, Maris learned she could indeed hear the whisper of the falls as they fell in the distance, and as she took in the sound of the falls she almost thought she could make out words on the water, like the whisper was not merely the sough of the water, but a voice. The woman—Noelani—Maris knew, was not in the falls but in a well in some forgotten place on the edge of a forest that she had never been. Perhaps she was calling to her, in a very literal way, from the water?

Maris groaned loudly and let her head fall into her fingers. Rubbing her temples, she told herself to get it together. She was starting to question her own sanity. A naiad calling to her inside the sound of water? *Please.*

"You're awake." Simon's voice spoke over the water's.

"I've had the weirdest dreams," Maris spoke from inside her hands. She inhaled a few calming breaths before parting her fingers so her eyes could find Simon's in the space in between. "You were in them. And now you're in my room." Clarity finally arrived, and with it, shock. "Why are you in my room?"

As if such a thing were completely normal, Simon yawned,

stretching his legs to their full length out before him. "You fainted," he said simply. "Michaela thought such a sight might be bad for business, so I carried you up. Put you in bed. Figured it'd be better that you didn't wake back up alone and confused, but I must have fallen asleep waiting. Sorry if my being here is weird for you."

Dropping her hands, Maris sighed. "It's not. I mean, it *is*. Everything is." She stared at the temporary tattoo on her wrist, choosing her next words carefully before she spoke them. "Is it true? The story Addie told me—is it really just a legend, or . . ." Her words trailing off, she waved her hands in the air in front of her as if to say, "Is it all true? Did my father really murder someone? Are there really such things as naiads?" and the most frightening question of all, "What is my part in all of this?"

Simon nodded as he pulled himself upright, then rose from the chair and, with a quick look out the window, relocated himself to the corner of Maris's bed. He raked long fingers through his unruly curls again before patting his hand gently on the bend of Maris's knee. He opened his mouth as if to say something, reconsidered it, and started again.

"Havenwood Falls is a unique place," he began. "There are many legends here—many of which are true, many of which are not, and many of which are only half known and still mostly mystery. I can't say with any certainty exactly what happened at the well, or to the creature that lives within it, or even whether the story as we know it is anything more than fiction. But there is a reason you are here, Maris. Something brought you to Havenwood Falls. The biggest question is what are you going to do now that you're here and you know there's a reason you found this place."

"I don't know," Maris admitted, her eyes moving from the man at the foot of her bed to the glimpse of water in the distance outside her window. She laughed, and the sound was hard. "I want to believe this is all a fantasy. Maybe I got into a car wreck and I'm in some kind of coma or something."

Simon smiled. "Maybe."

Maris's second laughter was softer when it came through her lips. "But part of me knows I'm not dreaming. This is real. Whatever this is, it's real." She felt the truth of it as she spoke it, and another thought occurred—a question for which she desperately needed an answer. "Is she real? The woman—the naiad—Noelani? And . . . is she really a naiad?"

"Yes. She is real, or at least she was. And she was a naiad. I'm afraid I don't know much more."

Maris stared intently at the man on her bed until her eyes found her way to his—blue and iridescent and slightly glassy. "So if naiads are real in this place, then what are you? Your eyes don't look human."

Again, Simon smiled, and as if by way of answer, he blinked. It took Maris a moment to comprehend what she'd seen and then he blinked again and she saw it clearly this time—an inner eyelid sliding over his pupil so that it wet the eye underneath without fully closing, similar to a cat's eye, or a reptile's.

"I'm a dragon shifter." He grinned, and Maris could see it. It was hard to define what *it* was exactly, but there was something distinctly dragon-y about him.

She swallowed hard. Maris had always been the type to believe human beings were not the only creatures to walk the planet, but meeting one was . . . different. "And what am I?"

To her relief, Simon's eyes blinked like a human's this time, and the chill that had seeped into her bones dissipated. "That remains to be seen."

Maris muttered "Okay" under her breath about a dozen times before replying. *Cool.* So not only were supernatural critters real, but she might be one herself. Actually, it kind of made sense. She'd never quite fit in anywhere, no matter how hard she looked. Maybe that was why.

"Can you take me to her well?" she asked.

Simon shook his head and in one, smooth motion, rose to his feet and extended a hand. "No, but I know who can."

"Is she a dragon . . . or a naiad . . . or whatever, too?" The fact that she'd said that sentence was too weird for Maris to think about.

"Oh, no." Simon laughed as he gave Maris's hand a gentle squeeze. "She's something much worse."

CHAPTER 9

*O*dette Alverson was tall, elegantly beautiful, and completely intimidating. Maris could feel the other woman's pale blue eyes follow her every move as she made her way behind the bar in Fallview Tavern & Grille, listening intently as Simon instructed her on both the town and the operations of the restaurant. There was a sharp, curious look in the proprietress's eyes, and every time Maris caught a glimpse, she wavered in her assessment of whether the look was curious or cruel. Something about Odette Alverson was deeply unsettling and, simultaneously, totally alluring.

Simon had directed Maris to Odette as a source of information, but thus far Maris had been unable to summon the courage to speak to the woman. It was rare that she was overawed by anyone, and even more rare that it would be enough to make her keep her distance when her insides were burning with questions. Still, while Odette had given Maris a friendly wave when she'd arrived and done nothing to dissuade her questions, Maris had clung behind the bar instead, milking as much information as she could from the only person in Havenwood Falls Maris might actually consider a friend. It helped that he was a man, too. Usually, men found opening up to Maris irresistible. In

OF SALT AND STARS

fact, she'd learned more than she wanted to know from the lips of overly chatty men. Unfortunately, no matter how many smiles she gave Simon or how she accidentally let her arm brush up against his, this dragon man remained frustratingly tight-lipped. They'd been at the bar for hours—indeed the setting sun was already tinting the sky pink—and she didn't feel like she'd learned anything more than she had that morning in the inn.

Maris found it helped to temper her questions—and Simon's perpetually cryptic answers—about Havenwood Falls with brainless chatter about bar operations, a subject Maris suspected she might actually know more than Simon about. She couldn't tell if Simon was being vague on purpose when he deflected her incessant questions about the town, the well, or her father, or if he simply didn't have any good answers to give. It was either a very big secret, or information was shared strictly on a need-to-know basis, and Maris was on the wrong side of that need.

"Okay," Maris said finally, waving the bar towel in her hand over her head in a sign of surrender. "Is there *anything* else you can tell me?"

"No," Simon insisted, for what must have been the millionth time that evening, though he'd never once shown he was anything other than patient with her questioning. He tossed his head back over his shoulder, nodding toward Odette, who was busy not listening as she sorted menus at the hostess station. "But *she* can."

Maris flung the towel down on the countertop with an exasperated sigh. "*Fine,*" she relented. Then, summoning her courage, she made her way to the other side of the tavern.

Odette turned as Maris arrived, brandishing what looked to be a genuine smile under critical eyes. "Maris," she greeted her coolly.

"Hi . . ." Maris stammered, then collected herself. "Look, I know this probably sounds crazy or whatever—"

"Your tattoo," Odette cut in, holding her hand out to accept Maris's arm. "May I see it?"

Maris didn't know what else to do but comply, and so she did, holding back a shiver as Odette's fingers—which were as cool as her voice—traced around the star Addie had added to Maris's wrist.

"I had thought," she whispered, speaking as if to herself, "but I wasn't sure to believe. But it is true. You are the child of Peter Heilen, and, it would appear, bound to his fate as well."

Maris gulped, retrieving her arm from the woman's grasp. Her touch gave Maris the shivers, and she'd been having a tough time feeling warm already. "So it's true then? The legend of the naiad in the well? That my father . . . murdered someone?"

"It would appear so." There was no emotion or judgment in Odette's voice when she said this. It was simply a statement of fact.

"Are you"—Maris cleared her throat to push through the insanity she was about to say—"are you a naiad, too?"

"No," Odette answered in a voice just as cool and emotionless as before. "I have a very different relationship with the water."

The way she said it told Maris in no uncertain terms that further inquiry on that particular topic was off limits. There were a few beats of silence, and then Odette asked a question of her own. "Tell me, have you ever been in love before, Maris?"

Maris blinked at the strange question, which was not at all in line with where she thought this conversation was going. "In love?"

"Yes, in love. Have you ever truly loved someone? Anyone—a family member, a friend, anyone?"

Maris didn't have to think of an answer. She knew it already. "No," she said, shaking her head with a derisive laugh. "Lust, yes. I've had a lot of that. I've cared about people, but I can't say I've ever really loved anyone. I just have never been able to bring myself to be able to. Except . . ."

Her voice trailed off, and Odette's eyes widened, anticipating an answer. "Except?"

Clearing the way for another crazy thought to take form in her throat, Maris sighed. "Except her. Noelani. I love her. I don't know how, or why, and I'm not even sure I know what love feels like, but . . . I love her. It's ridiculous, really. I'm not even attracted to women, or at least I never have been—not in that way. But I see her and I think of her and I get this movement in my chest that sort of hurts but feels amazing at the same time, and all I want to do is *be* with her. It's like a sickness that I don't want to get better from. It's not infatuation. It's not lust. I know what those feel like. This is . . . different. I don't even know if she's real, but I love her."

"Oh, Noelani is very real," confirmed Odette, who breezed over the particulars as she continued to home in on her point. "But tell me, what do you know of her?"

Maris shrugged. "Only what Addie told me, really, and I can barely believe that. It's all so strange—no offense." Unfortunately, Maris had no idea who or what she was talking to anymore when she chatted up the residents in Havenwood Falls.

If any offense to what Maris had said was taken, Odette didn't let it show. "No. I don't mean what you've *heard* of her, or the stories you've been told or what you might have read about naiads and rusalki in a storybook, but what you know of *her*."

At first, Maris wasn't sure she understood what the other woman meant, and then it dawned on her. "I dream about her," Maris said, feeling warmth creep up her cheeks and color them red. "A lot, actually. I have for as long as I can remember, but lately the dreams have been . . . different."

Nodding, Odette confirmed this was an appropriate answer. "And how is she in these dreams?"

"Beautiful. Kind," Maris said automatically, the blush crawling its way down her neck in a wandering sort of trail that was not missed by Odette's gaze. "In my dreams, she loves me back."

"Then there is hope."

"Hope?"

"Yes," Odette breathed, drawing her hand to her chest. For a moment, she seemed to let her thoughts percolate on a conversation that mostly just confused Maris, her fingers drumming against her breastplate, then her hand dropped to her pocket, and she pulled out a crinkled piece of paper. "Like Simon, I don't have all the answers"—Maris bit her lip, feeling slightly guilty for how much she'd pestered the guy and how shamelessly she'd tried to flirt her way to answers—"but I can add what I know about Noelani's curse. She was, as Addie said, once very beautiful, and very loving. But when Heilen—when your father—drowned his bride-to-be in her well, the rage and suffering of it cursed them both. For Noelani, it blackened her heart and made her vengeful and cruel. For your father, well, he saw this when he looked into her eyes. Whatever capacity he had to love and be loved was lost until his own emptiness overtook him. And, it would appear, some of this curse spread to you as well."

"Me?" Maris blinked back her surprise. "But I wasn't even born yet."

"Magic has a way of being passed. It's in your blood," Odette confirmed, unfolding the slip of paper. "You are called to the water, yet removed from it. You are flanked by people who love you, but unable to return their affections. You suck people into your light and snuff them out, and eventually, should you continue down that path, you will find yourself as dry and dead as your father—the life quite literally sucked from your bones—unless you can undo what your father has done and unravel the harm he inflicted upon Noelani."

The softness in Odette's voice hardened over, like liquid turned to ice, as she said this, and Maris took a step backward, her own hand rising as if to shield her from the sting of Odette's words. It was true, unfathomably true, and Maris knew that—she could see the truth of it in her history of wanderings, of broken hearts left behind. Of Graham.

And it hurt.

Odette held the paper out to Maris, and she took it, careful to avoid the other woman's fingers. On it was a grainy black-and-white image of two people. The first, with his pale hair the same shade as hers and an eerie resemblance throughout the nose and mouth, was her father when he had been a young man. The other was a woman. It was not Noelani, but someone else—an exotic beauty with dark, wavy hair and the lengthened eyebrows and almond-shaped eyes of someone who carried the other side of the Atlantic in their genes, although in the blurry image it was hard to tell if she might have been of African descent or perhaps of Middle Eastern heritage. Regardless, she was distinctly beautiful, with a softness in her eyes and smile that signaled she was as lovely of spirit as she had been of face. Underneath their pictures was a more recent addition: a sketch of Havenwood Falls, with a makeshift map that led to Noelani's well. Maris saw that it was connected to, yet totally removed from, any other source of water in the town—a thing set apart and distinct.

Maris ran her fingers over his father's image, feeling him now as much a stranger to her as the woman pictured with him. "My father never mentioned this place. Never mentioned anything about this woman, or any of it. He always seemed haunted by something, but never gave the impression that he even knew what it was."

"He couldn't have," Odette returned. "Our town is protected by magic, and there are memory wards that erase the town from memories, both for the humans that come and visit and the other things that, well, aren't so human, when they leave. It is a necessary precaution, you understand. But sometimes the truth has a way of making itself known. The same magic that makes people forget has a way of making some return, or calling some anew."

A thought struck in Maris' head. "Things that aren't so human? You mean there are more than naiads here? I've heard"—she fought not to glance in Simon's direction—"but I thought . . ."

Odette gave a brief, tight smile, the sort that looked like it had happened by accident. "Yes. Havenwood Falls acts as a sort of haven for supernatural beings—like me and like Simon. Like Addie and even Michaela. Like you."

"Me? I'm not . . ." Maris scoffed. "I'm not *supernatural.*"

"Oh, but indeed you are. At least half." Odette's fingers wrapped around Maris's arm and gently turned the tattoo on her wrist upward. "All supes are marked, even if only temporarily.

Those that are approved to stay have their marks made permanent."

Maris had that strange feeling of otherworldly vertigo she'd had when she'd reawakened from her fainting spell, and had to laugh. "So Addie really is a witch."

Odette did not confirm nor deny this. Instead she said, "There are many different creatures in Havenwood Falls, and they all have their secrets and enjoy their privacy. It would appear that the legend was true in that your father took some of Noelani's magic when he left and it has passed to you. Your just being here is testament to that. What happens from here on out will determine if you are part naiad or part rusalka, and what sort of consequence your arrival might have on the legend of Noelani, because that much is inevitable." She gave Maris's tattoo a meaningful tap and then released her arm, adding, "We will see if you are here to heal Noelani's broken heart, or if she will simply pull you down into the darkness with her. It is you, Maris Heilen, who will determine your fate."

Her eyes returning to the paper, Maris gazed again at the woman in the picture. She knew that many women had passed through her father's life—women whom he'd been unable to love every bit as much as Maris herself had been unable to love any of the men who had passed through hers. The fact that she'd been born at all was really nothing more than a nod to nature finding its way, and she'd never know why her father had stuck around, particularly after her mother's death. Thinking on it a bit too hard, she decided to abandon the thought. There was no train of thought that would take it to a happy ending. "What was her name?" she asked. "The woman he killed, what was her name?"

"Stella. Stella Malley."

"Did you know her? Did you know my father?"

"I knew them both, for a time. They were visitors, passing through."

"Was she a . . . a supernatural, too?" Maris asked.

Odette's lovely faced produced a patient smile. "No, she was not. Just an ill-fated star, it would seem. Her destiny was written in her name." Odette paused as her thoughts returned to the past and her voice took on a bemused tone as the woman's name slid from her lips. "Stella. A lovely, bright thing, burned out by someone else's darkness when she might have enjoyed the mist of heaven." Odette's gaze quickened and returned to Maris. "Have you ever given any thought to what your name means?" she asked, as another patron walked through the wide double doors of the tavern and began making their way to the hostess stand, marking the end of the conversation. "If not, you should."

Taking one last glance at the portrait of the doomed Stella Malley and completely at a loss as to how she should feel, Maris refolded the piece of paper and slid it into the back pocket of her jeans. She turned to make her way back to the bar, her thoughts weighed down by riddles and legends.

"Oh, and Maris," Odette called. She turned back to the woman, not sure if she wanted to hear more or not. "Be careful. Don't venture to the well on your own, at least not at first. The forest is a lot more complicated to traverse than you might expect."

Desperate to get her thoughts back to somewhat normal, Maris slung drinks at the bar while Simon cooked during the dinner rush, but the map in her back pocket felt like an anchor in her jeans. It pulled her thoughts with it as she sunk deeper and deeper into her reverie, her mind a tangled web of betrayal, love, and magic.

CHAPTER 10

The arms of long, dark shadows wrapped themselves around Maris as she entered the forest. Jakeel had only taken her so far, to the farthest recesses of the edge of the wood, before insisting that he'd go no farther, and she was utterly alone now. She checked her phone and wasn't the slightest bit surprised to see that it had no signal. It had battery life though, and that meant she had a flashlight.

For now, that was enough.

The tattoo on her wrist burned as Maris made her way deeper into the woods, alternating between rubbing the mark with her free hand and using it as a makeshift divining rod that she hoped might lead her toward water. It was cold in the forest, and growing colder as Maris ventured deeper, trying to match the marks on the hand-drawn map to her surroundings under the unsteady light of her handheld, makeshift flashlight. There was no trail or other sort of marker to guide her, and so she simply kept walking as if compelled to do so and hoped she was heading in the right direction. The forest was barricaded by mountains, so if she bumped into rock, she'd gone too far. A warmer jacket would have been nice to shield her from the cold, but she only had the light jacket she'd brought with her and a knit cap she'd found in the backseat of Jakeel's car. Luckily, Maris had her resolve to keep her warm, and that alone had gotten her through tough spots before.

Around her, the woods were cold but not as quiet as she'd expected it to be. Nor were they filled with the usual sounds you'd expect in a forest. There was no patter of animal footsteps nor cry of birds; no scuttling of insects. Even the leaves on the branches of the trees stayed still, their branches muted and unswayed by psithurism. But the forest wasn't silent, either. There was something—a high-pitched sort of gurgle, as if someone had opened their mouth to scream and then stopped, the sound only barely breaking through the silence—a ringing tinnitus that formed an unsettling soundtrack to Maris's journey and filled the space between her footfalls. It was dark, too, darker even than a forest should be at night; the tree canopy was so thickly webbed that not even moonlight nor the twinkling of stars could break through its barriers. The trees themselves cast layer upon layer of shadows, so that things that might have been green or brown or other colors in the daytime were recast in various shades of black —ink, oil, raven, pitch. The only signs of life Maris found in the forest were the eyes she felt focused on her back as she moved, their gazes so intent that she felt them stabbing holes into her body in the darkness.

Cold and shaken, her resolve giving way until she was left clinging to the verge of hysteria, Maris trekked deeper and deeper into the woods until, after a while, the possibility of turning back was every bit as daunting as moving forward. She began to feel the consequence of her impulse coming back to bite her. No matter how desperate she was to find the well or how many questions she had—how much her desire outweighed her fear—it would have been better to wait until morning, when at least she'd have daylight as an ally. Pushing thoughts of the legacy her father had left for her and of what had become of Noelani out of her mind, Maris considered that it had been her impulsive behavior that had gotten her into these sorts of messes in the past. Blaming herself provided the only protection she could muster from the fear that was seeping around the edges of her thoughts as she stomped deeper and deeper into the woods at the very edge of Havenwood Falls, into a place even Jakeel had had to think about before delivering her. It was impulse that had led Maris to Colorado. To Graham. To leaving Graham. To Grand Junction. To here.

But it might also be impulse that saved her, a tiny voice added. Like Odette had said, even forgetting magic had a way of calling you home. Even a curse could be broken. Even darkness could still be lit if someone brought enough brightness.

And so she walked on, mumbling and shivering.

Until she heard footsteps behind her.

The distinct sound of crunching leaves shattered the heavy silence of the forest inches behind Maris's back. Following it came a rumble that might have been mistaken for thunder had it not been closer to the ground and marred by an undercurrent of ragged breathing. Maris froze as the inevitable source of the noise registered in her thoughts, and she heard the growl, her thoughts immediately racing through every beast—real and imagined, because there were apparently no limitations on what might lurk in the shadows of a place like Havenwood Falls—of which she'd ever known: wolves, both the regular kind and the were kind; bigfoots; trolls; the Penghou; hellhounds. Spiders that might weave her into their webs or nefarious tree sprites that feasted on women. Dozens more monsters for which she didn't even have a name, but all of which bore claws and fangs and would very much enjoy the taste of her flesh.

A second growl followed the first, and Maris's fear bled instantly into panic. She ran, the flashlight on her phone shining unfocused light on things she only half saw but which were sure to visit her in her nightmares for years to come. She tore through the bramble, stray branches slicing at her skin as she flung herself through them, tearing through the flimsy fabric of her jacket so that small beads of blood mixed with her sweat. She fell once, but scrambled back to her feet and kept moving as whatever it was that chased her closed the distance between them, its ragged breath and rumbling growl nearly indistinguishable from her own as she tracked the progress of its movement behind her. Maris ran so furiously and for so long that she didn't notice the forest turning to frost around her, or that the darkness had become so dark it had taken on a blue sheen from the cold, or even that she'd completely stopped trying to follow the map at all.

Just when she thought she could not go on—that whatever was pursuing her would surely win—Maris shoved her way through a final barrier of branches and lost her footing as her shoes slipped on the slick ground of frozen meadow, the space bright and cold and silver under the steady glow of the moon. As she broke free of the forest, the creature behind her screamed, and the sound twisted Maris's head backward as if of its own accord, and she was forced to face her pursuer—a sight she would have much preferred to never see.

Maris's scream matched the beast's as the two sounds joined together in the otherwise silent wood. The thing that had followed her was not a wolf or any other monster she could have imagined—not a bigfoot or a troll or even a spider. It was not a monster at all—or, at least, it did not appear as one. Standing not ten feet from her, tucked within the shadows and spindly branches of the black forest, was a woman. Her jeans were caked in mud and her jacket torn; the knit cap on her head askew and the pale hair beneath it littered with leaves and pieces of bramble that had knit it together to form a bird's nest of tangles. At first, the woman appeared familiar, but completely normal—flesh and blood and as mortally human as Maris herself. But when the woman's face moved from the shadow and Maris could see it clearly, she screamed again, and she was grateful to be on the ground already as her knees gave way beneath her. The face Maris saw staring back at her was her own, only it was twisted and misshapen, its eyes blank black holes and its toothless mouth agape, as if it were nothing more than a crude, unfinished mannequin of herself.

For the second time in as many days, Maris fainted again, her head falling into cold and total darkness as it hit the frozen earth beneath her.

$$\sim$$

WHEN MARIS OPENED HER EYES, the creature in the woods was gone, its figure swallowed up by shadows in the blank space where it had previously stood. The air around her had grown still, and it was now so cold that Maris could see her breath form little tufts of vapor in front of her as she breathed herself back to a state of calm —or something as close to calm as she was currently able to achieve.

Her eyes still locked on the space where that *thing* had been, Maris pulled herself to her feet and patted herself down. Desperate to reclaim her senses, she ran her hands over her head, her face, her chest, her stomach, and her hips, her pulse slowing as she let herself sink back into the familiarity of her body. Odette had warned her that the woods were unfriendly, but nothing could have prepared her for that. Whatever had chased her had been her, but not her, like it was a manifestation of the darkest side of her, or something like that. She didn't want to think about it just now —or possibly ever.

She stared into the darkness once more, but seeing nothing except darkness there, Maris tore her eyes from the forest and, turning, swept her gaze across the meadow she now found herself in. The feeling here was no less terrifying than the woods. If anything, it was more unsettling, though it was hard to explain how. Woods, after all, particularly at night and particularly when traveled alone, are meant to be scary. Meadows are not, but this one was.

The meadow was small, but wide, and had obviously once been lush and beautiful, like a secret garden protected by a ring of forest. Now it was a frozen wasteland, covered in a layer of unnatural permafrost. Everything here was iced in place, but not even as beautiful as that. It was darker, duller, as if it were not frost at all but cobwebs and dust—a sprinkling of gray over perfectly formed wildflowers and thistle that still held their bloom and promise of color underneath a film of decay. There was utter silence here; not even that eerie gurgle pervaded the air. Even the frozen grass that crunched to shards beneath Maris's feet did so soundlessly as she pulled herself up and moved deeper into the meadow, following a beam of moonlight that directed her to the place she'd been seeking. The cold eclipsed any other scent, except the smell of cold itself, and one other thing—salt.

She stuffed the tattered remains of the map into her pocket and—with a steadying breath—retrieved her phone from the forest floor and focused its beam in front of her.

In the center of the meadow stood the well Maris had dreamed about, only like everything else in this place, it was dark and dismal, sheeted in a thick layer of ice that didn't dare so much as sparkle in the moonlight. This version of the well had a slightly familiar feel to it, too, and Maris did her best to swallow the fear that was rising in the back of her throat. She'd seen this before, but the memory was vague and mercurial, and she couldn't quite catch it long enough to decode it. But even if its appearance was not that of some haunted landmark, it was also the same well she'd seen in her dreams for decades—the one in which she'd laughed and loved and kissed the woman she'd been waiting for her entire life. Maris had always assumed that when—*if*—she ever found this place, she'd run to the well and thrust her hands in the water, calling her beloved's name, a name so delicious she could taste the sweetness of it when it crossed her lips. But now she approached the well carefully, guardedly, and wasn't sure if she should be approaching at all.

"Noelani?" Maris called, or at least she tried. The name stuck in the back of her throat and only a small squeak made its way out of her mouth. Maris cleared her throat and took a deep breath, squinting in the darkness. "Noelani?" This time the word was clear, and the sound of it echoed and reverberated, like a noise caught in a wind chime.

Something stirred in the well. Maris could hear the sound of movement, but it was trapped—the sharp sound of something sliding across the ice from underneath a frozen barrier.

"Noelani?" Maris called again, this time sounding brave and natural and almost insistent. She was only a few feet away from the well now, so she could hear as the frozen surface of the water was broken. She could see, clearly, as ten long white fingers with mottled black tips curled around the edges of the stones that lined the well's outer ring. She could see as the top of a head rose above the water and well stones, and she could see the figure that appeared bore a face the pallid gray of a corpse, which was in turn hidden beneath a thick mass of gnarled black hair that snaked around the body that rose beneath it and poured over the sides of the well like hungry seaweed. She could see the white gown that in her dreams had appeared lovely and enticing on the woman's body, but now lay like a burial shroud over a pile of old bones.

She could see Noelani, but she could also plainly see that this creature that rose from the well was entirely changed from the woman she had known in her dreams.

But, as frightening as the wraith she saw rising from the water was, Maris also saw the star tattoo on the inside of its wrist, so she stood rooted to her spot like she, too, had been frozen to the ground as she watched the thing that had once been Noelani lurch and pull itself out over the edges of the well, moving slowly but deliberately as if every contorted thrust of its wrecked body was painful. Dragging her long, water-logged hair behind her, Noelani —though it was hard to call her that—began to emit a low sound as she moved. It was a sound lost somewhere between a scream and a song—not a moan but a word. A single, strained transmission that started softly and began to grow, until, by the time Noelani had pushed herself beyond the boundaries of her well and was making her painful slog across the ground, it was a piercing screech.

"Heilen," the rusalka was screaming. "*Heilen!*"

"Noelani," Maris attempted. "Noelani, it's me. I've come to save you. I've come to—"

Maris's words were cut short when the writhing thing on the ground finally snaked its long, skeletal, black-tipped fingers around her ankle. Through the heavy fabric of her jeans, she could feel their cold, clammy touch, hard and greedy on her leg. There was a pause, as if for a moment perhaps the touch had elicited another type of connection, and then Noelani's hand locked into place on Maris's ankle, the grip tight and unrelenting, and in one smooth motion jerked her so hard she toppled onto the ground as the wraith began to inch her body—wet and clammy and oddly brittle—on top of hers.

"Heilen," Noelani screamed, her voice a strangled, urgent, guttural sort of call—a death howl heard only underwater.

Maris struggled, trying to throw the other woman off, but she was so strong, so forceful, so unremitting as her hands pinched and pulled. When her face loomed only inches above Maris's, she saw a face more horrible than even that of the creature in the woods, for there was nothing but cruelty and malice in the blackened features of the thing that had once been the naiad.

"Noelani, it's me," Maris attempted, but her breath was forced out of her lungs as Noelani snarled above her. Long tendrils wrapped around Maris's body, twisting around her throat and choking off the ability for Maris to do anything other than splutter as the rusalka moved away, her hair acting like a net that drug Maris along with it, toward the well. Panic rushing over her, Maris kicked and thrashed, screaming soundlessly for Noelani to hear her —to *see* her—but it was of no use.

Maris scrambled when the tips of her shoes bumped against the stones of the well, and she thought she heard the sound of the water as Noelani began to descend back into her dark depths, pulling Maris down along with her. She thrashed harder, terror rising within her as a torrent of tangled thoughts spun inside her head and her heart beat itself furiously against the confines of her chest. She was terrified, angry, and desperate . . . and yet there was a strange urge to allow herself be pulled into the well, to not let go of the thing that was dragging her toward a certain, unending darkness. It was a crazy thought, but insistent, and the confusion of it stalled inside Maris's mind, freezing her body along with it. She felt resigned, suddenly, as the first touch of water breathed coldly across her skin, and then, just as she thought that she would drown after all—sucked beneath the water like her mother had been and her father had tried to warn her of—there was a flash of light, blinding in the darkness. This was joined by the sound of wings and the feel of something sharp as it sliced through the bonds that held her, and then Maris was lifted as if by the jaws of life out of Noelani's clutches and airborne, held in the talons of what was undeniably a large blue dragon.

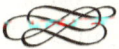

*M*aris didn't say anything when Simon—because that was the only dragon shifter she'd met thus far—delivered her back to the parking lot at the edge of the forest. She didn't say anything while she used the Luber app on her phone and then waited for Jakeel to collect her in his orange hearse and ferry her back to Whisper Falls Inn. And she didn't say anything when Jakeel himself had to help her out of the backseat and into the building, where Michaela and Addie received her with warm blankets and even warmer drinks—the kind that heated you from the inside out.

She didn't utter a single word until she was completely thawed, completely calm, and then—an hour later, when Simon finally returned in fresh clothes and human form—it all came rushing out.

"What the actual fuck," she started. "She didn't even hear me. She didn't see me. She didn't *know* me. I thought I would be able to . . . I don't know, to *fix* her. To make her remember who she was —who she *is*. But she didn't care. She was going to take me into the water with her, to what—drown me? And that *thing* in the woods. What the hell was that? I don't. I can't. I—"

"Maris, take a breath," Simon cautioned, leaning forward to

tighten the blanket around Maris's shivering body. Gently, he coaxed the coffee mug in her hand back to her lips. She took a sip, and immediately felt a rush of relaxation flood her.

"Odette did try to warn you," Addie, who was dressed as if she might have been attending a heavy metal rock concert rather than doing disaster intervention at midnight, reminded her. "Any of us would have gone with you had you asked. We are here to help."

"You're here to supervise, in case I'm capable of the same kind of evil my father was," Maris snapped, and felt instantly guilty. "I'm sorry. I didn't mean that. I mean, maybe I did, but I didn't mean it to come out so rudely. You all have been so kind to me." She looked at Simon and gave him a half-hearted smile. He smiled back.

"The 'thing' in the woods was a changeling," Addie continued, unperturbed. "When the light left Noelani's forest, such dark little beasties were able to creep in and make it their own. They are a type of fae—devious, quarrelsome things that prey on those they perceive as weak. They will try to trap you, so they can steal your place in the human world."

Maris gawked at her. "How are you supposed to beat something like that?"

"Changelings aren't beaten," Michaela interjected. "They have a place in this world as much as we do. But you can guard against them."

Addie nodded in agreement. "Faeries can't stand iron, so carry that with you. Changelings, in particular, avoid fire, so having that on hand will ward them off as well."

"Great. So I'll carry a hardware store in my pocket. Anyone know where I can find a blowtorch?"

Simon raised his hand and winked mischievously.

Maris nearly dropped her mug. "You can literally breathe fire?" she asked, but Simon only shrugged. Maris took another sip from her mug and this time felt almost entirely relaxed—as if she hadn't just been chased down by a soul-snatching changeling and then drowned by the woman she loved. Raising the mug to her lips for a third time, she suddenly stopped and considered her company. "I'm sorry, but I can't drink this," she said.

Addie laughed. "It's just tea with a little bit of brandy, I promise. No funny business. Besides," she winked, "it's not my style to trade in potions."

Maris looked at Michaela and decided it would be rude to ask what type of supernatural she was. If she'd wanted Maris to know, she'd have volunteered the information. "Okay. So, tonight was a disaster. How do I get through to Noelani—is it even possible?"

The other three traded glances, and Maris's heart sank. If a witch, a dragon, and a . . . whatever didn't know how to save a naiad from her own darkness, how in the hell was a cursed maybe half-supernatural chick supposed to do any better?

"We don't know," Addie finally admitted. "That is your magic, not ours."

Maris scoffed into her just herbal tea with brandy. "I don't have any magic. A curse, maybe. But that's about it."

Addie rolled her eyes. "Have you ever thought about why you chose the tattoo that you did?"

Maris hadn't. Not really. She wasn't even sure she'd chosen it. She just got it because it was the same as the mark Noelani had on her own wrist, and she said as much.

"But that's not true—at least, not totally," Addie countered. "See, I did some looking in the town archives. All supernaturals have a tattoo—Odette told you that—but Noelani's wasn't a star on her wrist. At least, it wasn't always. Before the event that . . . changed her," Addie said delicately, "her tattoo was something else —a clam with a pearl on its tongue. The star appeared later. After."

"What does that mean?" Maris asked.

"It means," Simon cut in, "that the symbol you chose is important. It's the missing clue to how to break the curse."

Maris shook her head. She sipped more tea and wished it were a potion. She'd take just about any clarity she could get right about now. "Odette said something similar earlier tonight. Something cryptic about my name, or about the power in a name anyway. But

I have no idea what she meant. She said Stella Malley was an 'ill-fated star' and that she could have enjoyed the 'mist of Heaven' had it not been for my father, and she said that I should know what my name meant. Does that mean anything to you?" She directed the question to the group.

"Yes," Addie said wisely, and then winked behind her librarian's glasses before pulling her cell phone out of her back pocket. "It means we should consult the almighty Google on name meanings and see if we can connect the dots."

Typing quickly into her phone, Addie launched a series of short investigative bursts, clicking and scrolling and responding to each with facial expressions that ranged from boredom to enlightenment and back again while Maris let her thoughts wander to the last dream she'd had of Noelani—days ago and worlds away in Graham's apartment in Denver—and ignoring the strange nightmare that had come to her on her first night in Havenwood Falls. She remembered the feel of Noelani's lips pressed against hers, the sensation of the water in her well as her body slid inside of it alongside the wet kiss of Noelani's form against hers. Her heart quickened at the need to slip beneath the water and descend into Noelani's world, the place of hers that was hidden away from the rest of the world where the two could be together, alone.

"Got it!" Addie announced, interrupting Maris's daydream.

"What?" the trio asked in unison.

"Odette was right, although it might have saved us all a lot of time—and sleep—if she'd been a wee bit less cryptic about the whole thing. Okay. So, the name Stella does, pretty literally, mean 'ill-fated star.' That got me looking. Maris, your name means 'to heal; of the sea.' Joined, Stella Maris is 'star of the sea'—a phrase symbolized throughout the ages, from ancient interpretations to modern-day religions, with the North Star. It's the one that would act as a guide for those that found themselves upon nighttime waters—a beacon of hope. Noelani has the symbol on her—it's the guiding light calling you to her—and it found you in your dreams.

You are the North Star, Maris—the star that can save her, just like the legend says. We just have to figure out how."

"No," Maris said, her lips curving into a smile as she shrugged out of the blanket. "We don't have to figure out how. I just realized I've known how all along." She looked at Simon. "Will you go with me to the meadow in the morning—be my blowtorch, just in case?"

He nodded. "Absolutely."

"Then daybreak," Maris decided, rubbing her wrist as she stared out the window and judged the number of hours until dawn. Five maybe, give or take. "I don't know how, but at daybreak we go and break the curse my father left on Noelani and her well, and see if there's anything to this *pure of heart* thing after all."

CHAPTER 12

*M*aris didn't sleep that night. Instead, she lay in bed, staring at the ceiling and considering if the next day might bring her death or her salvation, and how she might survive a second trip inside a haunted forest filled with changelings and other creatures of the dark that, until yesterday, she would never have even considered to be real. She never did decide—nor did she let herself get lost in the thought that she might fail and find herself resigned to a similar fate as Stella Malley: breathless at the bottom of Noelani's well.

Nevertheless, she had been called by the water, and to the water she would go. So, true to her word, when the first light of dawn crept over the horizon, Maris quit her idle thoughts, flung herself out of bed, and dressed as quickly and warmly as she could manage with her meager supplies. If she survived today, she'd find a way to fetch her car from Grand Junction. If she didn't, well, then it wouldn't really matter, would it?

Addie had loaned Maris a warmer jacket. Michaela had provided her with a pair of soft wool gloves that someone left in the inn's lost and found and a pair of women's hiking boots whose tread had worn dangerously slick, and Maris added these to her jeans and knit cap and called it good. She washed her face, swept her hair back into a low ponytail that wouldn't make the cap crawl up her scalp, and, summoning Simon—who had enjoyed another snooze in the armchair in her bedroom—boldly set off in the direction she'd traveled last night. She didn't need the map this time, which was lucky because it had ripped and smudged when Maris had run in the woods, ending the prior evening in poor shape. Now it was mostly useless, unable to serve as anything more than a painful reminder of the legacy passed down to her by her father. She left the piece of paper on the bedside table and hoped she could undo the damage her father had done. If she couldn't, then someone deserved to pay the price for his sins, and she supposed it would have to be her. It's not like her dreams would let her escape that fate anyway.

THE MORNING WAS BRIGHT, lit by a blazing sun that washed the scenic landscape of Havenwood Falls in a faintly golden glow, as if the town had been dipped in oil and set ablaze, the tips of the treetops pinnacles of reflecting light against a backdrop of white-hot mountain snow. Maris and Simon did not speak as they rode in his pick-up truck to the patch of forest on the outermost edge of town, but it was a comfortable silence—Simon at the wheel, his curly hair twisting out from underneath the brim of his cable-knit cap and fleece-lined denim jacket, and Maris beside him, daydreaming of the woman she hoped to rescue from the other side of darkness.

Jakeel had delivered Maris to a trailhead that joined a large expanse of property to the untamed forest. As Simon killed his truck's engine in that same space this morning, Maris realized she'd never thanked him for saving her the night before, nor asked why he'd been in the forest to begin with.

Staring at the dense patch of woods before them, Maris zipped up her jacket and turned to Simon. "I never thanked you for last night," she began. "How did you know where to find me?"

"It was my pleasure, and"—he tapped the side of his nose with his index finger—"dragon senses." When Maris gawked at him, Simon laughed so hard he had to tap his palm against the steering wheel for emphasis. "It was an easy guess. When you disappeared from Fallview, Odette and I knew there was only one place you could have gone. She sent me after you. You couldn't have been ready to face that—not the forest or Noelani. Not on your own. Not the first time."

Maris had to laugh. "Honestly, I'm not sure I'm ready to face it all again. But I have to. I have to save her." The thought occurred that she'd never really asked Simon if he wanted to join her—she'd just heard fire, thought dragon, and volunteered him along. "You don't have to come with me. I'm sorry, I just kind of forced you along, as if my problems were any of your concern."

Simon winked and swung the driver's side door open, bending down to speak to Maris through the parted space. "It's always handy to have a dragon on your side. Besides, I've got my own beef with this forest. Being here is helping me, too. And if we succeed, having Noelani back will help a lot of people."

Maris wanted to ask what kind of creatures in this forest would have been enough to give Simon pause but decided she didn't really want to know. She opened her door and slid out onto the ground, then moved around the truck to settle in beside Simon in front of the vehicle. Hesitating, Maris rubbed her hand over her tattoo anxiously. "You know," she confided to Simon without looking, "I have absolutely no idea what I'm doing. I'm about to go marching into a haunted forest and try to break a curse I barely know anything about. My ex would have had a lot to say about this, and none of it would have been good. He always said I was too impulsive, and reckless, and that it would probably get me killed one day."

Simon settled his hand on her shoulder and turned her to face him. "Sounds like now's the time to prove him wrong."

Maris looked into Simon's kaleidoscopic dragon eyes and wondered if it was possible to fall in love for the first time with two different people, neither of which were entirely human, or if this was simply what it was like to truly find a place where you belonged. "I think you and I are going to get along just fine."

Letting his hand slide down her arm, he gave her hand a reassuring squeeze. "Come on, Maris Heilen, let's go see if we can't get some darkness out of the woman you love—and maybe kick some changeling ass along the way."

CHAPTER 13

*E*ven the blazing morning rays over Havenwood Falls could not permeate the darkness that hovered inside the dense patch of wood. The heavy feeling wound itself, snakelike, in lengths that ran dark acres around the areas that surrounded Noelani's well, ensnaring those that would cross its barriers in gloom as easily as a spider's victim might be caught in its web. The moment Maris and Simon entered the woods, the shadows and silence and cold descended upon them, marking passage inside a world that was simultaneously both Havenwood Falls and a place separate from it. For better or for worse, they had left the safety of the town—though Maris had to seriously question how safe a town that was home to leagues of supernatural beasties could be—and were moving steadily in the direction of where darker things lay in wait. The worst part of it all, Maris debated, was a toss-up between the fact that she was in love with the darkest of those dark things, or that the darkness was hers, an inherited curse passed down by a father she'd only barely known.

There was also the fact that if she failed, she'd take Simon down with her, and she'd be just another name lost to a bad legacy. Her father had taken his bride; she'd take someone who was very possibly her only friend.

OF SALT AND STARS

Then again, her only friend was a *dragon*. Maybe the odds were slightly in her favor this time around.

Shaking off the shivers, Maris let the tingling in her wrist that had begun as soon as she'd crossed the forest's threshold act as a beacon, pulling her toward her fate. It insisted she veer left, toward a particularly menacing clump of trees carved out of sharp angles and shadow. Steeling her nerves, she, along with Simon, began moving in the direction Maris hoped would lead them to Noelani's well.

The movement through the forest seemed slower going today than it had last night. The sound of their footsteps was lost in the frozen hush of the wood, and cold air settled on their shoulders as they trekked deeper into the eerie darkness of the forest. Everything in the forest seemed to be reaching toward them—the spindly branches of the black trees that reached with long, skeletal fingers; the sharp, snaring bramble that clung to the bottoms of their pants and stabbed its way up their legs; even the cold, penetrating wind that sliced through their clothes and burned their skin.

Maris's body was tensed and on alert, and the silent shriek on the air seemed to swell in her ears with every thickening shadow and darkened passageway. Beside her, she could feel energy radiating off Simon that mimicked her own—waiting, uneasy, and on edge. She thought of asking Simon if he could hear the stilted scream she heard but thought better of it. Of course he could hear it. He could probably hear more than she could, and she really wasn't interested in him sharing. She didn't need anything else to add to her nightmares; they had a full cast of scary things already.

"How far did you walk last night before you got to the clearing?" Simon asked, his voice husky and hushed above her.

Maris continued to scan the darkness, torn between anticipation of finding the well and fear of seeing any movement whatsoever that would remind her they were not alone in the woods. "I'm not sure. Not long, I don't think. But I kind of lost track of things when that changeling showed itself. I just ran and sort of stumbled into it."

Simon produced an agreeable sort of noise but didn't produce judgment for her poor planning. "They're known to give a fright, that's for sure."

A harsh laugh pushed itself out of Maris's mouth. "That's an understatement. Those things were scary as hell."

"They can be."

"Does that mean there are times when those things *aren't* scary?"

Sucking in a deep breath, Simon used his arm to hold back a branch that looked like it was made out of claws so they could pass under it unmolested. "They're fae. Neutral. But can be swayed by light or dark. Once, they might have been nothing more than wood sprites, but when darkness took over this patch of wood, it covered them, too."

Great, Maris thought. *More bad juju to add to the Heilen name.*

"But we really shouldn't talk about them. Not here," Simon continued.

Maris was just about to ask why when the little hairs on the back of her neck stood on end.

"Because they'll hear you," Simon finished, as a small band of figures emerged from the depths of the shadows behind a gathering of particularly menacing sharp-leaved trees.

The changelings were figures carved out of midnight, but Maris could make out the shape of Addie's trademark glasses and the small stature of another she recognized as the diminutive stature of Jakeel. Worse, she realized as a hard knot curled in the pit of her stomach, she saw her own low ponytail on one of the shadowy figures and, on the final form, the curled ends of Simon's hair under the brim of a something pretending to be a cap. They moved silently as they filled in the blank spaces between the tall shapes of the trees, but even coated in darkness Maris could make out the jerky, unnatural movements, the strange, waxen faces.

Maris and Simon stood rooted to the ground as the band of

changelings pushed silently through the wood. "I think they heard us," Maris said. "What happens if they catch us?"

"I don't know," Simon admitted, and the shock of this was enough to swivel Maris's head away from the changelings and to the man at her side.

"You don't *know*?"

He shrugged. "I could tell you what the stories say, but you wouldn't like that either. Truth is, no one has dared venture into these woods since . . . the event. They stay in, we stay out, and life goes on. Call it a truce."

The changelings were growing in number around them and had now taken on a mass so numerous that Maris found it nearly impossible to distinguish their forms from the brush around them. It was like they were coming out of the trees themselves, or that the trees were changing shape and molding into the forms of her friends in town. A hundred terrifying scenarios flashed through Maris's mind, her psyche suggesting even darker and more twisted outcomes than she would have thought herself capable of, as the band of changelings closed silently in around them, pulling and stretching the darkness with them until it felt like all the air was being frozen out of the wood and Maris worried she might lose consciousness.

Beside her, Simon had begun to radiate heat.

"There are too many," he surmised, and Maris noticed that he seemed larger, thicker somehow, as if his body were expanding. It was hard to tell in the dark, but she could sense that he was changing—no, *shifting*. A swell of panic rose in Maris's chest as suddenly she found herself in the presence of monsters: a band of changelings taking on mutated forms of people she cared about at her back, and her single friend morphing into a fire-breathing beast at her side.

"*RUN!* Find her," Simon bellowed, his voice no longer smooth and masculine but harsh and raspy—a man's voice emerging from the snout of a dragon—and, as soon as the command from her brain reached her feet, she did.

Maris ran, crashing through the only open space in the trees she could find as her tattoo burned like fire on her wrist. She sped through the darkness, the branches of the trees once more slicing at her face as she screamed Noelani's name. Why she did this, she wasn't sure, but a cursed woman who lived in rage and grief at the bottom of a well somehow seemed safer than what Maris was leaving behind.

Crashing through another dense patch of trees, Maris emerged into the silent stillness of the meadow, too dark and cast in shadow in what should have been the brightness of morning. Noelani's well was in the distance, and already Maris could see the winding tangles of her black hair creeping over the edges and slithering like snakes along stones and frozen ground toward her. Maris took one final glance back and saw the wings of a great dragon, its scales glittering even in the absence of starlight. A blast of bright light erupted as a burst of fire cut through the darkness, and the resulting scream of the changelings was so immediately terrible and horrifying that it scarred itself into Maris's heart. She stood, her mouth agape as she gawked in the direction of the forest, her mind unable to fully comprehend what she had just seen as she felt the tendrils of Noelani's hair wrap around her ankles and pull her to her knees.

It's now or never, Maris thought, watching the dark black ribbons of Noelani's hair wind themselves like coils around her legs.

Maris did not resist. She let herself be pulled toward the well, and when her feet bumped against its edges and she saw the ghostly figure of Noelani wafting underwater, she grabbed ahold of the woman's hands as she pushed herself into the water. Icy coldness stole her breath as Maris slipped with Noelani into the blackness.

CHAPTER 14

$\mathcal{T}$he fall down the well was shorter than Maris would have imagined, not that she had given any particular thought to how long such a thing might take. Even more surprising than this, however, was the ease with which Maris found she could breathe. She'd half-expected to drown in some fathomless body of watery darkness, but she was instead sitting quite comfortably on what might have been a bed of soft moss in a large underground cavern. There was water above and beneath her, but in between existed a small plateau of dry land, the coast of an underwater lake that might have once been more beautiful than any of the places Maris had ever visited on her wanderings. Now it was as grim and haunted as everything in this part of Havenwood Falls. What's more, the feeling here was different than the forest. It wasn't frightening, not exactly, though it was certainly uninviting. The whole place was drenched in an unspeakable melancholy, so that the weight of it pressed down upon Maris, suffocating every bit of joy from her bones until—eventually—all that would remain was infinite sadness.

For the moment at least, Noelani was nowhere to be seen and Maris felt alone—utterly alone actually, which in itself was a distinctly unsettling realization. Taking a moment to return her breathing—and her pulse—to a state closer to normal, Maris sipped in stale, frozen air while her eyes adjusted to the dim. Gradually, her heartbeat slowed and her surroundings came into view. She'd expected this place to be a pitch-blackness even darker than the forest, but it wasn't—not completely. It was still dark— still almost unbearably cold—but Maris could clearly distinguish the boundaries of the new world she'd fallen into. There was no source of light that Maris could see, but nevertheless, the area around her was lit by a faintly ethereal kind of glow, gray and otherworldly, as if the place were formed from dust and ash. The only deviation from this somber setting was a mystical sort of sparkle, though even it seemed a possessed thing, the phantom light reflecting off the surfaces of the shapes around Maris as though everything was coated in a fine dusting of coarse sugar.

Using her hands to steady her, Maris pulled herself into an upright position. This dismal gray place, she saw, was an underground cavern situated at the bottom of a small waterfall, anchored in place by a shallow lake of murky gray water. Above her, Maris could see a tunnel that stretched upward toward the mouth of the well, and beyond that, Maris could make out the sky overhead, midnight blue well before noon. A fog had crept in, like a funeral shroud that eclipsed the stars, which only added to the gloom. In the space below where Maris sat, the cavern was stark and barren. Like the forest outside, what once must have been lush vegetation was frozen in various states of decay, the petals and blooms as delicate and brittle as spider webs. It was cold here— cold enough that Maris could see her breath in front of her face— but the air was stale and vaguely rancid, like a freezer left closed for too long. And it hurt to breathe too deeply, so that Maris could only draw quick shallow breaths, which only added to the feeling of despair. Even though she was standing in the open air on dry land, Maris couldn't shake the feeling that she might drown if she moved too quickly.

Reaching out to a rock, Maris rubbed some of the glittering substance onto her fingertips. She brought it to her lips and, tasting it, grimaced at the result. It wasn't sugar after all, but salt. Just like it had in her dream, salt covered every surface, glinting and gleaming at her as evidence of all the tears Noelani had cried in the decades since Maris's father had stolen her magic away and left her with nothing but pain. The salt crusted over everything—rocks and crags, the decaying corpses of plant matter, and even the shallow pond itself all were covered, no inch left immune to Noelani's suffering.

A faint slithering sound interrupted the silence, and Maris's heartbeat resumed its frantic pace as the moss—which Maris now realized was not moss at all, but a nest of matted, dark hair—began to shift and slide beneath her feet. It moved more quickly here than it had above the well, and the nest made fast work of entrapping Maris, twisting and curling around her in a nest of tangles. Fearing that if she struggled too much against it, it might swallow her like quicksand, Maris stayed as still as she could manage, trying to ignore the sensation of what felt like snakes wrapping around her body—the strands winding tighter and tighter as Maris grew ever colder and even her shallow breaths were reduced to little more than small sips. The tattoo on her wrist was hot—iron hot—and it burned from its place on her skin, every bit as scorching and painful as if someone had held a brand to her flesh.

When a final lock of hair coiled itself around Maris's neck and the tangle had grown still, the slithering noise of its movement was interrupted by a thick gulping sound. Maris watched as, in a heave, Noelani's face was born forth above the embryotic syrup of the shallow pond. Even with her gaunt features and black, soulless eyes, her thin-shriveled lips and pallid, waterlogged flesh, Maris could still sense the beauty underneath, and it was devastating. The creature's mouth curled around the shape of Maris's name as it groaned and lurched in a macabre dance, jerking and twisting out of the water as it made its way toward her.

"*Heilen*," Noelani the rusalka called in her strange, strangled voice. "Heilen."

Much to her own surprise, Maris answered, her voice calm and soothing even under the pressure of Noelani's hair and the fire in her wrist—even despite the weight of tears in her throat.

"Come away with me," she invited Noelani, using the same phrase she had heard her love utter so often in her dreams. Maris realized at that moment that this might have been a terrible mistake, but, she decided, if she were to die in this place, at least she would do so with her true love, and so she called the wasted beauty of Noelani to her. "Come to me, Noelani."

Maris watched as Noelani made her slow, contorted journey over the banks, her lovely white dress reduced to scraps of rotted fabric that tore even as she crawled forward and pulled herself within a finger's length of where Maris waited, nearly frozen from cold and fear. Swallowing her rising panic, Maris continued to invite Noelani closer, her words eventually giving way to a single one—*come*—as Noelani's rancid, bitter breath filled Maris's nose. Maris knew she should be horrified, that she should thrash and fight with all her might, that she should scream for help and do everything in her power to flee this monster coming to claim her.

But there was no time to do any of that. Something was changing.

As the thing that had once been Noelani inched forward, the tattoo on Maris's wrist began to glow softly, the light seeping upward through the cracks in her bonds as it spread warmth throughout her body. As Noelani crept into the ring of light shining from the star on Maris's wrist, she began to undergo a slow transformation, the darkness melting away as the light shone on the image of the woman Maris had seen so many nights in her dreams. Maris knew it was a trick, some kind of projection only seen when the creature came this close and not real—or was it?

Realization hit Maris like a bolt of lightning in the deep, dark cave. This dark version of Noelani was nothing more than a curse, and this ragged, monstrous form was a disguise—a mask— intended to hide Noelani's brightness behind a wall of pain, an exaggerated version of the same dark emptiness Maris had carried within herself. The darkness had consumed Noelani, had covered her up and locked her inside a degrading shell, but it was not her true form. The naiad's spirit was still there, hidden underneath. It was desperate and unchanged and crying out for help. The dreams Maris had been having were not just lovely fantasies, nor were they simple visions of the woman fated for her. They were cries for help, Maris understood, desperate pleas for salvation. For healing. For her not just to come find her, but to come and save her. The truth of this was more than the shape of Maris's tattoo; it was clear in the light that shone from it—the healing light that proved that Maris, and perhaps Maris alone, could see Noelani for what she truly was. And, more important than this, that in Maris's light, Noelani could be as she once was, if only someone could bring her out of the darkness she was trapped in.

If Maris could find a way to free her from the dark.

Noelani was now firmly encased in Maris's light, and Maris no longer saw the creature that had crept out of the gray waters. Instead, she saw a silken veil of hair the color of strawberries, a milky complexion. Noelani's eyes were the shade of springtime grass, her lips soft petals of blooming roses. She was a beautiful and lively thing, even though ragged breath still issued forth from her lips, and Maris knew, vaguely, that anyone else watching would have seen a monster hanging over her and not this lovely creature. But Maris didn't. Maris saw only the woman whom she'd fallen in love with over many nights and many years. She saw the nights they'd spent together; the constancy—the connection that had anchored her in a life spent flailing about always searching for something she could never seem to find. And then she realized something. Maris had thought she'd never been in love before, but knew now that she had been wrong—she'd been in love with Noelani this entire time, and had only been waiting for the chance to find her way back to her. And that sort of longing love changed everything, unshackling Maris from the need to run and inspiring the desire to fight. To hold on tighter than she ever had and never let go. To force Noelani back to her in the same way that she had been begging Maris to come to her each night in every single one of her dreams.

A new strength surged in Maris. "Noelani, look at me," she demanded.

"Heilen," came the strangled word again, the voice that came from between the rose-petal lips the sound of crinkling paper.

Maris felt the coils of hair squeezing her, the pressure growing tighter and tighter until she could barely draw breath. She was drowning, she knew—drowning in the same deep, consuming void that Noelani had been trapped in for decades—and she was simultaneously both the only one with the power to stop it, and powerless to do anything to fight against it.

With the last bit of energy Maris had left, she pushed her left hand through the hair that bound her. The star was blazing white light in the dusky darkness, and Noelani's eyes darted to it as Maris pulled her hand inward so that her fingers could embrace Noelani's face. The smooth skin was hard and clammy beneath Maris's hand, but she ignored this as she pitched herself forward so that her lips were only inches away from Noelani's. The other woman struggled against her touch, her mouth opening to reveal a swallowing darkness as she shrieked.

"Heilen," Noelani screamed, the sound of her voice at once so forceful and piercing that Maris felt her eardrums vibrate with the threat of bursting.

"Come away with me," Maris used her last breath to whisper as she pressed her mouth against Noelani's thin, cracked lips. Feeling herself slipping into darkness, Maris held the kiss, held Noelani's face to hers, tasting her own name as the light issuing forth from her wrist began to flicker and fade . . .

. . . but then something changed.

A TASTE like honey lit on Maris's lips, and she realized that

Noelani was kissing her back, her cool, smooth hands cupping her face as her kiss breathed life back into Maris, chasing away the encroach of waiting death.

Noelani's lips pulled away from hers, and Maris found that she could breathe easily again. She was warm, too, and the weight of sadness had been lifted from her shoulders so that it felt like she might float all the way upward, out of the well, and back into the world above. When she opened her eyes, the world had been recolored: the water in the pond sparkling and clear, the decaying vegetation restored to vibrant blooms—even the darkness above the well's mouth the crisp cornflower blue of mid-afternoon.

None of these could compare to Noelani herself, who was once again as lovely as she had been in Maris's dreams as she smiled down at Maris in her fully restored glory, a thing untarnished by darkness. There was an instant feeling of fullness that passed between them, an energy more full of excitement and anticipation than even the biggest of Maris's adventures. It was a dream made real, the current of an indescribable connection plucked out of a dream and into the solid reality of life, and Maris's entire body felt like it was sparkling, as if light was flushing out from her pores and she was a star made flesh.

The two women gazed lovingly into each other's eyes for the space of a few heartbeats, but it was Noelani who spoke first. "You found me," she said in a voice that was like the sound of bells. "You pulled me back from the darkness."

A blush crept into Maris's cheeks. "No," she insisted. "You found me. You've been calling me to you for as long as I can remember. I've dreamed of you every night."

She touched Noelani's cheek, marveling at her beauty, her familiarity, at the sense of wholeness Maris felt for the first time in her life. With Noelani in her arms a void inside of her had been filled, the deep craving she had tried for a lifetime to fill with scores of nameless people and places now utterly full. She had been driven to find something, someone, and she had wasted so much time looking when everything she'd ever needed had been here all along.

"I never knew it was you I was looking for." Maris smiled, drawing Noelani's face into hers. "You are my Water."

Noelani nuzzled her cheek against Maris's as their lips met. "And you, Maris Heilen, are my Star."

EPILOGUE

*T*he next day, Addie retraced Maris's tattoo with permanent ink and made her a resident of Havenwood Falls. Maris had never counted on permanency, either on her skin or in her life, but now that she'd found Noelani—as well as new friends who had become the first family she'd ever really known—she had no intention of ever leaving. Her father's crime might have earned him banishment from the magical little town in the Colorado mountains, but it was the only place on Earth that Maris felt truly at home.

Just as her shuttle driver had promised on the evening she'd arrived in town, the tow service retrieved Maris's car from the truck stop in Grand Junction and delivered it to Whisper Falls Inn. Until plans could be made to build a more long-term structure near the well, Maris planned to split her time between the inn and Noelani's forest. She never slept in the turret again, though, preferring to spend her nights in the company of her love in the cave beneath the well, where they lay in each other's arms and stared at the stars, no longer held apart by the space of dreams. When she wasn't with Noelani, Maris tended bar at Fallview Tavern & Grille, where she and Simon continued to build their friendship, and Addie promised to help her learn more about any magic she might have inherited from what her father had stolen from Noelani's eyes. Maris was human, but her call to the water and the residue of Noelani's magic in her blood might mean there was more to Maris than met the eye.

Light had once more returned to the dark forest, the changelings that had crept into the woods had disappeared to wherever it was that changelings disappeared to, and the warm sunshine soon recolored the meadow in vibrant hues of new life. The weeds shrank and flowers bloomed, and within days, the area surrounding the well was as lovely and fragrant as ever. The cold and salt melted away, so that the meadow was warmer and brighter than before. Finally, when water once more lapped at the top of the well, Noelani's sweet voice again filled the wind of the forest with song.

For the time being, Noelani's well would remain a secret in Havenwood Falls, both to allow the naiad's magic to restore and to give the privacy that was due to her and Maris. Only Simon and Addie had visited the well, where on a particularly sunny afternoon they helped construct a small grave marker in memory of Stella Malley, the woman who had died in Noelani's well so many years before.

On Noelani's instruction, the marker was made of a white crystal, a star etched on its surface above the woman's name.

"I can't believe my father was capable of something so evil," Maris reflected, as she and Simon secured Stella's gravestone in a patch of thistle not far from the well. She traced her fingers over the star before rising to her feet, using the fabric of her jeans to wipe away the last remnants of dirt that had accompanied the burial. "I feel so ashamed of the legacy my family's name brought to this place. I don't know how to make it up."

Beside her, Simon placed his hand reassuringly on Maris's shoulder. He didn't have any words of comfort to offer, but he had none of judgment either. That was one of the things Maris liked most about Simon—that he could say so much without saying much of anything at all.

"There is darkness in all of us, Maris, my love," Noelani reminded her, a serene smile playing on the corners of her lips while she sat next to Addie on the rim of the well. "Only the darkness in some is stronger than the light. It is up to each of us to choose which side we fall on, but there must be those on both sides, I'm afraid. There is a balance that must be kept. Without the darkness, the light would never be as bright."

Addie nodded agreeably as Maris and Simon rejoined the pair at the well, the foursome settling easily on the soft grass. Maris slipped her hand inside Noelani's as the naiad leaned her head on Maris's shoulder.

"Tell that to poor Stella," Maris said with a sigh.

"Can you tell us more about Stella Malley?" Addie asked. "No one truly knows what happened that night. Maybe it would help us all to be able to move on if we knew the whole story."

It was Noelani's turn to sigh. A wistful look passed across her face, but it was gone in a blink as she turned her eyes toward Maris. "Yes, I will tell you that story one day, but not yet," she said. "For now, I need to heal, and I need to know the woman who saved me."

We hope you enjoyed this story in the Havenwood Falls series featuring a variety of supernatural creatures. The series is a collaborative effort by multiple authors. Have you read them all?

Find the full list and sign up for our reader group at www. HavenwoodFalls.com

Subscribe to our reader group and receive free stories and more!

ABOUT THE AUTHOR

Seven Jane is an author of dark fantasy and speculative fiction. Her debut novel, *The Isle of Gold*, was published by Black Spot Books in October 2018. She is represented by Gandolfo Helin & Fountain Literary Management and supported by Smith Publicity.

On Facebook, Twitter, and Instagram @sevenjanewrites or at www.sevenjane.com.

ACKNOWLEDGMENTS

Many thanks are due to Toni Miller, Lynn Shaw, and Jenny Bynum, three wonderful ladies whose eyes and insight I would not trade for anything in the world.

To Kristie Cook and the team at Ang'dora Productions, LLC, who have welcomed me into the magical world of Havenwood Falls.

AN EXCERPT

A Havenwood Falls New Adult Novella

HAVENWOOD FALLS

REDEFINED

USA Today Bestselling Author

MORGAN WYLIE

Redefined (A Havenwood Falls Novella) by Morgan Wylie

From *USA Today* Bestselling Author Morgan Wylie - She's a lead witch assassin—until he leads her to question everything she's ever believed.

Hollis Blackstone is a lead assassin for her father's rogue band of witch hunters. For longer than she can remember, her father, Dante, has had two missions: rid the world of witches and locate his estranged family kept from him by his sister's rebellion. Working off a lead, Hollis finds her way through the mysterious borders of Havenwood Falls. Her father's orders were to gather intel on the whereabouts of all the Blackstones, all the witches, and the seat of their power. But then she meets the irresistible Ryne Calloway.

Half witch and half phoenix, Ryne hasn't been in Havenwood Falls for long. Rejected by his father's clan because of his witch heritage, he knows all about suppressing who he really is. In town for a fresh start, he hopes to relax and have fun. And that's exactly what he plans to do with the pretty new girl who strolled into town with a stick up her butt.

Ryne opens Hollis's eyes, widening her perspective beyond the hatred she's been taught. But when her father seeks her out, everything begins to unravel. She's finally found someone who loves her for her, but she's about to lose him before ever having the chance to love him back.

REDEFINED

BY MORGAN WYLIE

Hollis Blackstone stared at herself in her bedroom mirror, seeing only the assassin she had been created to be, wondering if there was anything else she might ever become. She had quickly gained the position as one of the lead assassins for her father, Dante Blackstone. Being a witch hunter was more than her job; it was her entire life, day and night. Hollis had been training to be the best since she could remember. On nights when the teams ransacked home after home, she caught a rare glimpse of him smiling at her —at what she'd accomplished—and she believed him to be proud of her. The teams liked to make a mess of each witch's home they attacked, but Hollis preferred her team to be stealthy, more deadly. The lack of interruption to one's home seemed to send a greater message than a tantrum of violent proportions.

Her room was nothing more than an empty shell, a cavern of unrealized possibilities. Hollis didn't waste time decorating her rooms, for there would always be another, in another town. Her father's organization—her family—moved around more often than they stayed in one place, or so it seemed the past year or so. Plus it was just one more thing to have to worry about, to take her focus away from her job—her obsession.

Pulling on her black leather jacket, despite the early May warm weather, she covered the multiple tattoos on her shoulders stretching down toward her elbows. Hollis fluffed her long dark hair in the mirror, checking to ensure the scar at her hairline was hidden, and made sure she was presentable. She had been called in to see her father, and he didn't tolerate sloppiness or tardiness. Dante always dressed impeccably to impress and to intimidate, and he expected nothing less from his teams. An inept capability to be present when requested was unacceptable to Dante.

They had only recently set up this home, and Hollis didn't even remember what city they were in this time, but she knew they were somewhere near Santa Fe, New Mexico. Dear old dad had been chasing a lead in his lifelong obsession to track down the other Blackstones—those he considered lost and in need of his guidance—and the secret place in which they lived. About a year and a half ago, they had almost found it, but somehow it mysteriously—most likely magically—slipped through their fingers, and they couldn't remember anything about where they had been or where they were trying to get. Her father had been infuriated.

He had been on a rampage ever since they had let Macy Blackstone—who'd been staying with them—get away. Macy had been the biggest lead they'd had in a long time. Her father received slight pulls in the right direction, which he could never describe other than to say he "sensed the spirit of his sister Marie and the rest of his family who *should* be with him." At other times, Dante would utter vague accounts of being so close to the name of the town in his mind only to have it slip away like a lost memory he tried to force to the surface. Somehow they still mysteriously received secret letters from Aunt Letti to Grace and the other old gals no matter where they were, but her teams could never trace the letters' origins.

Hollis strode down the hall with purpose and ownership, stopping only when she arrived at her dad's office. Knocking twice, she didn't wait long. He was straight to business as he called through the door.

"Come in, daughter mine," Dante called through the door, his voice strong and sure. It could have been one of several of the Blackstones who lived with them at the door, but he seemed to always know when Hollis was near. Dante had lived a long time and been quite prolific with reproduction over the span. Even Grace, who appeared to be in her seventies and was half hunter and half human, was one of his descendants. Hollis refused to consider them all siblings since the ages varied so drastically, but they were family just the same. Right as Hollis turned the handle, a young girl in her early teen years with golden blond hair skipped around the corner.

"Have fun, Hollis!" Sunny called with a singsong voice and a big smile.

Hollis didn't let anyone close, but if anyone could get under her skin and attach themselves to her, it was Sunny. Sunny had a way about her that would disarm the most hardened criminal. The family referred to her as their "little ray of caffeinated sunshine." Hollis reached out and tugged on one of Sunny's pigtails.

"Thanks, kid. See ya 'round."

"Maybe, maybe not," she continued in her singsong tone and shrugged. Sunny suddenly stopped and then frowned. Her expression sobered, then she stared into Hollis's eyes. "I'll miss you, but I'm happy for you." Sunny came in for a quick, unexpected hug, then turned without another word. She skipped down the hallway, leaving Hollis with a dumbfounded look on her face.

"What was that about?" Hollis wondered under her breath.

"Are you coming in, Hollis?" Dante asked with an edge in his voice. He didn't like to be kept waiting.

"Sorry, Father. Sunny stopped me," she offered as an excuse, the only excuse she would ever use, and the only one he would allow. He gave her a sharp nod.

"Come sit. I'm waiting on Nala and Rachel. And here they are now."

Hollis turned to find the two other hunters walk through the door. They sauntered in, their heads high and chins jutted out, proud to have been summoned. They were both exceptional hunters in their own rights, but Hollis was better. Their presence caused her to wonder why he wanted to see all three of them. Perhaps he had another mission for them, though they had each been out on a witch hunt last night.

"Take your seats," Dante directed as he stood, straightening his suit and refastening the bottom button. In his suits, he appeared dapper and put together like Pierce Brosnan in a James Bond movie, even down to the silver streaking his otherwise black sideburns. "It has recently come to my attention through a reliable source—"

"You mean snitch," Rachel sarcastically snickered.

Dante inclined his head. "Such a crass term. I prefer 'source.' Anyway, this source confirmed what a separate source had previously supplied. The town we have been looking for is, in fact, in Colorado. It is called Havenwood Falls."

"Weren't we just in Colorado, like a year ago?" Nala impatiently asked. She had been one of the main hunters first tailing, then keeping watch, on Macy Blackstone when she had inadvertently stumbled upon them.

"Indeed, but my memory of it has remained maddeningly elusive. No doubt a side effect of those damned witches the *other* Blackstones associate with."

"They shouldn't be allowed to use the name Blackstone," Rachel spat with disgust. Nala and Hollis both agreed.

"No, no. They are of our blood. Though they are misguided, we can bring them back into the fold, into our family, and redirect their purpose—help them see the error of their ways, so to speak," Dante clarified, looking each girl in the eye to ensure they understood.

"Do you know where in Colorado?" Hollis cut to the chase.

"No. That is the frustrating part. However, we know it is somewhere in the middle of the state. Most likely somewhere with a significant area of land where they could hide an entire town."

"How do we know your 'sources' aren't sending us on a wild goose chase?" Nala asked as she whipped her long blond hair behind her shoulder.

Dante sneered, and an evil glint entered his eyes. "I extracted the information from the witch myself. She couldn't help but tell me."

Nala and Rachel each swallowed hard. They knew what kind of methods the source would have had to endure for Dante to get the information he wanted. Hollis didn't flinch. She knew he did what he had to, to get what he needed.

"Well, it's about damn time. When do we go?" Rachel asked, readjusting in her seat as if she wasn't afraid of Dante's tactics. They all feared him. The ones like Hollis had the ability to hide their fear, which separated them from the others.

"No." Dante surveyed the girls slowly, taking measure of something they weren't aware of. "For this mission, I need to be able to completely trust the person I send. She would have to be able to go undercover, be skilled at listening, and have the ability to not act on instinct—to conceal her hunter side for the greater good. For this mission, I choose Hollis. She is the best suited."

Without reaction, Hollis simply nodded her acceptance. The other girls groaned.

"Then why are we here?" Rachel asked. She had a tendency to speak out of turn. Dante put up with it to a point. He had reached that point. The look he gave her had her shrinking back into her seat. Hollis couldn't help the glow of approval she kept hidden in her chest. Rachel got on her nerves the most.

"*That* is exactly why I chose her. Hollis can control her reactions and simply observe. Also, not to mention, Macy has seen you both and most likely would recognize you right away. She never met Hollis during her stay, as Hollis was out on an extended mission." Hollis realized he had called the other girls in to teach them a lesson and to, once more, instill competition amongst them by elevating one over the other. She didn't agree with his tactics for camaraderie amongst teams, but he did get results. He turned and looked to her. "Will you go, daughter?"

"Of course, Father. When should I be ready to leave for Colorado?"

"Tomorrow morning. I will have Grace get flights prepared. Pack light. Disguise yourself. I want you to blend in. Be a tourist, if need be. I want specific information on the town and certain people within it. I'll get a list together while you pack."

Hollis inclined her head in a half nod and half bow, ready to serve.

"How are you so sure she'll find it based on 'somewhere in the middle of Colorado'?" Nala asked, but Hollis could hear the tinge of jealousy behind her tone.

"Can you find it, Hollis?" Dante pointedly asked.

"I won't come home until I do."

Dante smiled. "That's my girl."

And that was how Hollis found herself at the private airport in Grand Junction, waiting for a shuttle to take her to Montrose, yet another small city in the middle of the Colorado mountains.

Purchase *Redefined* where books are sold.